D0466937

LADY THIEF

ALSO BY A. C. GAUGHEN

Scarlet

LADY THIEF

—— A SCARLET NOVEL ——

A. C. GAUGHEN

WALKER BOOKS
AN IMPRINT OF BLOOMSBURY
NEW YORK   LONDON   NEW DELHI   SYDNEY

First published in the United States of America in February 2014
by Walker Books for Young Readers, an imprint of Bloomsbury Publishing, Inc.
www.bloomsbury.com

For information about permission to reproduce selections from this book, write to
Permissions, Walker BFYR, 1385 Broadway, New York, New York 10018
Bloomsbury books may be purchased for business or promotional use. For information on
bulk purchases please contact Macmillan Corporate and Premium Sales Department at
specialmarkets@macmillan.com

Library of Congress Cataloging-in-Publication Data
Gaughen, A. C.
Lady thief : a Scarlet novel / A. C. Gaughen.
pages   cm
Sequel to: Scarlet.
Summary: Scarlet's true identity has been revealed and she has been forced to marry Lord
Gisbourne and participate at court, acting the part of a noblewoman in hopes of helping her
beloved Robin Hood's cause and forging a future with him.
ISBN 978-0-8027-3614-7 (hardcover) • ISBN 978-0-8027-3615-4 (e-book)
1. Robin Hood (Legendary character)—Juvenile Fiction. [1. Robin Hood (Legendary
character)—Fiction.   2. Courts and courtiers—Fiction.   3. Love—Fiction.   4. Adventure and
adventurers—Fiction.   5. Middle Ages—Fiction.   6. Great Britain—History—Richard I,
1189–1199—Fiction.]   I. Title.
PZ7.G23176Lad 2014   [Fic]—dc23   2013024938

Book design by Donna Mark
Typeset by Westchester Book Composition
Printed and bound in the U.S.A. by Thomson-Shore Inc., Dexter, Michigan
2 4 6 8 10 9 7 5 3 1

All papers used by Bloomsbury Publishing, Inc., are natural, recyclable products
made from wood grown in well-managed forests. The manufacturing processes
conform to the environmental regulations of the country of origin.

For my dad
Thank you for giving me the opportunities, love, and support to make an unlikely
career out of something I love. I never could have done this without you.
I love you.

LADY THIEF

CHAPTER
ONE

—o—

The fire breathed, the dying embers flaring and cooling in a hot pulse. I watched the cold black creep over the orange. The fire were going out.

The cold never worried me overmuch. We slept in the warming room of the monastery, and with plenty of blankets and a well-tended fire, a body never got too cold. I could see Much's head curled over his knees, his body in a ball nearest to the fire. His arm that were missing a hand were tucked in tight, like he were trying to protect the thing that had been taken from him so long ago. John sprawled out farthest away from the fire, laid flat on his back like he'd fallen down drunk. None of the fights, the battles, the trials ever seemed to pierce through him and leave holes behind like they did the rest of us.

A bare foot away, Rob lay nearest me. Always near, always far. He slept on his stomach now, and he never used to. It weren't many months since the now-dead sheriff had tortured him, laying him on a board fitted with spikes until they pressed through his flesh and tore. The holes on his back had been slow to heal, and the pains and infections they caused went so much deeper than his skin.

The embers went black, and then edges of gray started to emerge, and the light shrank full out of the room.

I never knew when it would happen. But it would happen. Few nights since the snows had forced us into the monastery were restful.

The noises came first—soft swishes. Thumps. Low gasps. I shut my eyes against it.

At the first yell, I sat up, moving close. My heart were too big in my chest, tight and hot and painful, and I felt water push behind my eyes. "Rob," I whispered, scared to touch him.

He yelled loud.

Pressing my lips hard together, sucking back my fear, I touched his head, stroking his hair, wishing each touch of my fingers could weave peace into him, like a spell.

His big shoulders eased, and he took a breath, still slumbering.

My chest didn't feel as tight but the tears weren't far gone, and I lay down beside him, still threading my fingers in his sand-gold hair. I pushed my head against his.

Breath and sleep came easier both, and my eyes started to slip down. I let them, unafraid. Tonight wouldn't be one of the bad nights.

—m—

I weren't sure if it were half a breath or most of an hour later, but I woke as Rob shoved me off him, hard. I rolled on the stone, and a moment later he were on top of me, his hands wrapped around my throat.

I couldn't see him in the dark. I couldn't see his ocean eyes, and it were too close to my every nightmare of Gisbourne. I clawed at his hands and tried to yell but it came out a cough.

"Robin!" John roared, and I could bare see his steel-roped arm come round Rob's neck, hauling him off. Rob's hands pulled me up till he let go, and I fell to the ground. The room filled with light as Much flared a candle, his face fair white even in the yellow glow.

Tears ran slick on my face, and I pushed them off fair quick before Rob could catch it.

Rob slumped against the wall, his chest heaving with breath, his hands pressed against his face. John stood above him, keeping him from me.

I scrabbled over on my knees, going round John and kneeling between Rob's spread legs. "*Scarlet,*" John grunted at me.

I paid him no mind as I pushed Rob's hands off his face. He were flushed, his eyes wild. "You . . . ," he whispered, clutching my sides, squeezing me so tight it pinched. His head fell on my chest, and he were breathing into the space between us like it were the only bit with air.

"Much," I said, turning a little. Him and John were just standing, frozen, watching. Not one of us knew what to do for Rob. "Give me the candle. You lot can go back to sleep."

Much did, even as John stood still.

Rob lifted his head, still touching me. "I'm all right," he said to John, his voice rough. "I won't . . . I'm not a danger to her." His fingers dug into my skin, and it felt like he were trying to crush me, make me shatter under his hands like an eggshell. A breath later, his fingers went gentle.

John nodded slow and wary, looking at me and turning back to his bedroll. It weren't a full moment after that Rob's hands uncurled from my skin and fell from me.

I stayed still, something stuck in my pipes that I couldn't swallow down. He weren't breathing as hard, and I reckoned that must have been a fair good sign.

His hands caught my hips again, but he didn't pull me near like I thought he might. He pushed, gentle, moving me away from him.

He stood, and without a word, he went to the door. He swung it open and the rush of cold air were like a slap.

John looked at me, but I just shoved into my boots and grabbed up an armful of Rob's things before going outside.

Rob were striding down the cloisters, and I ran to catch up with him.

I threw his boots down at his bare feet. "Don't run away from me," I snapped.

"Don't?" he growled. He bent over and shoved one boot vengeful on his foot. "I could have killed you, Scar!" he yelled. He put the other boot on and stayed bent over, crouching down low. "I could have killed you," he said again.

I sat on the snow-dusted stone, stretching my legs out and leaning against one of the stone pillars of the archway. "You didn't," I said, handing him a cloak. He stared at it. "Put it on. Anger may feel warm but it ain't going to keep you from falling sick again."

Rob's jaw rolled with muscle. "I didn't *fall* sick," he snarled, swinging the cloak round his shoulders and sitting on the ground across from me. "I was laid on a board with spikes on it, and I felt it as each one pushed through my skin. And those gaping holes didn't quite heal right, did they?"

My knuckles were rubbing over my cheek before I knew what I were about. He weren't the only one that Gisbourne and the sheriff had left marks on. The new scar I'd gotten for marrying Gisbourne to save Rob's life were harder than the last, like something were stuck deep inside it. It were longer too. "They never do."

He let a moment pass. "I don't want you out here."

"Yes, you do."

"You need sleep."

I just huffed at that.

"You'll freeze," he said.

"I like the cold," I said, tucking my cloak tighter around me anyway. He opened his mouth to try and shake me off again, so I asked the one thing I knew would hush him. "What do you dream of, Rob?"

He glared at me, but his eyes fluttered shut and he shook his head.

A. C. Gaughen

I rested my leg against his. He breathed a deep sigh, but his leg eased into mine.

We didn't talk more. We stayed quiet and wakeful in the cloisters till we were half-froze, until the sun came up and the monks walked their silent ways and I wondered if God were making Rob pay for his sins or just my own.

CHAPTER
TWO

John kicked my boot, and I jerked. It weren't like I'd been sleeping, just tucked inside a half-frozen stillness that had settled down on my skin. Rob kicked him back for it, and John stepped free. "You really want to take me on, Rob?" he asked. John were smiling, but he were standing between me and Rob again.

"Not at the moment," Rob allowed, standing and pulling me up, going round John to do it. He held me a moment, his hands on my arms, his face glowing heat onto mine.

John looked over his shoulder at us.

"Don't want to be late," Much said.

Rob let me go and I glared at Much. It weren't like me and Rob had more than our share of soft moments.

"What?" Much asked me, but I shook my head. The boy had less sense than a wooden post sometimes.

Rob led the way, and I followed behind him, with Much behind me and John at the flank. The winter forest were different for us; the snow covered the ground and made everything in the forest a lie, a trick. Holes were covered over, once-strong branches were brittle and weak. Everything looked beautiful and clear, like the world were at peace, but what it really meant was not a thing could live upon its frightful cold.

Not even me, and I were a creature meant for no warmth, no sun, no light. The winter forest wouldn't hide me in its branches, weren't strong enough for me to run along the trees, and it made me stand out against its snow.

My forest had turned on me.

The closer we got to Edwinstowe, the more the thing turned into a dance. In the winter forest, you could see farther than were fair good for a thief or her friends, so each step forward were a step to the side, stepping close to a tree to blend dark clothes to dark wood.

On the edge of Edwinstowe, the others stayed against the trees while I moved forward. I were still the best at this part, moving silent and unseen through a place. I taught the others what I could, but there weren't no teaching the shadows to welcome you in.

I stole through the rough rows of houses to the well in the center of town. I waited on the side of the nearest house, listening.

Their heavy footfalls were loud enough to announce them from far off. The knights strode through the town, the lane empty but for them. The villagers had learned to stay well below their notice; the knights were wont to take whatever they pleased.

I heard a door open in the quiet, and the footfalls stopped. "Sirs," said a breathlike voice, so oversoft I couldn't tell who spoke.

"Miss," the two returned.

"Why, I was just headed to the well for some water," the voice purred out.

"Allow us to help."

Quick moments passed before the two knights appeared, one holding a pail and the other holding the arm of Agatha Morgan, Mistress Morgan's redheaded eldest child. The first knight hooked the pail onto the rope and set to lowering it while Aggie leaned back against the well, batting her pretty lashes up at the second knight.

"How do the menfolk fare?" she asked sweet. "My father is one of the men rebuilding the wall."

"Is he?" the knight asked. "I'll ask for him and bring you news. The reconstruction goes well, and since we've come to town the vagabonds responsible for the destruction of the castle haven't shown their faces."

"Good thing," the first knight responded, heaving back to pull up the full pail. "We'd show them what a few good English knights can do to lawless rebels."

"Is it true the king himself ordered you to come look after us?" she asked.

"King's away," the first knight reminded her. He weren't quite noticing her game.

The second knight knew what she were about, and she arched her back from the well. He grinned. "The prince sent us. The castle, the wood, and the whole county falls back to his care without a sheriff. And we promised to take very good care of it in his absence." He stepped closer to Aggie, looking shameless at her chest as she smiled at him. "Have you good ladies missed having your men about?" he asked.

It were meant to sound saucy, I'm sure, but it were all I could do not to spit. Honestly, all the knights were pigs and Aggie were a damn fool. Not many women in Nottinghamshire— specially the married ones without their husbands—had slept peaceful and safe with their men forced to work for the Crown. And Aggie may have giggled when he touched her, running his hand up her arm, but I stepped forward.

"Morning, Aggie," I called. "Sirs."

Aggie's face dropped, and her body fell back against the well. She crossed her arms. "Imagine meeting you here."

The second knight took in Aggie's change and turned back to me, sauntering closer. "Why aren't you at the wall, lad? All able-bodied men were called—even small, rather flimsy-looking ones."

"Oh, for Heaven's sake, she's a girl in pants." Aggie pouted.

The knight took new interest in me, looking me over. "Well I suppose that's lucky. Look, one for each of us. I'll even let you have the pretty one."

Aggie looked wounded as the first knight put the pail down.

"Don't put your hands on her," I warned him.

The second knight grinned. "Jealous? I'll keep you busy, pet. Though it looks like you've already had a man's hands on you." His eyes hooked on my neck.

I put my hand over it, swallowing under the pain. I knew it were swollen, but it must have bruised up overnight.

"I'm right glad Rob finally taught you a lesson," Aggie told me with a sniff. "That's what you get for being so meddlesome."

The mood changed quick, and the first knight grabbed Aggie's arm. "Rob?" he asked. "Robin Hood?"

"The vagabond?" the second knight said, and took quick steps toward me. I stepped to the side.

Aggie had the sense to be sorry, even if it were late and little at that. "N-no," Aggie lied quick. "Her husband. Robert of Gisbourne."

"*Lord* Gisbourne," I snapped, and the knight halted his advance.

The knight laughed. "There's no way in hell you're Lady Leaford."

His fellow coughed, though, and the second knight looked back to see the first one leaving Aggie be. "We should go."

"She isn't Lady Leaford!" the second said.

"Didn't you hear *any* of the stories?" the first knight muttered to him. He shook his head and prodded his fellow farther down the lane.

As the knights disappeared, Aggie stomped her foot and turned on me. I frowned at her, going to the well and tying a scarlet ribbon to the hook. "How could you?" she snapped. "How am I ever supposed to get a husband with you interfering?"

"Go home, Aggie," John said, coming from behind a house with the others. "Or I'll tell your father what you're angling for."

She crossed her arms. "Oh, I'll tell him what you angled from me right back, John Little."

John frowned at her like he were losing patience. "Yes, Aggie, I'm sure you're eager to tell your father *that.*"

"Go," Rob told her, bare glancing her way. "And don't speak to Scar like that again, Agatha."

"I didn't mean to let it slip—" she started.

"No," he said sharp. "You meant to be cruel to the girl who saved your father's life. Who fed you when you were hungry. That's what you meant. Go home, Agatha."

She turned heel and left, and Rob came close to me and let his fingers brush over mine. My heart caught the sunlight and tried to tuck it in so close I felt near to bursting. I beamed at him, remembering again—*he loves me.*

He gave me a soft, small smile, but it blew off like smoke when his eyes dropped to my neck.

Rob turned from me, my fingers going cold where they had been warm, and I pulled my collar up tight against the bruises.

"Come on," Rob told us, and we continued on to Lord
Thoresby's manor.

Thoresby's loyal guards let us pass unbothered, and we went
to the barn. It were warmer in there, full of animals and horses
and wide-open space in the middle. There were three little
people waiting for us.

Jack and Will Clarke came over to us, trailed by the littlest
Morgan girl, Missy. She came and stood beside me, quiet, in a
way that always made me want to tuck her under my coat. Jack
went over to Rob and started yapping at him, and Will drifted
slow to me.

"Hullo, Scarlet," he said.

"Morning, Will."

His cheeks threw up a red flame, and he looked at me and
then away. His small chest puffed with breath and he looked at
me again, his face turning angry and sour. "Did someone hurt
you?" he demanded, his voice loud. "Was it a knight? I'll kill
him! I'm a much better shot now!"

At twelve, he weren't much shorter than me, but I felt
a need to kneel down. "No, no," I told him quick. "My coat
snagged on a tree and yanked me back, that were all." I saw
Rob turn away from me at the lie. "Besides, who would hurt
me when you're around to protect me?"

He looked at me, very solemn, and said, "I'll cut down the
tree if you show me which one. And if it's not too tall."

Trying to swallow my smile, I shook my head. "We can let
the tree live."

The barn door opened, and a few more of the children and women from the town came in. Will went to his brother, and Rob slipped up beside me.

"I hate to make you lie," he whispered, his breath rushing over my ear and making shivers trickle down my spine like water.

I shrugged. "I'm a liar. Besides, he wouldn't understand."

"Are *we* supposed to understand?" John asked, glaring at Rob and not looking at me. "Because I don't."

"Shut it, John," I told him with a frown.

"Will definitely wouldn't. All he'd understand is someone that claims to love Scarlet is hurting her. He'd probably kill you, Rob," John said, coming close. "Or happily die trying. I think the young man has a crush on Scar."

"You would know what that looks like, wouldn't you, John?" Rob asked, his voice iron hard.

"Rob!" I snapped.

But John just chuckled. "Well, who could blame me. I mean, you're the love of her life, but I'm the one who knows what her kiss tastes like, right?"

The boys were glaring at each other, not paying a lick of mind to me. Which were fair fine with me, for John didn't see it coming when I kneed him in the bits. He didn't fall, but he howled and twisted away from me.

"What the damn hell, Scar!" he roared.

"You are my *friend*, John Little, you do not wag your chin about any bit of me like that," I snapped. I whirled around. I wanted to slap Rob, but I didn't. "And you. John's trying to protect me from *your* dreams, *your* nightmares, something none of us fair well understand, so don't bait him like that. It's cruel and you know it."

He swallowed, and he looked at me, his face open and worn. "I am cruel, Scar," he said, like it were a confession. His eyes fell to my neck, and he shook his head. "Come," he called loud, his voice rougher. He stepped away from me. "Let's practice with the bows. John, are you well enough to help?"

John coughed and nodded to him. My heart twisted like a scrap of cloth, and I took the stairs two at a time to the hayloft. I sat on the edge, watching as the nine children and two women what had come lined up to listen to Rob teach them to defend themselves, and their homes, and their families.

Much came and sat beside me with a sigh.

"You have to know, with John—"

"I know," I said. "I know better than you think."

"He just wants to protect you."

"I know he does. And I'll always love him for it and many more reasons. But he and Rob are so awful to each other sometimes."

Much gave a soft noise, and I turned and took in his sad and mournful face. He saw me looking and shrugged. "They may be awful to each other, but only because they know they're brothers. And brothers can fight." He paused a long stretch. "They don't fight with me," he said.

"We're all family," I told him. "They just think of you like the baby."

He frowned. "I'm not a baby. I've grown a few inches, I think."

"I know."

He scowled. "You know?"

I laughed. "All your pants are short."

"Scarlet?"

I turned and looked to the stair where Missy Morgan stood, hanging back. She were as pretty as milk and sun, more short and quiet than her two sisters, but she were the jewel amongst them. She crowded the rail, her shoulders sunk in.

"I don't want to learn the bow so much. Can we practice more with the knives?" she asked.

Nodding, I stood from the ledge and pulled Much up with me. Looking at her, making herself small even in this place where she knew there weren't nothing to fear, my breath caught. "I reckon so. Much, will you run and snatch a few?"

He looked at my vest where I had at least three, but I met his eyes full and he nodded. He went past Missy, touching her arm a little, and she raised her eyes to him and held her breath till he passed.

Were Missy sweet on Much? That would be a match to be sure—though I weren't the sort to know if a love could survive with so much shy and kind in it.

I waved her closer, and she drifted up to me. "Did something happen, Missy?" I asked her.

A wash of color went all over her face, splotches of pink and red like fast-blooming roses. "Y-yes," she said. "Sort of. I was at market, and a man, he put his arms on my waist and he said something—something awful," she said, her gaze falling to the wooden floor and her hands shaking.

"Oh—" I started, but she weren't finished.

"And I did what you said. I stepped on his foot, and I hit him with my elbow," she said, wrapping her arms tight round herself. "And he let me go, and I ran. But I think I'd feel better with a knife."

My heart filled up hard and fast, bits of happiness spilling over the edges and slopping around inside my chest. Most nights it felt like God himself were punishing me, but seeing a girl protect herself instead of asking someone to do it for her felt like some kind of redemption. "Then we'll get you a knife," I told her.

—∞—

It were late in the afternoon when Thoresby came in, two servants with him carrying food for the children. He nodded to us and came closer, leaving the children—and John, the big hungry thing—to descend on the food.

Thoresby weren't a big man. He weren't an overstrong man, or clever, or young. But he were always fair, and I liked that about him.

"Have you heard anything?" Rob asked. His body turned a bit, leaning toward mine, like everything in him were pulling him closer to me and stopping just short of touching.

Thoresby nodded. "The prince is coming to Nottinghamshire. They're speeding up progress on the wall to be ready in time—a fortnight at the most."

I sucked in a breath. "Will he name a sheriff?" I asked.

"If he's decided, he hasn't let me know."

"But he received your petition for it?" Rob asked.

Thoresby sighed. "The messenger assured me he received it. Robin, I warned you not to rest too much hope on this. It's a very political appointment, and he has nothing to gain from appointing me."

"Nonsense," Rob said, waving this off. "You're well thought of at court."

"If I'm ever there," he said. "It's unlikely at best, Robin."

"He'll appoint you. Who else could he choose?"

"There are still unclaimed lands," he said. "Most of your old Huntingdon properties are still unentailed. He could easily bring someone into the county to make them eligible. And many minor landholders are eligible. There are a surprising number of possibilities."

Muscle in Rob's jaw flickered and bulged out. "Then gain his notice. Persuade him. Do *something*, Thoresby," Rob snapped.

"I know how much you want me to be sheriff, but you must prepare yourself—" he said, clapping his hand on Rob's shoulder.

Rob pushed it off. "No. No. What I must prepare myself for is defending the people again, because clearly I'm the only one willing to stand up for them."

Thoresby heaved a great sigh and looked round at the barn. "Things seem to be going well here, Robin. It was a good idea."

"It was Scar's idea," he said, flat. "Good thing they're learning to protect themselves—those children are growing up in a

world where not *one* of the people who are duty-bound to honor
and shelter them care for their well-being. Or don't you remember what they have suffered under the last sheriff? They were
taxed and tortured within an inch of their lives, Thoresby. Have
you forgotten?"

Thoresby looked at me. I shook my head and opened my
mouth to defend Thoresby, say something to allow for Rob's
short words and shorter temper, but Thoresby's eyes went to
my neck.

My hand ran quick to it, covering up where I thought I had
done. "It's not—" I started, but Thoresby shook his head.

"You don't owe me any kind of explanation." He looked to
Rob. "We all want to see these people safe and protected, Robin.
And evidently, we all fail in our own ways." He sighed again,
tucking his hands round back behind him. "Use the barn as
long as you like."

Thoresby left, and the children laughed at something John
said.

Rob turned and slammed his foot against the nearest stall
door. It wrenched with an awful noise, and the whole thing
shattered, throwing chunks to the ground and leaving rough
pieces hanging on the hinge. Thank God there weren't no
horse in there, or Rob would have been kicked something
awful.

The children stopped laughing.

"Go on home," Much said to them. "We'll be back again,
when you see the ribbon at the well. Be careful."

John started herding them out, and I crossed my arms. Rob snapped another bit of wood, color moving 'cross his face, wild and harsh. He bent down to grab another piece, and I cursed at him, rushing forward.

I hit the wood from his hands and pushed him, pressing him up against the wall, my hands on his shoulders. It weren't a fierce grip, not like John might, but it were enough to stop him. "What are you doing?" I snapped.

He pushed up, using my grip against me and moving me back with his shoulders in my hands, powerful and strong but gentle. My back nudged the other wall and he pressed closer, leaning against me. His breath were rough and hot and puffed over my cheek, my ear, my neck.

My hands curled slow around him, drawing him close to me, tight against me. "What are you doing, Rob?" I whispered.

He tucked his face into my shoulder and drew long, shuddering breaths. "We're not going to make it through this, Scar. Not another sheriff. Not another nightmare." His voice dropped, and if it weren't for the way the words slipped along my skin, I would have doubted he spoke them. "I'm not going to make it through this again."

I sighed against him, trying to think of the right thing to say. "Someone tried to hurt Missy," I told him soft. He went tense, but I twisted my fingers through his hair to keep him still and silent. "She fought him off. She saved herself." He looked at me, a tendril of hope like a deep current in his eyes.

"*We* will make it through this, because you aren't alone. I'm with you, the lads are with you, and now the town is with you. If Missy Morgan can fight a man, we will make it through this."

"What happened to Missy?" John asked, scowling into the horse stall where Rob and I were twined up against each other like ivy run wild.

"Nothing, and that's the point," I told him, pulling from Rob gentle.

Rob caught my hand and held it, tipping it up and pressing a kiss into the palm. He ran his thumb over the big vein there on my wrist, and it rippled through me like a shock.

"I'm going to go to the castle," I told them. "Thoresby said the prince is coming."

"I'll go with you," John said.

"No, I'll be well enough. Place is bare guarded now."

"Save for the knights," Much said.

I shrugged. "They're lazy."

John stared hard at me, even as Rob nodded. "You'll be all right. Go on so you're back before nightfall."

I broke John's gaze at that.

"Bring us news of the men," Much said.

Nodding, I said, "You lot headed back to the monastery?"

"You go. Much, will you help me tidy up a bit first?" Rob asked.

Much went to it, and I went for the door.

"You're not coming back before nightfall, are you?"

Lifting a shoulder, I saw John behind me. "I'll be back, John."

He met my eyes, dark and heavy. "Don't hurry."

I nodded, swallowing though it hurt my swollen throat. I went out the door and off for the castle, stealing myself some precious time to be alone and think.

CHAPTER

THREE

~o~

Even if the forest had turned, cold and dark were two things
that still had love for me, and by the time I made my purpose-
ful slow way to Nottingham Castle, both had fallen around
me like a cloak.

The snow made climbing the castle wall a bit harder;
sometimes the rocks were slick where I couldn't tell, and my
hands slipped and tore from the rocks, red and raw and sore. I
didn't mind it much—it seemed the one thing that were still
simple, that if I went slow and steady I'd still get what I were
after. Like much of the winter in Nottinghamshire, it had tricks
up its sleeve, but it weren't beyond my reach. On the wall, in
the wind, high above the earth, I still knew myself and what I
were meant for.

Cresting the wall, I felt the cold wind rush over me like a
victory song. I sat there for a moment, surveying the three

baileys at once. Three stacked, fortified courtyards; each one led to a better-guarded, higher part of the castle, surrounded by nothing but the sheer rock wall meant to keep armies out. The upper bailey were dark and quiet cold; it hadn't been much used these long months. After the day when life flipped on its ears, when the lads and I set explosions to crumble the Great Hall and the sheriff died and I earned myself a shiny reminder of my bond with Gisbourne, the castle had been empty. More than half of the middle bailey had been impassable from the wall what Much and John brought down, and the bailiff, the only person left to run the castle, moved his quarters to the lowermost bailey.

Then the knights had come. More than a month past, the knights had trotted up from London on the orders of the prince, to rebuild the castle under the charge of the bailiff, a man who didn't much want to hurt anyone. The knights took men from the towns to do the work, and food and drink besides to feed themselves; they were allowed to do whatever they pleased until the wall were finished and a new sheriff were appointed.

And so they occupied the low bailey, filling one set of barracks with their ranks and the other barracks with the men of the county. Including most of the men of Edwinstowe and Worksop.

I went to the food store on the lower bailey. I'd found it some months before, and despite the heavy lock on the front of it, I could sneak in through the high windows that weren't never guarded. Jumping and catching the sill, I hauled myself up and dropped inside.

It were a lick warmer than outside; the kitchens were near, and the heat from the fires kept the place a touch more livable. Wooden shelves stacked high to the ceiling were sagging with the weight of the fat of the land—grains of every sort, drying meat hung in great lines, stores of wine and oil and ale along with butter and eggs. They kept the milk in the kitchens day by day, but I sometimes managed to nick some of that as well.

Stealing through, I collected some flour, oats, dried meat, and meal, padding my shirt and thin coat with them.

The front door to the food cellar were locked, but there were a little back stair that connected up to the kitchens. I took it, twisting to the side to make it up the narrow steps. I slowed down, my steps turning careful near the door. There were a light shining on beneath the bottom edge of the door, and I heard voices, seeping through with the warm heat from the other side.

Tripping the latch, I eased the door open slow. In the crack I could see two cooks, bent over a flour-strewn table, pounding dough.

"Soon enough we will," one said, *pound-pound-pound.* She were tall and red cheeked and thin, a proper opposite to the one across from her, round and short with small eyes that never left her task.

The other laughed. "Not never soon enough!" she said. She tossed a lump of dough onto a pile.

"With any luck the prince'll bring his own cooks with him, and we won't be much use."

"Hush with that talk," the second said. "I need this coin."

"If the new sheriff is anything like the last, I won't need the coin *that* bad," the first said. *Pound-pound-pound. Pound-pound-pound.*

"There ain't no new sheriff yet, they said. Said the prince is coming to pick one."

"Well, don't that sound like a merry picnic," the first said, and they both had a laugh. Then she pointed farther than I could see. "Over there," she said.

The second cook went over to whatever she were pointing at, and as the first raised her fist to *pound-pound-pound*, I pushed open the door and ran past them, nothing but a shadow in the corner of her eye.

The kitchens were connected to the soldier's hall with a narrow walk, but I didn't want to go in there. There were a big fire in there, and knights were almost always lumped around it, talking and drinking and trying to charm extra food from the cooks.

Going back out into the cold were welcome and oversharp both. The night were clear and worth more than a single shiver.

I went round the soldier's hall to the first set of barracks, finding a window and sidling close. Propping my foot on a stone in the wall I jumped, grabbing the bars and hauling up to peer in.

The bit of light that were streaming in from the moon

behind me were eaten up by the fire in the room, red and glowing and catching on shining armor and velvet cloaks.

I let the bars go. Wrong barracks.

Going over to the next one, I did it again and looked inside. No fire and nothing much shining.

My arms burned but I held tight, scuffling my feet up the wall till I were all tucked in the window.

"Scar?" I heard.

I twisted a little so I weren't between the moon and the men, and the light came through the window. "Godfrey?" I asked.

He nodded, standing on his cot to come closer to me.

"How you lot faring?" I asked soft.

"Not well," he said. "Tired and hungry. A few men are sick."

"What sort of sick?" I asked. I pulled out the little packages, the dried meat and oats. They couldn't do much with the flour and meal; I'd save that for the town. I slipped it through the bars.

"Coughing mostly. Martin Dyer's been casting up his accounts for days."

Men were drifting toward the window, taking the food as others opened it and parceled it out. "What news?" called one man. "What of our families?"

"Everyone's well," I assured them. "We've been taking care of them. Food's a mite scarce but ain't no one starving, no one's hurt. How close are you to finishing the work?"

Godfrey sighed. "Close. They've been working us damn hard lately. I think they want it done soon. You know I don't think I'd have been so happy to see half the wall fall if I knew we'd have to rebuild the lot of it through the winter."

I looked up at the full, laughing moon, mocking me from its far safe perch. "I wouldn't never have asked it, if I knew," I agreed. "And these damn knights are eating the shire out of house and home and never pay a farthing for it."

"Just keep our girls safe, young Scarlet," Hugh Morgan called to me. "It isn't hardly wise to have knights roaming around who think they own everything without men at home."

"I promise," I said. I did as best I could. I didn't want to tell him that some of *his* daughters were the sort that fancied marrying a knight and didn't take my advice as much as I'd choose.

With most of the men taking their bit of food, they drifted away from the windows, and Godfrey leaned up closer. "How's Rob?" he asked.

Godfrey Mason had been with us in the caves when the nightmares had started. They weren't as bad then; the forest and fresh air had calmed him, I thought. But it weren't so in the closeness of the monastery.

"He's fine," I said, but the words caught in my mouth like it were mud.

"Any word from Gisbourne?"

We hadn't heard from Gisbourne in months. He'd left an animal for me in the forest, a fox staked out on a tree with a knife through its heart. Then he went to London, far as I knew. "No," I said.

"There's been talk around here," he said. "The maids said Gisbourne's things have been sent up to the castle."

I looked at him. "What?"

"And the prince is coming. Everyone's talking of it."

"I heard. Didn't know that Gisbourne were coming back." I couldn't stop a shiver from running over me like a wave.

His hands slipped from the bars like a creature going back to sea. "I'm glad I could do something, at least."

"Thank you," I told him.

I twisted on the window ledge and jumped down, holding the flour tight to my belly before setting off to the upper bailey. The middle bailey had been so long broken that no one much had been up here, and it were quiet and safe, the way I ain't never known this place to be. The Great Hall were full fixed, the caved-in roof patched over. The residences stood dark and empty, and I went in them slow like phantoms might guard the place.

The sheriff's room, the grandest in the place, were empty, but it were clear the maids had been through here, scrubbing floors and laying fresh rushes, putting up the heavy winter bedclothes and tapestries. Logs were piled beside cold fireplaces, and the whole place were clean and fresh.

Gisbourne's room looked just as it had, like time had frozen with the winter, only there were two large trunks now at the foot of the bed with a fresh stuffed mattress and newly tight bed ropes.

The thief in me wanted to go through his things, look at his treasures like he weren't someone I were so afraid of, but I couldn't. I sat cross-legged on the top of the trunk, as if sitting there and keeping his coffers closed could keep him from coming back.

We were supposed to have time. We'd paid dear, in blood and promises that took my soul with them. We'd tumbled the wall, we'd watched the sheriff die—it was all supposed to have meant something.

But it weren't better. It well may have been worse.

I twisted the gold band on my finger, hating it anew. My time had run out, and my husband were returning to Nottinghamshire.

CHAPTER

FOUR

~⚬~

I went to Tuck's, slipping in the back door, hoping for the noise and heat and familiar smell of the lot of the men. But it weren't so; Tuck were alone, wiping down the bar.

"It's late, Scar," he said, offering me up a smile.

As if I needed such reminding. I yawned. "Went to Nottingham," I said.

"Want some soup?"

Ever since months past when one of his pies had made me retch up, all Tuck ever gave me were soup and broth and the occasional stew. I didn't mind; my belly seemed to take it better than slabs of meat or sweets and such. I nodded, and he ducked into the back for a bit.

Right then, John came thundering down the stairs, and Bess were flying after him. "John!" she cried.

"No!" he hollered, flapping an arm like it were a wing.

"Leave off, Bess. Just give me a moment's rest from your torture."

She slumped her round hip against the banister. "Really, John. I just need more time."

"Or maybe you don't. Maybe needing more time is all the answer I need."

"That barely makes sense, John," she said. She shook her head and went back up the stairs.

He heaved out a sigh and turned, sat on the stairs, and shoved his big head into his hands. His fingers worked through his hair and he lifted his head.

"Christ," he grunted. "What the hell are you doing here, Scarlet?"

I lifted my shoulders, and he pushed off the stairs, coming closer to me. He sat beside me and stared at my neck.

I covered it with my hands. "Mind your business, John."

"Not going back tonight?" he asked.

"Later," I said.

"It's already later," he told me.

Tuck came back out with a big bowl of soup for me, and I set into it while Tuck laughed at John. "Kicked you out, did she?"

John just glowered, but I looked to Tuck. "You mean Bess? What's going on?"

"Mind your business; wasn't that what you said?" John snapped at me.

Tuck's belly rolled with his laughs. "You foolish young

things," he said, shaking his head. "So tell me of the menfolk, Scarlet."

I swallowed a mouthful of soup. "They're well enough. A few are taking sick, but they're not ill cared for. Most are just worried and eager to be out. Seems they'll be done soon enough. Wall's almost finished."

"Maybe then the louts they call knights will hightail it back to London," John grumbled.

"Not likely," said Tuck, settling himself into a seat. "They're settled and can live for free—very tough to shake them off. Not that I'm complaining; they still bring coin to drink here."

"Until they run out of coin and decide the Crown needs your ale," I reminded him.

He shrugged. "That day, I'll mind."

"Any other news?" John asked.

Gisbourne's coming back. I opened my mouth to tell him, but I didn't want to speak the words aloud. "The prince will name a new sheriff when he comes."

John whistled. "That's news."

"Who do you reckon it will be?" Tuck asked. "Has to be a landholder, right?"

"Right," I said. "It's meant to be a landholder in the county, but if there were someone the prince wanted for the job, it's easy enough to have it done. Rob got Thoresby to petition the prince, but I don't know if he'll choose him."

"At least Thoresby knows the people," Tuck said. "But I can't think he'd be so natural at being sheriff."

"He'd be fair," I said with a shrug.

"You mean he'd listen to Robin Hood," Tuck said.

"Rob's fair."

John's eyes went to my neck, and him looking made Tuck look. Tuck stood up, his body tight, making me remember how much of him were muscle. "Rob didn't do that to you, did he, Scarlet? Figured you got into a scrape, which ain't unusual for you."

"It's not like that, Tuck," I said, but I weren't much good at lying about it yet.

He looked to John. "John, tell me the truth."

"Rob's had some rough nights, Tuck. He didn't know what he was doing, but he did it," John said, staring at the bar.

Tuck's eyes were hard on John, like somehow it were his fault, but Tuck nodded. "Scar, you'll stay here till the morning. We've got extra beds."

Beds that were warm and safe besides. I wanted to—it would be so simple to just nod and go upstairs, but I shook my head. "I'll go back, Tuck. It's not the way you think."

His big paw fell on mine, and I looked up at him. "Scarlet. I've known my fair share of rough men, and I know Rob ain't that. But you don't give him the chance to do it twice, you understand? You'll stay here."

Being told what to do made me want to run out and do anything but. "Tuck, stay out of it," I told him sharp. "You don't know what's going on. And I wouldn't never give up on Rob because he's had a bad time."

Tuck shook his head. "There's no two ways about bruises, Scar."

I glared at him. "There ain't no two ways about loyalty." I sighed, shaking my head. "It's a bad situation, Tuck. We all know that. But I believe in Robin almost as much as the Almighty. And I won't give up on him."

Tuck turned to John. "She goes, you go with her."

John sighed and leaned back in his seat, but he nodded. Tuck tossed his towel down. "Drop the bowl in the kitchen when you're done, Scar. I'm going to bed."

"Can I make you stay here?" John asked.

"No. Can I make you tell me 'bout Bess?"

He chuckled. "Not a chance."

—⚊—

John walked me back to the monastery, quiet as we made slow work of the crunching, frozen ground. When we reached the grounds, he turned to the warming room and I just nodded toward the infirmary. He met my eyes, and they understood more than I liked. He nodded to me.

The infirmary were empty of needy souls, and so there weren't a fire in there. Still, there were blankets and cots and I took both, curling up in a corner and sleeping. It had been an awful long day, and I just wanted a few moments of true rest.

When I woke, the sun were up and I could hear the monks moving about outside and the bell ringing. I felt colder than when I went to sleep, and figured it might be worth the risk to go to the warming room now. Rob wouldn't be there still.

I went quiet from the infirmary, pushing on the door to see a body blocking the other side of it.

"Rob," I whispered. My heart started to pound, but it weren't like I were afraid of him. I only didn't want him knowing why I might choose to sleep in a cold empty room rather than with the band. Didn't want him even thinking on it.

"Morning, Scar," he said.

Slipping out the door, I let it shut behind me and sat beside him slow. The sun were fair warm, and it weren't as cold as most days. He looked at me, his ocean eyes stormy and wide. His hands went slowly up and he looked at my neck, wincing like I hit him when he caught it full. It felt worse. "Christ Almighty, Scar," he said, letting his hands fall.

"What's happening to you, Rob?" I asked. My voice fell so soft I weren't sure he heard. "I don't care about the bruises. I don't. I been bruised before. I'm just so frightened for you."

"These nightmares, Scar. I don't know what to do."

"Please, Rob, can't you tell me of them?"

He shook his head, slowly. "I don't even know how, Scarlet. I would give you everything I am, but I can't say these things."

I moved closer to him and curled against his body, and he rested his head on mine. "I love you, Rob, don't you know that?" I whispered.

"I know. I love you too. I wouldn't wish that on a soul, but

I love you more than anything, Scar. And I'd die if I . . . if I ever . . . ," he said.

"No dying," I said. Truth was, I didn't want him to finish that bit. I didn't want to know what he thought he might be capable of doing to me. Not with Gisbourne back, not with the prince coming. I couldn't lose the safety of Robin's arms. "We just need you to sleep. Maybe you should try Brother Ralf's tincture."

His fingers ran along my arm, and even through so many clothes it burned and made me feel like I was some delicate, precious thing. "I've seen men on such sleeping draughts," he told me. "It dulls everything. If the knights caused trouble, I'd be useless. I'd go sleeping right through."

"Rob," I whispered. "It ain't the nighttime we need to worry after. We need you to rest so you can lead. Nothing would happen to you while you slept." I turned a little and sniffed my nose against his cheek. "And if it did, I would defend you with my life."

Both his arms came around me, hauling me over him to sit a step lower than him, between his legs with his body tight around mine. He rested his head on my neck and I leaned back against him, resting my elbows on his knees. "I'll do it for you, Scarlet. I'll talk to Ralf today."

I trembled but I nodded my head, twisting my eyes shut tight. *Please*, I prayed. *Let this work. Let him just need sleep. Let me defend him and his hero's heart.*

"It's strange," he said low in my ear. "When night falls my

chest is full of fear, but holding you like this, Scar, I can't help but feel grateful. Joyous. By the light of day, I still cannot fathom that I'm the one you love."

I turned a little to look at him. "I do love you. I always will." I found myself staring at his mouth, my breath gone, desperate to kiss him and see what it felt like, to love a body so very much and have your lips touch, to taste him.

I ducked my head down, shutting my eyes tight and feeling a shudder like pain go through my bones. I weren't going to risk God's wrath more by having adultery added to my sins.

His arms squeezed tight around me, and I weren't sure if he knew my mind, but it felt like he understood.

—⁑—

I were on my way to Edwinstowe already when I saw a body darting through the woods. I hid and watched, but soon enough called out when I realized who it were. "Will!" I yelled. "Will Clarke!"

The fair-headed boy stopped.

"You running for me?" I asked, going over to him.

He nodded, red cheeked and huffing. "I saw 'im," he gasped. "I saw him!"

My breath flew. "Where?"

"On the road. To. To Notting. Ham," he huffed.

"How long?"

He put his fists on his hips, thinking. "S'long as it took me to run," he told me.

I nodded and set off running. He groaned and started running behind me. "Go home, Will!" I yelled. He kept on running.

"Mam says he'll kill you!" he shouted.

"He'll kill you first!" I yelled, and I heard his footsteps slow. "Thank you, Will!" I shouted, and ran on, leaping over a fallen tree.

Sure as sunups, Gisbourne were in Nottingham Castle. The whole place were in a tizzy for him too. Maids running every which way. Knights kitted up in full order. He left quick as he came, though, on a fresh horse and headed straight for Edwinstowe.

I tracked him with a wide berth. He didn't bother anyone in the village, and he just went straight to Tuck's. I were fair far back when I saw him go in, but I ran for the place then, slipping in the back and staying low.

No one were screaming, which were a fair good sign.

"—all. I trust you'll give him the message."

Someone touched my arm, and I turned to see Rob crouching beside me, John behind him. John pushed a finger against his mouth, and I glared at him. Did he think I were thick? What were I like to do, announce myself?

"Yes, milord," Tuck said.

There were footsteps, and a moment later Tuck called, "John? Rob? You still back there?"

They stood and I stood with them. "Scar too," John said.

"How much of that did you lot catch?" he asked.

We came to the front side of the bar. "None," I said.

"He said he wants to meet with Robin," John said. "After Vespers, at the well."

"Vespers? He said Vespers?" I asked. "Do you think he knows about the monastery? Or the ribbons and the barn?"

"Vespers is just faster than saying a little after sunset, and the well is a central place," Tuck said with a shrug. "He probably doesn't."

"What else?" I asked. "Did he say what he's about?"

"No. Just said he reckoned I knew how to get a message to Robin Hood."

Rob's hands settled on my shoulders, his body warm along my back. "It has to be some sort of a trap."

"He doesn't have men with him; I'm sure he's free to use the knights, but he doesn't have men of his own," I told Rob, turning to look at him.

He crossed his arms, frowning at me. "Oh? How long have you known he was back?"

My face ran hot. "I heard things. Just found out he were back today."

"And you didn't tell me." His eyes met mine, and I looked away. "Of course you didn't," he said, and this were low and sad.

Much burst into the room. "Rob! Rob! Gisbourne's back!"

We all just stared at him.

"Little late, Much," John told him. "He wants to meet with Rob."

"Well, all of us," I said. "It ain't like you're going alone."

"You're not going," John and Rob said at the same time.

"Of course she is," Much said. "Even if you ignore the fact that whatever he wants from Rob will definitely have something to do with Scar, don't be stupid and think she'd be at home knitting, lads. Better to know where she is."

"Thank you," I told Much. He grinned at me.

"Up high and well armed," Rob said.

"Fine," I said. "But don't think I'll sit idly by if he tries something."

"We wouldn't expect you to ever keep yourself out of needless danger, Scar. Don't worry," John said.

I glared at him.

"Am I the only one who thinks we just shouldn't bother? Who gives a damn what he has to say? I'll kill this or hurt that—doesn't that pretty much cover it?" John asked.

"Why come back at all?" I said. "He's been gone for months."

They all looked at me.

"Oh, for Heaven's sake, I don't think he cares that we're married."

"No man doesn't care that he's married," John grunted, looking at the stairs. "Much is right, whatever it is definitely has to do with Scar. Without a sheriff to hire him on as a thief taker, he doesn't have any interest in Nottinghamshire."

"Well, he can't have Scar. No matter what," Rob said, looking at me. "I think we have to find out what he wants. He

simply causes too much carnage for us to ignore him entirely."
I looked down and Rob came closer, catching my hand and
running his fingers through mine. "Can you do this?"

I nodded, meeting his eyes. "I'm not afraid of him."

Rob leaned closer and kissed my cheek.

"Let's get going," Rob said. "We need to get to the monastery and back by sunset."

—⁓—

After such strange quiet in the past few months, it felt fair
right to be walking through Sherwood, armed to the teeth the
four of us. John and I went high on rooftops and Much were
hidden behind a house while Robin stayed behind another
house.

Gisbourne rode in alone on a dark gray horse, and I gave
Much a nod. He started to move round the back to look for
Gisbourne's fellows. "Do I have an audience with the elusive
Master Hood?"

"Yes," Rob said, still hidden.

"And I imagine my darling wife is here as well. Missed me,
Marian?"

John caught my eye and shook his head before I moved. I
scowled evil at him.

"You can talk to me, Gisbourne," Rob said.

He smiled. "You can call me Lord Leaford now, Hood,"
Gisbourne said.

Angry heat rushed over me, and I raised myself over the

edge of the roof. "What have you done to my father, Gisbourne?" I yelled, even over John swearing at me.

Gisbourne looked up and touched his fingers to his forehead, mocking a bow to me. "Apparently it's easier than I thought to draw you out, my dear."

The sight of him made my scar itch. He looked well enough—a little thinner, but still tall, harsh, clothed entirely in black with spots of silver gleaming from his weapons, his fastenings, his sword belt. I had spent so long fighting this man, running from him, fearing him, and he were here, alone. He almost seemed unimpressive.

I couldn't help peering round him to look for some sort of ambush. I caught sight of Much, and he shrugged and shook his head.

"I'm alone," Gisbourne assured. "I called for Robin to speak to you, in fact."

"Speak."

"No pleasantries? Haven't you missed me, wife? Everyone at court was quite devastated to have missed the wedding. I accepted their best wishes on your behalf, naturally."

"Tell me what you did to my father, Gisbourne!"

"You needn't worry about him," Gisbourne said. "Lord Leaford is quite unharmed. I only meant that when I married you I assumed the land and title that were promised in our contract—something, you'll be delighted to learn, that gave me the right to petition the prince for the position of sheriff."

My heart went to lead in my chest. I hadn't thought of that.

"Which he is coming to Nottinghamshire to give to me, within a few days. And when he arrives, you will be living under my roof like a proper, dutiful wife."

"Like hell I will!" I roared.

He threw his head back and laughed. "I've missed this, sweeting. Witty banter. Well, I needn't remind you of the cruelty I can inflict upon your people as sheriff. Clearly it's even entered your mind what I could do to your parents, your home, and dependents as the rightful landholder. But I won't force you with violence, my love. I will entice you."

"I doubt that," I snapped back.

Even through the dusk, his dark eyes glittered fierce. "We can play these games all I want, Marian, but we both know you don't want to be married to me. You married me to save Robin's life, and I will offer you a bargain—perhaps the Devil's bargain, as it were."

He took a breath, still smiling at me.

"I'll annul our marriage as soon as the prince leaves if you live with me while he is here."

Hope rushed fast like a flood into my chest. An annulment? I could live with Robin without the cloud of sin over us. I could *marry* Robin.

"You'd kill me," I said. "There's no trusting you. The second I was close enough you'd gut me like a deer."

He shrugged. "My temper can get the better of me, of course, but I don't intend to kill you. Besides, I recall you telling me you were rather difficult to kill, yes?"

"Why would you even want this, Gisbourne?" I asked. "It's a fool offer."

"You have my word that I won't kill you, and that once the prince leaves you will have your annulment. Should you accept, you will dress, speak, act, and be fully disarmed the way a lady befitting your station should. These are my terms, and if you would accept them, you need only come to the castle and join me in my chambers."

"Tell me why."

"Why isn't important," he told me, smiling a little. "The only thing you need to consider is what you're willing to do to marry your dear hero. Because trust me, love, you'll never get an annulment from me otherwise. And if this doesn't go the way I want and you are not under my roof, when I become sheriff I will have no guarantee for what blood my displeasure will purchase. I'm being—what's the word—kind." He smirked at me in the darkness. "You're looking quite fetching these days. I can see your scar from here. Lovely."

I turned from him, hiding behind the ridge of the roof. He laughed, and it were ghoulish and echoed round me in the dark.

"Feeling shy, love?" Gisbourne taunted.

"She gave you her answer," Rob said. "You can go. Unless you would like for us to entice *you*."

"Think about it, Marian," he called. "All the red ribbons you could want. Though I imagine your hair is a little too short for them since our last encounter."

Frowning, I pushed my hair off my face. It were wild, never staying tied back since Gisbourne had thought he could use it to hold me and I'd cut it off to be free of him.

I reckoned he left then. I didn't hear nothing more, but I didn't move from the roof none.

John called up to me but it were Robin that climbed the roof, taking my hand. "You're not going anywhere near him, Scar. We'll find another way."

I nodded and sniffed, and he tugged my hand and we climbed down, side by side. He held fast to my hand the long way back to the monastery, and I loved it. I wanted him near me more than anything.

He showed me the vial the monk had given him as we took out the bedrolls and set them near the fire. "He said I'll sleep sound," he told me. "You don't have to be afraid of me, Scar."

I tucked close along his side as he drank it down. "I weren't never afraid of you, Rob," I said. It were a lie, I think. But it were truth in the notion that the fear weren't never what I chose to hold to. I loved him more than I feared his dreams.

When we laid our bedrolls out, I nudged mine closer to Rob, and he nudged his closer to mine till they slid together and looked like one bed. When we laid down, his arm slid over my hips and snugged me close, his chin hooked over my shoulder and his breath rushed over my neck, like every bit of him were slipping around me and binding us together.

This were what two souls merging into one were meant to feel like.

I wanted to stay awake, to treasure this, to roll it over in my mind till I had picked up every little bit of it, like baling hay. But it were just moments before I fell asleep, safe in his heart.

CHAPTER

FIVE

I woke in some strange form of hell. The fire weren't all out; it were glowing and red and making red glow around me. But Robin weren't behind me, he were on top of me and screaming. His fist crashed down over my face and I yelled too, finding my legs and bucking him off me. I reached for the knife I kept by my pillow when I saw it flash in his hand.

"Scar!" yelled Much as Rob lunged for me.

I swung my leg down and kicked his out so he fell. The knife skittered and Much ran for it. I jumped on Rob, pinning his arms down. "Robin!" I shrieked. "Rob!"

He roared like a gutted animal. He twisted his leg up and kicked me hard in the belly. I fell off him and he followed, slamming his bear paw on my face again. I rolled him, punching him back and hitting him so hard in the face it made pain rush up my arm.

"Scar, get him outside!" Much yelled.

Rob rolled me again, but I were ready this time and tucked both my legs up to push him hard back. I leapt up, dizzy and swimming, and grabbed Much's good hand and ran.

We ran for the door and the night and the snow, and Rob followed us, grabbing my hair as we opened the door.

I swallowed a scream but fought tooth and nail to get outside, letting him crush me into the snow.

The moment the snow hit us he sucked in a hard gasp and rolled off of me. "Scar?" Much called. "Scar?"

I pushed up off the snow, and it were stained with red where my face were. I were shaking hard and when I tried, my legs wouldn't hold me none, and I fell to the stone in the cloisters.

Much stripped off his overshirt and stuffed it with snow, bringing it back to me and pressing it to my face. Rob were down the row, huffing and trying to breathe and I couldn't help him. My bones were shaking so hard I thought they'd tear straight apart.

"Don't let him see," I mumbled to Much. "Please."

Much were whiter than the snow, but he nodded.

Rob turned toward us. "Scar," he said, like his mouth were half full of rocks.

Much stood over me, blocking me from him. "Just go inside, Rob," he said quiet.

"Where's John?"

"I don't know," Much answered. "Please, go inside."

I heard Rob's breath still huffing out hard. Then I heard his feet scuff over the stone and the door creak open.

Much turned back to me, but I were bent over my body, heartbroken and bleeding and letting rivers run from my eyes, cursing the day they tortured Rob and brought back whatever phantom he were fighting now. They had tortured him and now it were torturing me too.

—⁂—

Much went back in after a while. The monks filed past me for their prayers at sunup. Then John came along and found me, and his face went flat and he went into the warming room.

I heard raised voices and smacks and thuds. Heat and shame rushed up and I stood, wobbling on my legs, wavering toward the door that didn't look so fearful in the daylight. My body hollered at me, my stomach turning and rolling. I went into the warming room to find John and Rob with their shirtfronts caught up in each other's fists, bellowing in each other's faces.

"Stop," I said, and they both fair shocked me by obeying. Rob saw me and he went slack and more than a bit green.

John let him go, and Rob just hung there like God were a puppet master making a toy with his body. John could bare contain himself; he were huffing through his nose like a bull in pasture.

"You have to go," Rob said. I knew he said it to me; he were looking right at me, but I couldn't imagine he meant it for me.

We all looked at him. "What?" I squeaked.

"You have to go," he said again, swallowing whatever were stuck in his pipes. He looked at me and away. "All of you. I want you to go to Tuck's and stay there."

"No," I spat. "Don't be daft."

"*Daft?*" he growled. "Daft? I beat you within an inch of your *life* and you'd stay here, but I'm crazy? You want me to do it again, is that it?" His voice raised. "Do you want me to kill you?"

John pushed Rob hard, and he hit the wall.

"Rob!" I yelled, and it made me hurt everywhere. "We don't leave each other. You made me promise to stay when all I wanted to do was run, Rob, and that were the hardest thing I've ever done. Don't make me break that oath."

Rob straightened up, staying farther from me. "No," he said. "No. This isn't the same. This is your safety and my sanity, so you leave or I will, Scar. Tuck will take you in, but I don't trust myself there." He swallowed again. "I don't trust myself anywhere."

"I won't go, Rob," I told him. "Why can't we fight this together?"

"Because it's not your fight, Scar!" he yelled. "You can't fight this for me. And I can't fight this with you."

His eyes stared at me, wide and lost, and I felt like every rope tied between us were snapping. I felt bloodless, like I hadn't anything inside me but bones and air.

Rob's eyes dashed away from me. "John, you'll take her to Tuck's."

"I won't come back here, Rob," he told him. "Not for a few nights at the least. I can't even look at you right now."

My eyes dropped to the floor like my gaze were weighted with stone. There were nothing between us all but quiet.

"Much, go with them," Rob said.

Much swallowed, but he nodded.

John's big feet shuffled close to me, and he let me lean on him. "Come on," he told me. "We're going now. Much, can you gather everything up?"

Much nodded. "I'll meet you there."

I wanted to yell—to scream that I would stay, that I wouldn't leave him, that I didn't much care if it killed me.

But I didn't. I let John herd me out, and I didn't say a thing more, my voice tiny and trapped inside me.

John led me outside like I were a child, and he walked slow beside me, watching me.

"I'm fine, you big lug," I murmured.

"You're not. He beat you," he said, and it turned into a snarl. "Christ, I want to kill him."

"He weren't himself."

"I know that. I don't care about that." His fist went tight. "And I wasn't there to help. And I'm *furious* that somehow this is my responsibility, to be there when everyone is damn well sleeping so that the man *you love* won't beat you. This isn't fair, Scarlet. It is awful to somehow be part of you and Rob. To protect you from him. And I can't do that anymore. I can't." He threw a punch at nothing, batting away the cold. "I loved you, do you know that?"

He looked at me, but I fixed on the ground. "You never loved me," I told him soft. "You fancied me, but it weren't the same."

"No, Scar. I *loved* you, but it wasn't enough. Love isn't enough. There has to be other things there, like choice, and duty. I keep thinking these things, Scar—I think about having a family. What it would be like, to be a father. I want that more than anything. That role—it's more important than everything mashed up together."

I dared look up at him. "You'd be an uncommon good father, John," I told him.

His shoulders lifted a bit. "Do you think?" he asked, his voice awful quiet.

"I just said so, didn't I?"

"Bess is with child," he said soft. "My child—"

"John!" I yelled, and winced at the pain that shot through my face. "Ow."

He smirked. "Easy. I asked her to marry me—to make a right family of it all—and she hasn't said yes yet. And waiting for her answer, Scar, it burns. Every second burns. Because maybe she won't. Maybe all my sins have piled up so high I'm beyond saving, and I'm not supposed to have a family." I started to protest—of all the damn things!—but he shook his head. "And my point is that maybe if you have the chance to annul your marriage, you should take it. Rob's crazier than a bag full of cats right now, but he loves you. And it has to be killing him that he can't be to you what he wants to be, because love *isn't* enough. You have to choose that person. You have to choose them every damn day. I made my choice—you have to make yours."

That were it, the thing that had been rolling round my mind like a loose marble. "You think I should take Gisbourne's offer." Shivers ran through me as I thought of that day in the castle, when he had me by the throat, squeezing, and his growled words: *I want to see you die. I want to see the light tamp out of those devil's eyes.*

"No," he said, kicking a branch out of his path. "No. I don't think you should go to Gisbourne. I don't think you should go back to Rob. I don't think you're getting anything done by staying at Tuck's. There isn't a right way here, Scar, but if I were Rob . . . I'd want that annulment more than anything." He looked at me. "The monks said you were asking about how to get out of a marriage. Seems you want this annulment too."

"I do," I admitted. "And sometimes I think, there ain't nothing what I can't take, thinking on all we've already been through. What could Gisbourne possibly do that I couldn't take?"

"Kill you," he said quiet.

"He wants something. It's such a strange offer, he wouldn't make it just to kill me."

"He well might, Scarlet. But say he is telling the truth. There are other ways he could hurt you."

I remembered listening to the things my sister had to do in London, the way men touched her. It pushed blood into my cheeks and made me shiver. "Not if he wants an annulment."

"*You* want the annulment. What if *he* doesn't really want an annulment?"

My shoulders shrugged up, but I didn't answer him.

"You're already married, Scar. If he can't—or won't—swear before a priest that you're still a virgin, there is no annulment. That's all it takes. He outweighs you by more than a hundred pounds, at least. If he comes after you in close quarters, there isn't much you and your knives can do about it."

I were starting to sway, my head dizzying round.

"I know I'm scaring you, Scar, even if you can't admit it. You should be scared. You have a lot of fight ahead of you no matter which way you go."

Rubbing my arms didn't do nothing for the cold, for the hot swirl in my head. "I'm tired of fighting, John."

"We've all been fighting more than our fair share, Scar. Maybe both of us should start fighting for our happy ending."

My eyes shut and my eyeballs felt like ice behind them, like little bits of my eye had gone to frost. "What if there ain't an end, and it ain't happy besides?" I asked him. "How could it be, after all this?"

"I don't know, Scar."

"Can we stop?" I said. My stomach were overtight and rolling and twisting. "I think . . . ugh," I whined, bending over, ready to cast up anything that remained in my belly. Nothing came up, but the pain didn't ease and the world were sliding round me.

"Come on, we need to get you out of the cold," he said, tugging my arm.

I straightened, standing on wobbly knees. My head beat a

cruel tattoo, and it were choking me. "J-John——" I never got a chance to finish the thought, as the dark trees and bright day pushed together and changed to total dark.

—⚏—

My eyes were bare open before my belly twisted and I retched. I were in a bed, and the best place seemed to be off the side of it. Lucky there were a pot there, and someone set my face toward it.

When I were done, I looked, and it were Ellie, one of Tuck's girls. She petted the duck feathers left of my hair where I'd cut it off months before. "You all right?" she asked.

I shut my eyes and hugged the pillow, but the lumps Rob had put on me yelled in protest and I rolled onto my back. "Christ," I moaned.

"Sit up a bit," she told me. "Tuck sent some broth up."

I obeyed, though I didn't much feel like it. She pushed a bowl at me and I reached to grab it when I saw one hand was covered with bandages hard and stiff. "What . . . ?" I asked her.

She shrugged. "Brother from the monastery said you broke your hand."

My chest felt like it cracked open. My hand were broken? I couldn't throw knives. I couldn't . . . Christ, I could barely defend myself. My hands shook as I took the bowl from her.

Ellie leaned back on her hands. "So strange," she said, staring at me. "Never would have even thought you're a girl, but now that I know I feel stupid for not seeing it before."

I frowned. She were more stupid for hussing her bits at me so often.

"Robin's downstairs, you know," she told me. "Stalking outside like a lion. John won't let him in."

Coughing a bit, I shrugged. "He won't never, not with Bess in here."

Ellie sat up straighter. "You think? Do you reckon he's serious about her, then? I told her John is just a boy, and a stupid, disloyal one at that."

I didn't throw the soup at her. I felt right proud for that. "You don't know nothing, Ellie," I snapped at her. "John is the most loyal. The most protective. He chooses Bess and he'll love her till he rots. He deserves a family."

Now her eyes narrowed. "Have you and John fooled around, then? Living in the woods with all them boys, must be just like everyone says, isn't it?"

"Don't be a fool. I ain't never done nothing with John. *You* have."

She shrugged. "So?"

I put the soup down and tossed the blanket off. "I'm going to see Rob," I told her.

She didn't stop me. I went down the stairs and near the door, but I stopped. I went to the window, looking outside.

He were there. He were pacing, just as she said. Looking fair miserable.

I didn't want him to know what he'd done. Sure, he knew, but seeing me were a different thing. The hand were bad, and he'd know just how bad. He'd know what it meant for me. And he couldn't know.

Most because, as I watched him, sad and hurting and the kind of alone that I couldn't be a part of, I knew what I had to do. I knew what I wanted to do. And Rob wouldn't never rest if he knew I were going to Gisbourne and couldn't bare throw a knife.

Rob wouldn't never forgive himself, neither, if I died.

I went back from the window and asked Tuck where John were. John came up from around the bar, glaring at the door, where Rob were just beyond. "What?" John asked.

"Find out what Gisbourne wants," I said. "And find out when the prince comes."

CHAPTER
SIX

—o—

Three days later, I hadn't much moved from the bed Tuck had given me. I'd looked once in a glass, and my face were purple by half. My belly were yellow and black, and my hand had set to aching fierce. From what the girls were saying, Rob were outside most of the time, which were like to mean he ain't slept. Weren't nothing good coming from that.

It were dusk when Much came to me. I were downstairs, hanging back from the windows to watch Rob without him seeing me. He were just sitting now, waiting. Watching.

Much looked bigger to me, like his bones were growing, and it made me remember how young he were still. He were only half formed, half grown. A few years never seemed like much between us, but he still had changing to do. "John told me," he said. "What you're thinking of doing. And I tried to find out what Gisbourne wants—we both did—but we couldn't. And Rob's suspicious."

"You can't tell him," I said. "Even after I go, keep it as long as you can."

He nodded. "So you're going."

"Maybe. How long till the prince comes?"

"He'll be here tomorrow. They're releasing the men at the same time so a good crowd will greet the prince."

My eyes shut. Weren't there no luck for me in this world? "I can't go to him with no way to defend myself, Much. What am I supposed to do with a broke hand?"

Much frowned. He had such a serious face, so oft full of thoughts, but this were strange on him, like there were something he didn't understand—which happened rare enough. He'd spent most of the winter tearing through the library of monks' books that I could bare pick up, never mind understand. "What does your hand have to do with defending yourself?"

"Now you're just making fun," I told him, standing and drawing closer to the windows as Rob began to pace.

"No, I'm not," he said. I looked at him and he kept on frowning. "I think you're confused."

"My hand's *broke*, Much," I snapped, looking away.

"And you think that's how you fight," he said, like light just dawned in his head. "Christ, you think your knives make you what you are?" He came closer and put his hand on my shoulder, but I didn't turn to him. "You remember when you bought me the *kattari*?" he asked.

I shrugged under his hand.

"Why'd you do that?"

"Because you were whining and moping all about and complaining that you couldn't fight."

"So what did the *kattari* change?"

"Nothing," I snapped. "I just gave you a weapon that weren't hard for you to carry."

"It changed something. I couldn't fight without it."

I shoved his hand off, glaring at him. "Of course you could! You've fought every damn day of your life and the person who doesn't look at your stump of an arm and know it means you're a better, stronger, harder fighter than someone with two hands is a damn fool." He started to smile and I pushed him. "And if you're trying to say I don't need my knives to fight, it's different!"

"How?"

My chest felt like it caved in. "Because he *will* hurt me. Badly. And there won't be no band. And no Rob. And if he wants to make me every bit the scared, helpless girl, it won't be hard." My voice were gone, and the words were bare solid, like dust in the air.

Much stepped forward, looking into my eyes and I looked down. "Scar," he said soft. "Scar," he repeated, until I looked at him. "You learned to use your hands to fight for you. And you learned to trust the band to be at your back. You may have even learned to let Rob save you. But you don't need a damn one of those things. Your power, your great gift, is that you never give up. When something fails you make a new plan, and another, and another. You never accept defeat. You never give up."

"He'll kill me."

"He wants something from you, and I don't think it's to kill you."

"What if it is?"

The corner of his mouth twitched up, and I frowned hard before it turned into a full smile. "Then don't make it easy."

I ducked my head.

"You don't have to do this, you know," he told me.

I stood. My body hurt everywhere, and I hated that Gisbourne would see the proof of this shameful thing between me and Rob. I hated that I were going. I hated that I were going alone, for the first time in years without the band behind me. Without Rob.

"Find some way to distract Rob."

"Scar—" Much said, but he didn't finish the breath.

"Keep him whole, Much. Find something in those books of yours to make him better. Please."

Much caught my good arm and squeezed awful hard. "Don't die, Scar. He doesn't come back from this if you die."

That bit, at least, made me smile. "Neither do I. Go on. Make it good so he don't suspect."

Much nodded and let go of me. I hoped it wouldn't be forever.

—⚋—

John followed me to the castle. I told him to leave off, but
he wouldn't neither. He helped me climb with my hurt hand, he
waited on the wall beside me as I sat there for most of the night,
staring at the residences. There weren't no candles lit by then.
We didn't talk none. Me and John weren't the sort for that.

When light started to rise above the trees, I stood from the
wall. "Bye, John," I said to him.

Paying no mind to my bruises, he hugged me straight off
my feet, then let me go. "We won't be far. We'll be here if you
need us."

That weren't true. If I needed them, it would be quick and
done fast, before they could charge in. I were going, and I were
going alone. "I know."

He nodded, and just stood there. I went over the wall and
into the castle, and he just stood there still. Climbing up to the
residences were slow and awful, using one hand to climb up
while the other were useless. I sat in Gisbourne's window with
one look left for John. He were still standing there, watching.

I took a breath and looked into the room. Gisbourne were
sleeping, and my fingers twitched for a knife.

Couldn't I just kill him right there? While he slept. No
mess, just a knife in the throat and he'd wake up in Heaven
'stead of his bed.

Well, it ain't like I make such decisions, but in truth, I
doubted he were meant for Heaven.

But I still wanted to be. And that meant I couldn't honestly
kill him while he slept.

I dropped one leg inside the window and left it there. That were as far into the room as I were willing to go. I let my boot scrape along the rough stone, making a soft bit of noise, and it were enough. Gisbourne pulled awake, brandishing a short sword from under his pillow.

Heave-chested and wild eyed, he found me in the room, his mouth twisted in a snarl. He swore, putting the sword down. "Marian," he grunted. "You came."

"Why do you want me here, Gisbourne?" I asked. My heart were hammering but I wouldn't move none. "Tell me or I'm leaving."

"No you're not," he said, lying back without a care for me. "You want that annulment. You'd never have come otherwise. So shut up and be still and I'll tell you if I feel like it."

I pulled my leg back up, and I drew the shutter closed behind me but I didn't move. I just sat there, in the window, wondering what I had done.

―⁂―

My heart were thrumming like someone were playing it on strings. I didn't sleep, just took in as much as I could about the chamber. It looked the same as it had before: big chairs by the fire, the two trunks, a bed. A big bed. Gisbourne were sprawled out in it, and it were like watching a bear. It weren't something I'd step close to, but if it were sleeping there weren't no harm in looking.

He looked broader than I remembered. His hair were shaggy

in sleep and his big back were bare and muscled over. He were
built like John, all bumps and lumps and trenches in between.
He were strong. Stronger than me.

It were full sunlight before he moved, and then only when
a manservant came into the room. He looked at me and went
over to Gisbourne, calling his name until Gisbourne woke
with a growl like a beast.

"My lord, the prince will be arriving soon. You must dress."

"Fine. Eadric, find a lady to dress my wife as well."

"Wife, my lord?" he asked.

Gisbourne sat up. "The thing that looks like vermin in the
window."

Eadric looked at me, and scowling at him didn't make him
stop. "Yes, my lord," he said, leaving.

Gisbourne dragged himself up, standing naked before me.
My cheeks set to blushing but I stared at him and he stared at
me with a frown. "Christ," he muttered finally. He dragged on
a pair of hose and an undertunic with a grimace, striding over
to me.

My hands went to shakes and I balled the good one into a
fist to make it stop.

He reached for me, but I ducked under his arm.

Grabbing my shirt, he whipped me against the wall. "Be.
Still," he growled.

I tried to knee him in the bits but he blocked me, using
most of his big body to push me back against the wall. He
pushed his arm against my pipes and I whipped my head around

and some God-awful sound that were fair close to a whimper came out my mouth.

"Jesus Christ!" he roared in my face. "Stop moving!"

I stopped. I were shaking hard and hating every footstep that brought me here.

He looked at my bruises, it seemed, then let me go. My blood were moving too fast, making me shiver and shake, and I slunk away from him. "Who hit you?"

I spat a curse at him.

"You damn well better speak right when we're around other people," he snapped at me. "It's bad enough that you have the hair of a boy. The bruises, however, I can't say I mind."

Eadric and a young woman came back into the room without so much as a knock. I had forgotten this bit of noble life—there weren't never a moment to yourself, never a moment alone.

Which, considering my husband were like to kill me, maybe it weren't such a hardship.

The servants threw open the trunks, and my cheeks filled with blood. One of his godforsaken trunks was full of women's clothing. For me.

He'd known I would come to him.

The lady's maid had a pot of white and a brush with her, but when she went to paint my face, Gisbourne looked up from where Eadric was dressing him proper. "No," he called. "Don't paint her."

"My lord, the bruises—"

"Do not make him repeat himself, Mary," said Eadric.

Mary bobbed and set to dressing me instead. First she pulled off my clothing, taking my knives from me one by one, and I felt blushes burn over my whole skin as Gisbourne kept his eyes on me. I shook and felt water in my eyes, but I just glared back at him. She put the long linen dress over my head, then the first kirtle, a heavy tunic that spread to the ground. She put a second one over it, heavier still and lined in fur, that only went to my knees. Then she tugged tight sleeves up over the linen to match the first kirtle, tying them to the tunic.

She clucked over my hair before deciding on a velvet band and gold net that covered my whole head and hair besides. Gisbourne smirked at me, and it were all I could do not to tear it all off and stomp it in the fire.

"Come along, *love*," he sneered, offering his hand to me.

I walked past his hand without so much as a glance his way.

He lashed out, grabbing my neck like a dog and dragging me backward, fingers biting hard into my skin and making me twist. "You will observe proper etiquette, Marian. You haven't forgotten it, I trust?"

This time I managed to get him in the bits, and he howled and dropped me. "You want me to be some proper thing, you take your damn hands off me," I snapped at him.

He straightened with a snarl and took my good hand, squeezing tight and leading me out of the room.

—⁂—

Sometime after I had latched the shutters in Gisbourne's chambers up, it had started to snow. It were something of a blessing, truth be told, because the world weren't near as cold when it were snowing. The servants brought us heavy cloaks lined full with fur, and as little as I liked any of this, I found myself snuggling deep into the cloak. It were uncommon warm and soft and felt like the first thing in months what were kind to me.

We didn't have far to go. The upper bailey were full of nobles in bright, expensive things, all assembled and waiting for their prince. Most were lords and ladies from the royal court, I reckoned, for none had shown their faces round Nottingham before.

The castle weren't the same, neither. It were clean and tidy, and if there were some of the wall unfinished still, I couldn't see from where I stood. Pine garlands and streamers of cloth were decorating the place, swinging in the breeze to catch the notice of a prince.

The snow were blowing right for my mug, and I kept blinking and sneezing against it.

Gisbourne squeezed my arm overhard. "Be still, you *animal*," he growled.

I tore my arm away from him.

There were knights that came up the bailey first, causing an awful ruckus with their banners and their armor and their swords clattering around. They parted, and this were a set of two huge snow-white destriers, draped with silks and royal emblems. A man and a woman sat on top of them, and they

stood, letting their horses hoof about while more knights came
behind them and the "common folk" flooded in last. They
were the men from the wall, women from the kitchens, all the
castle workers—a captive, adoring crowd.

The bailiff stepped forward, made small by the prince's
display. He said words of greeting to him that I couldn't hear,
and then he turned to the people and shouted, "Lords,
ladies, and all those assembled, I give you Princess Isabel and
Prince John of England!"

People cheered and clapped for him. I didn't. I weren't the
cheering sort. The people weren't cheering for him in truth,
they were just yelling to have something to yell for.

And then the big horse shifted again, and I saw across the
space to where people had parted and someone stepped to
the front of the crowd.

Rob. It were Rob, and he were staring at me.

"My dear people," the prince shouted, with much more
effect than the bailiff had. "I have learned of the grievous
wrongs done to you by my former representative, the sheriff of
Nottingham. It shall not stand. I have come here to rectify the
situation and personally ensure that the man I choose this
time is the best for my interests, but most of all, for my people.
For you!" he shouted, raising his arms.

The people cheered back at him. He were young, a few
years past twenty at best. Younger than I thought of a prince.
I knew that he were more than ten years younger than King
Richard, but seeing him were strange. You heard so much

about a body in legend and stories and song, it were odd to see him true.

He lowered his arms, and the people lowered their cries. "So I shall judge this, fairly by all accounts, and have a contest to ensure the fitness of your lord. In two days time, a tournament shall begin. There shall be three parts—first, a joust, to prove to you his valor. Second, the melee and contest of swords, to prove to you his strength. Finally, there shall be the crowning event—an archery contest, to prove his most sound wisdom, his keen eye, and his superior judgment. To the winner of this final event shall the title fall."

My mouth watered to do it but I didn't much dare to spit on the ground. A game? He were choosing the next sheriff based on a *game*?

The people didn't agree with me. They cheered and cheered, and I looked at Gisbourne, with a fair smug look on his face.

Maybe it weren't even much of a game after all.

CHAPTER

SEVEN

—o—

The prince dismounted and were led inside. He looked at Gisbourne and motioned him forward, and so Gisbourne grabbed my hand vengeful hard and dragged me forward. I looked back at Rob, standing there still, staring at me. I couldn't see his heart on his face. I couldn't know if he were angry, sad, or hateful toward me.

Gisbourne tugged so hard I nearly fell off my feet, but I were held up by the rush of people, closing like a wake to follow the prince.

Knights set up in the halls, blocking people from passing, but we were let pass at every point.

"I can damn well walk!" I snapped as Gisbourne kept his hold on me.

"It's so much more entertaining to drag you, my love," he said, tossing the words over his shoulder.

He stopped sharp at a guarded door. I knew where we were—this were the sheriff's old quarters, the nicest room in the place. The guards opened the door to an antechamber with still more guards and we went in.

A young lord in an overpuffed green velvet tunic stood there. "Gisbourne," he greeted, with a smile so thin I could bare see his lips, "so good to see you again."

"My lord de Clare," Gisbourne greeted, bowing. "May I introduce to you my lady wife, Marian of Leaford. Marian, this is the future earl of Hertford."

They were both fair staring at me, so I dropped a curtsy and made a face.

De Clare coughed. "Charming," he said with a bow.

Gisbourne's lip were curling. "He wished to see me."

"Yes, well, now he's decided to keep you waiting," de Clare said, sitting on a bench and propping one ankle on his knee. His eyes stayed on me overmuch. "So she doesn't look half as wild as they say. Damn near domesticated, even." He tapped his eye with a laugh. "I see what inspired the change."

"You should see what I did to *him*," I spat back.

De Clare laughed and I had half a mind to make him think better of it when Gisbourne's heavy paw slapped across my face.

Pain were hot and blinding and I weren't quite sure how, but I ended up on the floor. De Clare were laughing still and Gisbourne had turned away from me. A knight stooped and offered me his hand with a clatter of armor. Shamed, I pulled away from him and stood up on my own.

"She's still learning," Gisbourne said.

Annulment, I said to myself. I said it so many times the word
lost its taste. It made me think of my Rob, and the thought of
him and the pain pulsing through my mug suddenly made
water push up behind my eyes.

I sucked in a breath and pushed away the tears. I weren't
never going to cry in front of Gisbourne.

Something wet were on my chin and I licked the side of my
mouth. It stung and my mouth tasted like copper.

"You look pretty in red," de Clare told me with a chuckle.
I wiped the blood from my mouth and stared ahead at the
door.

The door opened and a taller, immensely broad-shouldered
man stepped forward. De Clare swallowed his laugh at the
sight of him, and he spared bare more than a glance for de
Clare. He took one long step from the door and stopped, bowing and catching my hand. His sheer size made me think
he were older than me by far, but he smiled and the light
that caught in his eyes made him appear far younger. He
couldn't have been more than twenty-five, younger even than
my husband.

"My lady Marian," he greeted, kissing my hand. "Forgive
my impudence; I know we have not been introduced, but your
father has always been a great adviser to me. I am the Earl of
Winchester. It is an honor to meet you."

He straightened up and I gave him a curtsy. He frowned as
he looked at my face.

"Gisbourne, someone has done injury to your wife," he said, his voice granite-like.

Gisbourne smirked. "Your Grace," he greeted with a deep nod. "I'm hunting the rapscallion down."

"Good," Winchester said, still looking to me. "Any man that harms a woman ought to be flogged." He gave me the littlest of smiles. "Though I hear some women have their own ways of answering such harm."

"Some women do, my lord," I agreed, bowing my head as I were meant.

"I will tell the steward to seat us together at supper, my lady. There is much I would like to discuss with you."

"Your Grace," I said, curtsying.

"The prince will see you now," he said, gesturing us forward.

The room weren't the same—weren't nothing the same round here. It looked lovely and warm, covered in coffers and fabrics and servants. The pink-cheeked princess sat in a chair by the fire, and the prince were lounging in a chair beside her, picking at a plate of food.

Gisbourne pulled me in front of them like he were presenting me, and I stood there, looking from the prince to the girl and back. "Your Royal Highnesses, may I introduce Lady Marian of Leaford," he said.

"It's traditional to make obeisance, young lady," the prince said.

I swept into a curtsy, the heat of the fire on my back making me sweat.

"Very good," he said. "Gisbourne, I see you've been disciplining her."

Gisbourne nodded his head. "My prince."

"So, you're the girl who is helping Huntingdon cause so much trouble."

I eased up on my knees, starting to pull up.

"Did he say you could rise?" asked the princess. I stopped, frowning at her.

The prince chuckled.

"Yes, your Highness," I said to him.

"Yes, what? Yes, you acted as an outlaw? Yes, you betrayed your loyalty to your country, to your king? Yes, you defied the sheriff, my sworn representative?"

My knees set to burning. "Yes," I repeated.

"Yes, *what*?" he said again. "Are you sorry for your actions?"

With a grunt I stood straight, rubbing my aching knees. "No," I snapped. "I ain't never going to be sorry, neither. The sheriff were a sorry excuse of a man and I'm more 'an happy he's dead."

The prince's face folded into a sneer. "You're an impudent thing," he told me. "Perhaps you should be on your knees as you beg my forgiveness."

He nodded to Gisbourne, who swung out with his boot to kick the back of my knees. It were a hard target in skirts and I jumped away. "I ain't begging," I snapped. "I never did nothing wrong."

"Kneel, or you will gravely insult the Crown," the prince

growled at me. Gisbourne stepped forward to make me, but the prince snapped, "Gisbourne, heel."

Gisbourne's face twisted, but he retreated back to give me room to kneel before the prince.

I could kneel, but I weren't about to *beg*. Slow, and fair awkward because of my skirts, I took to my knees, staring the prince down. "Your Highness," I grunted.

"Let's try that again. You acted as an outlaw and disrespected the Crown in so doing. Do you admit this?"

"Yes and no," I said. "I defied laws to be sure, but I acted for the people and that is always meant to be in respect for the Crown."

The prince sighed. "Good Lord, Gisbourne, how on earth do you suffer this? Lady Leaford, you hadn't the right to take action, and acting as an outlaw will always be unlawful, naturally." He sniffed. "That said, in marriage your sins fall to your husband, and I have absolved him of them. You are free to earn my good graces."

"Grace may well be beyond her grasp, my lord," Isabel said soft to him. It weren't near soft enough, and I glared at her.

The prince chuckled. "Perhaps indeed, my love." He took her hand, playing with her fingers before drawing them to his mouth to kiss them. "Gisbourne, isn't my princess very wise?"

"Yes, your Highness."

"And beautiful too, isn't she?"

I couldn't much see Gisbourne, but Isabel were looking at him, and her face didn't look so pinched and catlike now. She blinked her eyes wide.

"Always, your Highness," Gisbourne said, and his voice were rough.

The prince sniffed again and waved his hand, leaning forward a little to meet my eyes. "Now, Lady Marian. This is my land, and as such, I will be the one to act for the people, do you understand?"

I stared back at him.

"You are a noble lady, and a wife. If you continue such flagrant disregard for my royal authority, I will punish you and my forgiveness will be beyond your reach. I strongly encourage you to cleave to your husband, be a good little girl and be dutiful and pious in all things. And Gisbourne, you might want to think about how the behavior of your wife reflects on your authority. Particularly the authority provided by certain positions?" he said, raising his eyebrows.

Gisbourne made some kind of a grunt.

Prince John smiled. "Now, Lady Leaford, you may kiss my ring and go."

Kiss my ring—like he were the damn king. He weren't even his brother's heir, only third in line to the throne, and he could sit here like a monarch. I stood still, but Gisbourne's fingers caught my elbow to drag me up and were grinding the bones like he were trying to make bread with them.

Finally I stood and stepped forward, kneeling before the prince to kiss the Angevin seal imprinted in gold.

He smiled at me, but all I saw were teeth.

Gisbourne dragged me out into the antechamber. As soon as we were there he raised his hand to hit me again and I slammed my good hand into his throat and my knee into his bits. "Don't you *ever* strike me," I snarled at him.

De Clare were still there and he strode over to me, grabbing my injured hand and squeezing. A scream bubbled up but I shut my mouth and it came out a yelp. He did it harder, twisting, and I fell.

"Trash," he spat at me. "How dare you hit a lord!"

Gisbourne were grunting but I couldn't even see him. De Clare squeezed again and I couldn't stop the scream from coming.

The door burst open with Winchester filling it, but it weren't needed. Gisbourne had his sword out, and I were fair shocked to see it weren't pointed at me.

"Unhand her," he rumbled.

Winchester crossed his arms as de Clare stared at Gisbourne. "I was helping you give the little bitch what she deserves!" de Clare said, his fingers still mashed in my broken hand.

"She is a lady of the court," Winchester told him.

He dropped my hand, and one of the knights caught me up before I fell. Lot of good they were when he were squeezing.

"Apologize," Gisbourne said.

"You've lost your mind, Gisbourne," de Clare said.

"No one ever said I was sane, de Clare. She's my wife and I'll be the one to show her discipline."

De Clare folded over to give me a mock bow. "My apologies, my lady."

Gisbourne sheathed his sword, satisfied, but Winchester's

mug were still storm-filled and dark. "Come along, Marian," Gisbourne said, and Winchester's glare twisted to de Clare.

Gisbourne said nothing until we were back in his chambers. Then he let me go, pushing me forward, and he yelled out the door for some ale. He slammed the door shut, and I sat in the window, opening the shutter a space and trying hard to keep the water in my eyes.

"You're a stupid, foolish peasant," he growled at me, sitting before the fire. "I told you to speak right to the prince. I *told* you to behave."

"The prince!" I snapped. "With his *royal authority*. What authority? He ain't the damn king. He's a spoiled *boy*."

"He's a *prince!*" Gisbourne roared.

"He's your master," I snarled. "And what, five years your younger? Were you taking orders before he could even hold a sword?"

"You idiot girl," he growled. "Just shut up, be still, and do what you're damn well told. I wouldn't have to hit you if you'd just do what I tell you."

"Keep hitting, see what happens," I snapped. They were brave words, but they weren't as honest as they should have been. My arm felt like it had splintered apart like a block of wood.

His eyes were fixed on the fire. "I can hit harder, Marian."

"I'm fair shocked you didn't let de Clare snap my damn hand off," I spat at him. "Doesn't matter to you none."

He whipped round in the chair, his eyes blazing hotter

than the flames. "Doesn't matter? Are you daft? For him to strike you is an insult to my honor. A grave insult that I will not allow."

I spat on the ground. "You have no honor."

He lunged from his chair, coming to me to loom over me, all darkness and hulk and shadows. "My honor is the only thing that means anything to me."

I stared back at him. "Then you have no thought as to what it means. I'm no innocent, so I can't say I ain't earned whatever pain you put me to. But you've killed children. Without a sin to their name. Honor knows nothing of that."

"I protect my own. *My* name. Nothing else matters."

Turning my hand, I looked at the new spots of blood on the bandages. "Damn fine job of protecting me you're doing," I told him.

He caught my chin and dragged me up, looking full in my eyes. His were dark, like oil skating over midnight water, and looking in them felt like falling into black. "Are you mine, Marian?"

My body set to trembling. "You know that answer, Gisbourne."

He let me go, looking away, the black waters drying up. "I do. And yet, you came. With bruises on your face, when all of Sherwood defends you."

"For the annulment."

His lip curled. "Naturally. And yet I wonder if it wasn't your sweet Huntingdon who has been dishonoring you the same way I'm wont to do."

"Rob wouldn't *never* raise his hand to me. Rob wouldn't never hurt me," I said, my mug hot and my blood running fast. "Rob loves me more than he loves his self." It were all I could manage to say the words clear and true.

My eyes set to leaking and I went for the door, near knocking a servant with a tray of ale. I passed her and bare made it another bend in the hall before my mug burst with water. I ran.

I ran through the snow. I made it to the gates, to the towering walls of stone what kept me from Sherwood, from Rob, from the forest that kept some shadow wraith of Scarlet while Marian were here and skirted and chained. And I stopped.

"My lady?" called a knight, coming close to me. "My lady, it's freezing. Allow me to see you back," he said.

He reached for my arm, and I whipped away from him. "Don't touch me," I told him.

Much's words rang in my ears: *you never give up.* It seemed like a curse more than anything.

If it were true, and Gisbourne were set to be the winner before the competition even began, then I weren't sure what I could do to stop him being sheriff. I didn't have a plan, much less a second plan.

All I had were fear, and worry, and faith. Faith that when the time came, I would know what to do.

My feet were cold and heavy as they climbed back up through the baileys. When they stopped, I were in a dark, cold room of stone. I moved past the pews like a ghost and fell onto the kneelers by the dais in the old chapel.

It didn't seem right to cry while you prayed. It seemed self-ish to talk to God in such misery. My only sister had died so long ago. My band were in a forest that didn't feel like mine anymore. My love were kept from me by an awful ring on my finger, and it seemed God were the only one left to cry to.

CHAPTER

EIGHT

—o—

I went back to Gisbourne's room after night fell. He weren't there; I had passed the main hall and knew most of the gathered court were there to feast with the prince. I felt like a shadow in the halls, and it weren't something I could stand.

I searched the room for my knives, but I couldn't find where the lady servant hid them. I reckoned Gisbourne had a hand in that. Course, it weren't hard to figure out where he kept his money, either, and I took a fair bit of that and stashed it behind the shutter where the lady servant couldn't strip it from me.

Fetching new linen wrappings from the dry storage, I peeled the old ones off my hand and tossed them in the fire. It were bleeding a fair bit, the stick that had set it broken. I used the fire poke to hack off a bit of a fireplace log and set that in its place. My hand were double-thick and raw and sore as anything.

Cradling it to me, I curled up in the chair by the fire with one of the furs from the bed and went to sleep. He were a loon if he thought I'd be sleeping in the bed with him.

—⚬—

Gisbourne slammed into the room late and well drunk. I woke but didn't open my eyes none. I stayed quiet and still as I felt him loom over me, blotting into dark the light of the fire.

He didn't touch me. I heard noises, and him moving away, then the bed creaked and the curtains rushed over the bar.

I opened my eyes. His clothes were strewn on the floor, and the bed were covered over with drapes. I shut my eyes again, clutching my hand to my heart, trying to remember what all this hurt were for.

Waking early seemed the best way to skirt round him. I tried to put on my own things but it were damn difficult and I had to call for the lady servant. I bid her hush and do it quiet, and she obeyed me.

It would be a few hours yet before Gisbourne rose, and it felt like the closest I'd get to freedom for a long stretch. I retrieved the purse and went for the marketplace.

Even the market had changed. Nobles were still arriving, trailing behind the prince in a progress, and with them came merchants and sellers of every sort. The market were jostling and full, and slipping into the people put me at ease.

I bought knives from a merchant I liked that most days were up in Leicester. I got two sets of cheap ones for the coin

I'd filched, and as I were paying and the merchant turned, I caught a wrist with his fingers around a blade hilt.

"Don't," I warned soft, my eyes flicking up to the man who owned the wrist.

His face flickered into a grin, and with a quick twist from him I were a step away from the merchant's shop, held tight against the thief.

"Can't you let me have my fun?" he asked, his Irish brogue low in my ear as I aimed my knife to drive in his thigh. "Scarlet?"

I stopped before I stabbed him, wriggling out of his paws. I turned and looked at him—tall and shift-footed, with too-long hair and too-bright eyes—not a lick of which were known to me. "I don't know you."

He swept into an awful proper bow. "Allan a Dale, my lady thief."

Tucking my new knives into their proper places, I frowned at him. "You know me?"

"I came up in London behind your legend. And still it grows," he told me, tossing me an apple from a stand. He waved me forward. "Walk with me?"

"Dangerous prospect," I said, but I did, and I bit the apple. "I miss London every now and a bit."

"Filthy, pest-ridden, hard-scrabble, beautiful city," he said, grinning.

"But how did you know me?"

He looked cut. "A knife-wielding lady who cut off her own

hair to fight a thief taker? There aren't many of you in the world, my lady."

I snorted. "Don't have to call me lady, Allan."

"Dressed like that I think I do." He cast about in the marketplace. "So where is Robin Hood?"

"Where he ought," I said. "With his people." We passed a shanty of a house on the edge of the marketplace, and two children were there, filthy and still, watching all the people go by.

Frowning, I turned back to the nearest bakers stall and gave the rest of my coin for bread. "You're *paying* for things?" Allan said.

Lifting my shoulders, I went back toward the children. "Not my coin, so that ain't quite so."

He laughed. I gave a loaf to the two children and quick enough others came, and Allan were quick to take bread from my stack and rip it apart to spread round. "I've heard this is what you do," he said. "Stealing to feed people." His head went to the side. "It's so . . . strange."

"It's what nobles do," I said bitter. "Prince John feasting every night—he's taking the game and the crops from the people of the shire, putting them to starve in winter. Least I ain't stealing to feed myself."

"Don't be ridiculous," he said. "He's stealing to feed his ego, not his belly. It hasn't been so well tended these days."

"His ego?"

Allan kept the last bit of bread for himself, and with the

food gone, the children went too. He nodded, chewing. "You didn't hear?"

I frowned. "I ain't much for gossip."

He stopped, swallowed, and then did a turn with a tuck of his cap, winking for show. "This is the royal court, fair thief. It lives on gossip, perception, and hearsay." His hands spread wide. "Let me spin you a tale, then."

He bowed and I crossed my arms.

With a shrug, he stood. "Well, when Richard left for the Holy Crusade, he kicked John to France. Told him to stay out of his country while he was away, and named his wee nephew his heir. Because God knows, Richard knows how to steal a crown—it was taught to him in the womb, so they say. Eleanor of Aquitaine herself incited her sons in rebellion against their father. And if he didn't learn violence from her, then maybe from the Devil that bore them all."

"Devil?" I asked.

"Oh aye, you haven't heard that one either? Richard loves to boast of his Devil's blood, begat when his ancestor wed a serpent."

My eyes rolled. "Christ, you're a fool."

"Don't let a few silly truths muddle up a good story," he told me sharp.

I looked Heavenward, but there weren't no help there. "What's this about John's ego?" I reminded.

He frowned. "Can't appreciate a decent yarn. Something wrong in your head, Lady Scar. Richard kicked John out of

England, and the bishops were bickering as bishops are wont to do, and Eleanor petitioned for John to come back. So Richard allows it, right, and John's been setting up his own royal court outside of the bishops meant to rule in Richard's stead. The two courts have been rising, both powerful, and fighting each other in petty ways. So Richard sends in the Archbishop from Rouen to keep the peace—and knock John's legs out. Prince John makes his stand and he's expecting everyone to rally to him, but they don't. They keep Richard's orders and leave John. So John runs north at Mummy's command and is trying to win back the people's hearts."

I gawped at him. "So it's true, then? He wants to change things around here?"

Allan laughed. "He wants . . . to make England his very own high-priced whore. He wants to feel loved without ever caring what it takes to earn the real thing. A little coin, a little bread, and watch England do her merry dance."

My shoulders lifted. "So long as the whore is paid and eating, what's the difference?"

He tossed his apple core onto the street. "Ask the whore."

—m—

We were near the edge of Nottingham, and I saw the market and the castle beyond in one direction. I saw forest in the other, and my heart ached so fierce I almost set off for it, like wading into the ocean with no hope of swimming for distant shores. Allan were talking—for a thief he yapped an amount I could bare fathom—and I thought how easy it would be to just step over the road and into the forest.

"Scarlet!" he yelped, grabbing my dress and yanking me back as a carriage thundered past.

Landing on my backside, I stared up at the blue coach, hung with gold and the royal seal.

"You don't want to be crushed by the Queen Mum," he told me, giving me a hand up.

"That's Eleanor of Aquitaine?" I asked.

He shrugged. "Her carriage, at least."

"Scarlet," said another voice, and this one were farther. The dust from her carriage cleared and Rob were there, looking dark and shadowed and haunted.

My blood ran fast to beating and my mouth hung open. I fair thought I'd know what to say to him, but I didn't.

"Don't tell me you're Robin Hood," Allan said, crossing his arms. "I thought you'd be taller."

Robin strode across the road, stepping close to me, so close Allan weren't even in my world anymore. I blinked and stared at him. Good Lord I couldn't look at him but for thinking he held everything in my heart. It were a terrible power to keep over me.

"Who are you?" Robin asked, looking to Allan.

"Allan a Dale," he said. "You sure you're her man, because I'll tell you, the stories I hear put you at about seven foot tall." He paused, but I didn't look to see his face. "And the stories I *tell* have you much more game for a laugh."

"Allan," I said, breathing in the smell only Rob had, of pine and ash and ocean. "Go now."

"My lady," he said, and that were the last of him.

Rob's eyes were fierce and hard and they glittered down at me. "Please explain in some small measure, Scarlet."

"Allan? He's a thief, from London. Kindred soul," I said.

"Gisbourne."

My eyes shut. "Rob, I had to."

"No, you didn't. You told me you would never go back to him. You told me you understood that he would kill you. And what is wrong with your hand? Is it broken? You went to him with a broken hand?"

"Rob," I said low, not daring to open my eyes. "My hand'll be right again. And as for killing me . . . well, he hasn't yet."

"*Scarlet.*" My eyes flew open and his were shut tight, his head bent. Hurting, I pushed my forehead to his. His hands came up and held my face, leaning as if he were 'bout to kiss me. His eyes opened a sliver and met mine, and he let me go, swearing and turning from me.

"That's why, Rob," I told him soft.

"Why what?" he snapped, turning back round.

"Why I went to Gisbourne. Because I need to kiss you, to touch you, to hold on to you through your awful dreams. Without us both wondering if we're doing a sin."

He turned back to me and caught me, one arm round my waist pulling me off my feet and the other in my hair tugging my head back. I caught his eyes, fixed on me in a way that made heat rush over me in a breaking wave, and I couldn't breathe.

Our lips touched. His were dry and rasped over me a bit, like it were so chaste it weren't even there. Then his mouth opened and it weren't dry anymore. His lips were perfect against mine, more soft than I would have never guessed, and warm like the sun hitting the water.

My blood ran hot and fast and I felt more than human, like I were powerful beyond every measure. His mouth opened more and his tongue ran against my lips, and my whole body sparked like tinder. I bare had a thought, but I wanted more of him, so much more, and my hands were desperate for it, fingertips running like they could keep whatever they touched.

My back nudged up against a wall, somewhere shaded from the sun and prying eyes, but I didn't never remember moving. His head twisted and our lips broke for a bare instant before he touched them back again, twisting his head the other way. His lips pressed my bruise and I jerked.

His arms went tense and hard around me, and the kiss broke apart. His nose nudged me like a dog giving orders, and I obeyed, moving my face to one side. Hot hands running my sides, his mouth touched impossible gentle to the bruise by my mouth from Gisbourne. Rob's lips left, then dropped soft small kisses on the bruises that he had laid. He kissed my closed eyes and without wanting it, water dripped out from my eyes. He kissed that away too.

"I'm sorry, sweet," he whispered into my ear. "I'm sorry I pushed you to this."

My hands twisted to fists in his shirt. "I never should have married him, Rob. I should have found another way."

"We'll get out of this," he said. "I'll get better, and you can walk away."

I shook my head a tiny bit. "I'm getting that annulment. They call me Marian, Rob, and they act with so little honor it's a horror to call them nobility." I pushed my head to his. "They took my name, Rob."

His lips touched mine again, more puffed and soft now, burning against mine. When he stopped he didn't go nowhere, speaking straight into my mouth. "They can have your name. I know who you are, with or without it. And I won't ever let you lose that. My love. My Scarlet."

I pressed a kiss to his mouth. "Say it once more?" I asked.

He kissed me. "Scarlet," he breathed. Another kiss. "Scarlet."

I didn't need strength. My heart were so full to bursting that I could have run to London and back without food, drink, or rest. My body were burned over and over with the feel of him, and it were all I needed to stay strong.

It were an awful sin, and I didn't care. Kissing Rob made me an adulterer, but wedding Gisbourne when he weren't the one in my heart made me an adulterer too. I didn't for a breath believe a kiss would make Robin better, but it were all I needed to hold on to everything I were doing this for.

Church bells rang out, and I broke the kiss, listening for the hour. "I have to go," I whispered against his mouth.

His nose rubbed mine slowly, then his mouth pressed against mine once more. "Do you know how often I've imagined kissing you?"

My breath stopped, and I opened my eyes to search his. "And?"

"You cannot tell me to stop now and watch you walk away," he said, his breath running into my breath. Another kiss. "Especially to him."

My ring felt heavier then, and I pulled back from Rob. I stroked his cheek slow with my good hand. "I'll make it right, Rob. I'll get the annulment and then I can kiss you in public. All day long. Till the village wives wring their hands at us."

He smiled, leaning into my hand. "We've always been good at causing a bit of chaos."

I stepped away from him with a sad smile, but he tugged my good wrist and brought me back for one more kiss. Then he let me go and I walked back to the castle, every step dragging and slow like I were fighting against a tide.

CHAPTER

NINE

∼o∼

The servants were laying out a fancy dress and brushing it flat and free of dust and dirt when I came back to the room. The long bit were gold, shimmering and bright, and the shorter bit that fit over it were tufted red velvet, the same color as my old ribbons. It were an awful expensive thing, and it felt like soft moss beneath my hand.

"You would like to dress now, my lady?"

"No," I said quick, pulling my hand back from it. "Where can I bathe?"

"We'll fetch the bath for you, my lady."

I forgot about this—the silly labor of baths. Fair shamed by it, I stashed my knives by the shutter as they left, then watched as the servants first brought the basin to the chambers, then pail after pail of water warmed in the kitchens and sloshed cold by the time it made it to me. I didn't mind that much—I were used to bathing in colder waters—but I were meant to sit in the half-empty basin while they poured it over me, slow and waiting for more water.

Then the lady servant set upon me with soap and cloths, and that part were a far cry better than bathing in the lake.

Course, Gisbourne walked in half through this ordeal, and I weren't none too pleased by him seeing all my bits again. And he just folded his arms and watched me. I covered myself in the water as best I could with my knees and such, but it didn't make me feel much better.

"Quite a gentleman, aren't you," I spat at him.

"What?" he asked. "A man can't look upon his wife? From what I'm told it's the same as looking upon my arm, or my foot. You belong to my body, Marian, and I shall look at you how I choose."

Blood were creeping up my neck and cheeks, and I stared at the water as the maid finished, fetching a sheet for me.

"You were missed at supper last night," he said.

"I'm sure."

"I realize I wasn't specific about this before, but court suppers are part of our bargain. Every function you are expected to attend as my wife you shall attend, or our deal is off. Do you understand?"

The servant shook the sheet open, standing off to the side. I motioned her over, to stand between me and Gisbourne, but she just looked confused.

Gisbourne laughed, damn him.

Full of hate and shame, I stood, wrapping the sheet round me as quick as I could. Gisbourne came forward as I stood there, putting his hand on my stomach where the big bruise lay, pulsing and sore under the thin cover of the sheet. My whole skin shivered with the touch of a hand through so little fabric.

He looked at me, his eyes dark. "Seems you know a lot of gentlemen."

It should have shamed me, but that weren't the way of it. It made me think of Robin, of his mouth and his hands and his body all along mine.

"Hold on," he ordered abruptly, and without more word he grasped my middle and pulled me from the bath. Swallowing a gasp, my hand shot out to his shoulder as he lifted me up over the edge and set my feet down.

He let me go immediately, and I pulled away from him, holding the sheet tight to me.

He pulled the tunic off over his head. "Send up more water," he said to Eadric. "No reason to let this waste."

I dragged the long, loose dress over my head as more of his clothes came off. He bared his chest, staring at me. I looked away, but I felt his eyes on me as he stripped down completely.

"And here I thought what's good for the goose is good for the gander," he goaded with a laugh. "Don't want to peek, love?"

Rob's kiss burned over me again. "Don't call me that. You don't love me. It's a mock."

"Yes," he said. "It is. *Love.*"

I shook my head, keeping turned away from him and letting my maid tug and pull and tie me. I heard the splash of the water and the sounds of washing, and I felt like I were fair pinned in the corner of the room, unable to move.

The servant sat me on the edge of the bed and brushed what there were of my hair—long bits in front that fluffed about my face, and the short bunches in back that didn't lay flat. It behaved a bit more for her, and she did some trick with pins and it stayed back, like it were all gathered about the bun that weren't there anymore.

"Thank you," I murmured to her.

Gisbourne stood from the bath. "Last chance," he said before his manservant put the cloth around him. I stayed still, and he laughed at me. I sat on the bed while his manservant dressed him in black velvet, stark and fine against the white of his shirt, his body big and wide and hard with muscle that seemed odd to be dressed in velvet.

I looked away. He weren't ugly.

Not liking the thought, I went to the window, retrieving my knife when he weren't looking and hiding it in the back of the shorter overdress.

Finished, he held out his hand and I took it, letting him pull me in front of him. He stared me over, but not the same as when I wasn't dressed. "Perfect," he said. "The dress suits you nicely. Now if you just don't open your mouth, we may be able to pull this off."

"What is there to pull?" I asked, taking my hand back. "It ain't as if we're fixing to steal something from the prince." I looked at him. "Are you?"

"I'm trying to convince him that you're a well-bred lady instead of a heathen," he told me. "It's a little bit harder than stealing bread."

"Why should he care?"

"I care. You *should* care."

"Why?"

"Christ, you're little better than a toddler." Shaking his head, he came toward me till my back hit the wall, and he leaned close to my ear. "You want an annulment, Marian, yes?"

My hand curled around the knife I had hidden, but I nodded.

"Do you know what the only thing is that will allow for our marriage to be annulled?"

My mug went hot and red but I didn't say nothing to him.

He leaned even closer so his lips touched my ear. "Lack of consummation."

Stepping back a pace, his eyes went over me in a different way, a way that made me hold my breath because breathing made my chest move too much. Though my heart were hammering hard enough that it might have been a fair exchange, the cloth beating with the pulse of what lay beneath.

"You'll be a good girl tonight, won't you?" he told me with a sneer.

He moved away. I looked at the window, at the sliver of dark night I could see, and I turned and followed my husband.

I weren't full aware of how many nobles had come to Nottingham. The Great Hall were filled to bursting, with huge long tables running the length of it. There were one larger table up on the dais, with fewer seats than the rest.

Gisbourne led me to the royal table and a breath fluttered within me. Were my husband so favored that we would have to eat with these people? Gisbourne did the dutiful bit and pulled out the chair till I swept into it, and pushed it forward for me. I reckoned that the tradition were for the damn weight of the things—I were strong as girls came, but I couldn't have lifted such a chair.

Seated in the wooden trap that kept me at the table, I stared at the spectacle. There were huge plates of animals in garish display, giant turkeys sitting golden and steaming, platters heaped with cuts of meat the like I'd never seen. Antlers of the stag they had killed were draped with jewels and pearls above the meat from his body. There were a whole table of falsely colored sweets.

Flour. Sugar. Eggs. Game. All this belonged to the people of Nottingham, who were starving while these people fatted themselves.

Horns blared out into the hall while the men stood, welcoming the prince and princess to the table. The prince were meant to look handsome—with his fine clothes, and the certain bearing and surety that handsome men had—but he weren't. He were more than ten years my elder but he looked like a spoiled, milk-faced boy.

"Welcome, lords and ladies, to the humble supper I have been able to give to you. Please enjoy, and let us first drink to the health and safe return of my brother abroad. To King Richard!" he bellowed.

"King Richard!" we all answered. That I was fair fine with drinking to.

A cup touched mine to my right. I looked and nodded to Winchester. "Your Grace," I greeted.

"My lady," he said. A servant stepped between us with an offering of venison stew, and Winchester ladled a bowl for me and then himself. "I am grateful to see you much improved from last night."

"Last night?" I asked.

"Your lord husband informed me that you weren't well."

I looked down. Gisbourne hadn't cared, but it were close to truth. "No, I wasn't."

"My lady," he said quiet, so much so that I had to lean toward him. "I'm more than aware of your husband's ungallantries. Should you ever wish for my assistance, you shall have it upon a moment."

My eyes lifted. "Thank you, your Grace."

"Now, I believe you know another dear friend of mine."

"I do?"

"The former earl of Huntingdon?" he whispered to me.

My blood ran fast. "You know Rob?"

He smiled, tasting his soup. "So I imagine the stories are true, then. It's him that truly has your heart."

Allan had said as much before. "Who the hell is telling these stories?" I asked.

He chuckled. "More than likely, Eleanor of Aquitaine and her minstrels," he told me, nodding down the table. I could see past Gisbourne and the princess to the prince; he leaned back and gave glimpse of an elegant grayed lady.

"That's the dowager queen?" I asked.

He nodded. "There is no fairer personage to serve in the royal court," he whispered to me. "Her youngest son may know little of what honor and grace truly represent, but trust me, she is the font of such qualities."

Like a cloud, the prince blocked my view of her again.

"And she loves nothing more than a well-told story. She encourages such amongst the royal court. Courtly loves are always her favorites."

"The love me and Rob have ain't so courtly," I told him.

He laughed. "God will judge you, not I," he said. "But I would love to see him again. We knew each other well when we were boys."

Perhaps he were true, and he loved Rob, but it were equal as likely that he weren't, and this were some trick to find Rob—another wolf in the royal court. "I'll speak of it when I see him, your Grace, but as he's a bit of an outlaw he ain't so easy to find," I told him.

"Thank you," he said, patting my hand.

"What are you two whispering about?" Gisbourne asked, but his eyes were on our touching hands.

Winchester released me. "The lady was assuring me her bruises didn't hurt overmuch," he said. "I had inquired after her welfare."

"Your gallantry is misplaced," the prince fair shouted round a mouthful of food. "The lady isn't some delicate flower in need of chivalry, but rather the firmness of her husband's hand, Winchester."

"Surely no woman should lack for chivalry, my son."

The prince looked to his side and I reckoned it must have been Eleanor that had spoken.

"Hardly a woman at all, is she, though?" he said, and a bit of food spat out. Even the princess made a stuck-up little face at that. "She's a thief. A criminal. An outlaw—hardly falls into the same category."

"The gentility befitting her sex should be inalienable," Winchester said.

"Don't be silly," the prince railed on. "I suppose you bow and scrape for peasant women too, Winchester?"

"My wife is no peasant," Gisbourne said.

I frowned. Honestly, why bother piping up at all?

"No, of course not. She elevated you, in fact, didn't she?" the prince crowed. My husband's face went dark. Didn't much think he liked to be reminded of that.

The far ends of the tables were still talking amongst themselves, but the closer bits were listening to the prince make sport of me. "But my prince," someone spoke up. "Surely you must take deportment into account. If anything, dear Gisbourne has lowered himself by his association. It's like mating with a wild animal."

"And what should we take into account about a person that so lowers the conversation during such a lovely meal, my lord de Lacy?" the queen said.

"If you can call de Lacy a lord, my lady queen," said another man.

"Lord enough to see you on the field, Wendeval!" de Lacy roared back at him.

"My dear mother," the princess said. "You must forgive him. We are all so confused about what to do with such a curiosity in our midst. We have all heard such stories about her, and now it seems she cannot even muster the words to speak. You must understand how this lends a certain air of savagery."

"And yet the court's ability to discuss a young lady as if she were an object seems savage also," the queen said. "Most unbecoming, Isabel."

I saw the princess flush at this rebuke, and Gisbourne looked to her.

"My dear mother," she tried again, "I only meant to allay his thoughtless words. I, of course, have been eager to get to know the lady Leaford and am eager to hear what must be such . . . colorful stories. In her own words."

"Ah, yes, you do love a good story, Mother. Come, Lady Marian, regale us," the prince sneered at me.

Gisbourne's vengeful gaze settled on me, and I licked my lips, pressing them tight together. I pushed up my chin and clutched my hands tight. "I won't perform for you," I said, pushing the words careful through my teeth. God knows they weren't natural on my mouth. "Perhaps you think me a fool, and who could blame you, as I sit here and listen to you call me a wild animal, a peasant. But I am wise enough to know when my words will only be met with derision and scorn." I looked to the side a small bit. "So no, my prince, I would prefer not to regale you."

My husband's hand settled on mine, his fingers clawing in and cutting. I didn't much dare to look at him, to breathe.

Out the edge of my eye I saw a pale face lean forward. Her blue eyes were bright, and there were a stark, harsh beauty to her face. Eleanor of Aquitaine inclined her head to me, and I flushed.

"Well said, my lady Marian," she said.

Gisbourne released the bear clamp on my hand and I tucked my head down to the dowager queen.

CHAPTER
TEN

───o───

When supper were over Gisbourne caught my elbow and held me in a fair wolf's trap, dragging me out the hall, moving faster than the rest. It were a few twists and turns before we weren't in a crowd, and he pushed me ahead.

"God damn you!" he growled. "You and your filthy, proud mouth! I will be made to pay for that, and by hell so will you."

"I did what you asked!" I snapped. "I spoke well, didn't I? I didn't stab no one."

He pushed me again and I tripped over the skirts, hitting the wall, and he slammed his whole body behind mine so it stole away my breath. I reached out to fight him, to grab my knife, but he trapped my arms. I struggled hard, fair panicked now, but it didn't matter, didn't make him move.

"I could take you, Marian," he threatened low in my ear. He bit my neck and I shook and struggled more, trying to be free of him. I ain't never felt so trapped, so weak. He had my name, and every moment more he were taking my courage from me. He were taking everything I had from me. "I could bind you to me forever with the duty a husband is entitled to from a wife. I could give you a scar to match your wedding present. I could beat you until you remember your place, your promise." His teeth sank into my ear and I cried. "Pick one."

"Is this what your honor means to you?" I asked, but my voice weren't much there and shaking besides. "Will this make you feel bigger in the eyes of the prince?" I drew a breath. "Or is it the princess you want to impress?"

His hand slammed the wall beside my head and he roared, "Pick one!"

Moving his hand meant he let go a bare shadow of a bit, but it were all I needed. I jerked out from him and pulled my knife. He stopped himself quick when he saw it, and his eyes went narrow.

Good. If all I had were his fear of a blade in my hand, that were enough.

Voices rose up in the hall behind him, and Gisbourne turned.

I ran for the nearest window, ready to fling myself out if need be.

It weren't needed to fling. Gisbourne were at least a few moments behind, and I climbed out on the ledge and onto the posts that stuck out the side of the wall. I hated that my hand meant I weren't much good for climbing. I hated the skirts that twisted up my legs. A few shaky leaps more brought me over to a stone trough and I jumped onto that and down.

I went for the wall and stood at the base of it, staring up. It were high and I were already weak, the shivers that Gisbourne started not nearly out of me yet.

Coming round the side and bitter with cold, I wondered what to do about the guards. I couldn't much climb past them, and my head weren't working proper enough to figure out a better plan. Moments came and went, and I were just colder and colder yet.

Looking to the residences, I wondered if I had to go back. If I had to return to him in his foul temper in that thimble of a room. I stepped forward, then stopped. Weren't nothing that way but pain and trouble. How could I go back?

"My lady," the guards said.

I turned. They stepped their heels together in an awful clamor.

I walked toward them slow, careful, and they kept their watch.

Walking past them, every step got more quick as I realized they full meant to let me walk out unbothered. It seemed there were something I could like about being a noblewoman after all.

The guards at the base of the castle opened the gates for me, and gave me a horse and a cloak besides. I could bare stammer out my thanks, stunned stupid with surprise.

I rode out into the night, heading straight for Edwinstowe.

The horse bore me more quick than my feet would, and the beast took me through the narrow wooded path that led to the monastery. I dismounted and left the horse in the yard, going to the warming room.

I stopped at the door, my hand trembling near the latch, remembering the last time I were in there.

My hand made its decision and the latch tripped, the door opening and the warmth running over me. The three boys stopped. They weren't asleep yet, and for one horrible breath, I wondered if in skirts and a noble's kit I didn't belong here.

"Christ, it's good to see you, Scar," Much said, bounding over to me and hugging me.

John were next, lifting me off the floor with his big arms.

Then he let me go and Robin were there, and the part of me that weren't much tough at all, the part that loved him and were terror-struck at Gisbourne rose up, and tears jumped from my eyes.

He caught me close, tucking me tight into his chest till it felt like my own chest, till it felt like he drew breath and it ran through me to make me strong. "They can't see," he whispered in my ear. "Cry as much as you need to, Scar. I won't let them see."

His arms strapped closer around me and gave me their strength. "I am so scared of him, Rob," I whispered soft, rubbing his neck with my words.

"You're all right," he murmured, his hands like running water down my back to draw my pain away. "You're with me now. And if you want, you don't ever have to go back there."

"Just hold on to me a bit longer," I breathed into his neck, the skin hot and damp with tears.

He nodded, and I thanked God for his calm heart.

I held him till my breath ran steady and I could bear to untwine my arms from him. As I let go, I looked at his face and I knew in a heartbeat he weren't calm at all. He were furious, rage and steel and hellfire in his eyes, but he were calm for me. He gave calm to me so I could be strong.

"So," I asked, giving a bare smile, "what's the plan?"

"Thoresby's been allowed to compete," Much said, "but he can't beat much of anything in an archery contest. He's truly a terrible shot."

"The obvious thing is just to dress Rob up like Thoresby," John said, "but he doesn't want to do it."

"I'm working with him," Rob said. "He's getting better."

"He's not really," said Much. "But I'm trying to figure some sort of arm band to make his aim better."

"Why won't you just stand in for him?" John asked. "You'll be in a coat and scarf and such anyway. We could make you pass. Dammit, Rob, it's the simplest plan."

"No, it isn't," Rob said quiet. "We all know what's happening to me and I can't be counted on for much. Besides, if they catch me, he's disqualified entirely. And I'll be killed."

I threaded his fingers through mine and squeezed. It weren't like I would ever let that pass.

"I'll see what I can pick up about the others," I said.

"Gisbourne's a good shot," John said. "We know that."

I nodded. "I think that's why Prince John chose this. Gisbourne claims it were promised to him, and I think the prince is just making a show and giving it to Gisbourne anyway."

"All we've got is Thoresby," John said with a sigh. "I don't think it will be enough."

Gripping Rob tight, I stepped forward. "It has to be enough. Our people have gone through hell and more under the last sheriff. If Gisbourne is sheriff we won't never be free."

"*We've* gone through hell," John growled. "And we have nothing to show for it. I'm beyond weary of all of this."

"We're close, John," I told him. "Things will be different with Thoresby."

"Things are never different," he said, and stared at the fire.

"You lot go to sleep," Rob said. "Scar, are you going back tonight?"

My pipes ran thick, and I swallowed. I had to, didn't I? "Yes," I said soft.

"I'll walk you back."

He let go of my hand for a moment to pull on a cape and boots, and even that small bit of him I wanted back. It returned swift, and his fingers pressed into mine, gloveless and warm.

He tugged a slight bit and I followed him.

"Bye, Scar," Much said.

"I'll be up at the castle for the tournament tomorrow, Scar," John said. "I'll look in on you."

I wanted to snap that I weren't a baby or some small thing that needed looking after, but it weren't the truth. I missed the band. I missed feeling safe and looked after. I nodded at John and left, tucking Rob's arm closer to me.

We stepped into the cold dark and it felt sweeter with him beside me, like instead of dying the world had made space for the two of us. Going to the yard I took the reins of the horse, pulling him along with us as we walked.

"What happened tonight, Scarlet?" Rob asked me.

I turned my face into his shoulder against the thought. "Not worth thinking on, Rob. Are you still not sleeping?"

"I've slept a little," he said. "Never for very long at a time. The monks said that might help."

"And it has?"

He nodded. "The nightmares start and I wake up. I don't slip into them."

"But they're still there."

"They've always been there, Scar. I cheated them for as long as I could."

"I had nightmares when I were younger, when my sister died. They went away after a time." *After I met you,* I knew with a start. I hadn't put that together before. And now he had nightmares, and I couldn't put a balm on his mind the way he had mine.

His arms rubbed along me, warming me like fire. "I'm trying for you, Scar. I'm trying to find a way out of them." His voice were whisper soft and the night ate it up. "I keep thinking about that night, when I hurt you. How much worse it could have been. And if we ever—I mean, in the chance that we ever have a family—" His voice stopped, and he were swallowing, over and over, like whatever were stuck wouldn't go down.

Family. That meant children, didn't it? Babies. It made shivers and gooseflesh run over my body. For so long I had never thought I were meant for that, but *Rob* . . . I could see our family clear as water. Strong sons with Rob's eyes and moppy little girls with my sister's gold hair. Rob with them all bundled up in his arms.

"Rob," I said soft. "You tried your damnedest to kill me, but you didn't. You couldn't, and I wouldn't let you. So if this thing is always chasing you, I wouldn't never let you hurt a family. But you will fight this. Can't you tell me what you see, when you dream?"

He shuddered. "Tell me what happened tonight."

"You'll lose your temper," I told him soft.

"And if I tell you the nightmares," he said, pulling me close and tucking his head to mine, "you might lose your love for me."

"Never," I swore.

"It's always the Crusades," he whispered into my ear. Despite being so much like what Gisbourne had done earlier, this made my skin blush warm and my heart beat fast. "There was so much fighting, Scarlet. So much death. And so much of it I was responsible for. And when I dream, I'm fighting still."

I knew that weren't but a bit of it; he would never fear to lose my love over such a thing. I knew he fought. I knew he killed. But it were enough for now.

"Tell me what happened," he said, his lips brushing cold onto my cheek.

"I'm afraid of Gisbourne," I said, my voice twisted and small. "He threatened me, and it were pure awful, Rob. The court made their cruel words, and Gisbourne were more than bothered by it." I shook my head. "People have talked foul about me for so long, Rob, I bare notice it anymore. But he hates it. And he makes me pay for it."

"People who don't know you, Scar. Those that know you wouldn't ever speak badly of you."

"You don't think?" I whispered.

He drew my hand up, kissing my fingers. "No."

I held tight to his hand but pulled away a bit, tugging him to walk. "You didn't lose your temper," I noticed.

"Love," he said soft, his thumb running over the bumps of my knuckles. "If I can keep my temper when you come to me and cry and I want to kill anyone that's ever wronged you, trust me, I can stay calm when you just need someone to tell about it." He pulled me closer again and kissed my temple, my cheek. "Besides," he said, "something tells me you're not explaining the worst of it."

"I just feel lost," I said. "In skirts and trying to talk a way that ain't natural. Trying to be something I'm not—for *him*."

He pulled me to him, hands running 'neath the guard's cloak and over my sides, my hips. My body felt different in a dress, in the castle; my legs weren't for running, my arms weren't for climbing, my waist seemed important in a way it ain't never been. In the forest, my middle were the part of me that were most soft without muscle or bone, so it needed to be protected, covered, hidden. In the castle it were on display, but it still felt like a weak spot. Vulnerable, which weren't a thing I much liked.

But Rob's hands on my waist felt like a thrill, like it were close and hidden, a secret place for him to touch. I let the reins drop as he kissed me and my body sparked over with fire like dry kindling. I pushed him back a bit against a tree, my hand desperate to touch a single part of him.

My hand slipped under his cloak, under his tunic and his shirt to bunch them up a bit. My hand were cold as it went, but I pushed it flat over his heart and let the heavy beat push warm into my hand. That was what I wanted from him.

His hands overcame the little pins in my hair, and he ran his fingers through the long bits, through the short fluff in back, over and over again.

I had heard enough girls—most yapping about John—say that a kiss made them stupid, blind to the world with every sense fair gone. And true, I hadn't kissed enough to well compare, but Rob's kiss made every bit of me thrum with life, with hot and blood. It made me feel brighter and taller and in these dark days, it were like a magic draught to shore up my strength.

I left his lips to press a kiss by his heart. "I love you, Robin," I whispered to him.

His arms pulled tight round me, pressing me to him, forging us like metal. "Don't go," he whispered to me. "I can't do it, Scar, I can't send you back there to him. To more hurt."

Shivers ran over my spine. "I don't want to go," I told him. "But Rob, I want to marry you. And that's more than the rest."

"He'll never give us an annulment," Rob breathed. "We can't trust the likes of him."

"No," I told him, gripping him tighter. "We can't. But God knows I weren't meant for him, Rob, and we'll get this annulment somehow."

I nudged his face with my nose until he brought his mouth down to mine for another kiss like magic potion. I needed some unholy kind of strength and courage to walk away from him.

He broke it off with a heavy sighing. "I love you, Scarlet. Go on, now, before you steal my sanity too," he said.

"Too?" I questioned.

His grin by the moon were wicked and handsome. "Thief of my heart."

I tugged him close and kissed him once more. "Thinking better of walking me back?" I asked him soft, a little sad.

He sighed 'gainst my mouth. "You'll be faster on the horse, and honestly, I don't think I can watch you walk back into that castle."

"They just let me come and go. It's mad," I said, smiling.

His thumb ran over my cheek. "You're a noblewoman. They can't keep you out. Or in."

I shrugged. "I were a noblewoman before, they kept me out just fine."

He laughed. "Yes, you were very clear about that fact before."

Rob kissed me once more and helped me on the horse—it weren't half as easy in skirts—and stood back 'gainst the tree as he spurred on the horse. I watched Rob as the horse trotted on, his white shirt bright in the moon and standing like a light in the trees.

Soon the forest covered him up, and I went back to Nottingham, alone.

CHAPTER

ELEVEN

The morning were bright and cold, fierce and harsh. The castle's deer park to the west had been cleared and made into tourney grounds. The field were clear of snow and tree bits, and horses were all round the grounds, stamping the hard earth and pluming white breath like smoke from their nostrils, their backs steaming with heat in the cold like they were ghost horses.

I were tucked in a great big chair plush with cushions, fur wrapped about me and servants with hot wine at the ready. And yet just across the grounds in fair shaky stands that weren't never cleared of snow there were the people of Nottingham-shire, shivering in their boots and bare coats.

How had I gotten to this side of the ground?

The knights went to their places, and I watched. Their phantom horses wheeled in the back part before the run. The flag dropped and the riders spurred forward. The horses stretched, their legs massive and corded round with muscle and power, and the knight rode it, a chipmunk on the back of a dragon. But the knights did have their own kind of grace. It weren't much in the way of valor to play at fighting like it weren't something that the people at their sides had to do every day for their food and life, but the knights were a grand vision. Their armor were fitted in a way that made steel mock the way the body could move, but still, the shining plates twisted and moved together and made the knight a faceless thing, a warrior.

And when they crossed, their heavy lances looked not for each other, like a sword might, but for the blank open space in front of a man's chest. That were the spot the lance longed to fill, a hard strike dead center. It were a strange game. In a knife fight, I worried first about what my opponent might do with their weapon, but it weren't so in a joust. It were as if you had to forget that the other might strike you; he became nothing more than a place to land your lance, and you had to trust that you would either strike first or your stance would hold you through a blow.

I liked that. You weren't never fighting an opponent. You were made to hit a target, and forget all else.

Sitting back, I thought I'd do fair well in a joust.

The crier, a silly little man that kept yelling titles and such, rapped his stick on the ground twice but didn't shout. I looked up and noble ladies ushered the queen mother to sit between myself and Isabel.

I stood double-quick and curtsied, though Isabel just gave a nod to the queen. The queen sat and her ladies tucked furs about her, and then with a wave of her white hand they left and found other seats.

Feeling foolish, I got back into my chair, pulling my legs up beneath me and my fur over me.

"How are the fights?" the queen mother asked.

"Dreadful," Isabel said. "I so wish during these times of war that England's noble sons would not so mock the practice of it. Why, it is as if they spit upon Richard's Holy Crusade." I saw her cast her eyes slight to the queen.

"Hm," the queen said. "My lady Leaford, what do you think of the practices of tournaments?"

"I think it's foolish and lovely," I said overquick. There were probably a better answer, but it weren't in my head.

"Oh?" she said. "Please explain."

"Fighting like this is beautiful, in a fashion," I said, slow now. "No one is hurt for true, and there is grace and power in it. The horses, the riders, I even like the armor."

"But you said foolish too."

I swallowed. Fool tongue. "Yes, my lady queen. These ain't—" I coughed hard, blood rushing my cheeks. "These aren't the men that would ever be called upon to fight. There is a war and they are not part of it. And the men that watch them, shivering from the far side, will fight and die as soon as King Richard has need of them. And yet they do not have the money to practice, and not the money to protect themselves from such fates."

She pulled her fur closer to her neck, and its hairs stood

tall like the animal had its hackles up. "Such a difference is not just in the poor and wealthy, Lady Marian. It is strange as a mother to see one son play at war while the other wipes blood from his face each night. But I can see the beauty in a joust as well, and as a mother I wonder if this is what young men see when they dream of war. We women often don't see what the appeal is, but they crave it."

"You know yourself in a fight," I told her. "There's no lying about your skills. About what you can do. It's a good feeling."

"You can't feel if you're dead," Isabel said. "There's nothing good about fighting."

"Then you utterly mistake the role of women, Isabel. We fight for different things, but women are the most natural of fighters." The queen inclined her head to the princess. "Something I have liked about you from the first, Isabel, is that you have defiance and pride within you. That is a form of fight."

Isabel's cheeks went to blush but I weren't so sure she liked the compliment. "In my experience women don't get to fight for what they want," she said, her voice low and careful. "We don't understand war because we are not allowed to."

"You can always fight for what you want," I told her, over-fierce, sitting forward. "Always. People try to take that from you no matter your station, but you can always fight."

She gave a snort. "If I were some peasant heathen I'm sure I could," she said.

"I ain't no peasant," I said hot.

"Just a heathen, then," she said, peering past the queen to smile tight at me. "How does Guy put up with you?"

It took me a moment to remember Guy were Gisbourne's given name.

"I'm *not* a heathen," I ground out, careful to say the words right. Christ, I were out of practice with this. "And you bare seem to know what the word means. I make no apologies for the way I talk—I only started doing it because nobles and men with power and heavy fists don't bother with a lowborn churl, and I chose safety over fancy words when it came to the streets of London. And I don't look the part of some noble truss, but I spend my life trying to help people that can't help themselves. People hurt by the cruelties of their lords. Say that I'm a heathen like I don't serve God, but all you're doing is making yourself look the fool."

Her face went fair sour. "Oh, this is how you help people? From up here on your high chair in your expensive furs, watching your husband tilt?"

"Perhaps I ought to be lower," I told her, standing. I dipped to Eleanor. "My lady queen."

I heard Isabel make some tittery noise behind me, but I turned my cheek from her and walked down from the dais.

Stepping from the stage for nobles felt good, but there weren't nothing normal about walking through people in skirts, in fine clothes, watching them step away from me to let me pass. I couldn't fade to shadows; I couldn't not be noticed. I hated it.

"You look a little lost."

I turned to see Much steps from me. He smiled under a big farmer's hat in his crooked, half-sure way, and I hugged him.

He hugged me tight with a laugh. "John and Rob are awfully boring without you around."

I mussed his hair with a laugh. "I'm certain they are. So what do you reckon, will someone make me a widow today?"

We went and leaned on the fencing that were meant to keep the common folk from the grounds. We were low, back, and to the side, and from there the whole thing looked vicious and fierce, less like a game and more like gods stomping about for notice.

"I doubt it," he said, honest as ever. "Gisbourne is a very good fighter."

I rubbed my still swollen lip. "I know."

"He slept, you know," Much told me. "Last night, whole way through."

This thrilled my heart like a holy fire. "It's fair strange, talking about Rob like he were an infant or such."

"It's good news."

I shivered. "It's perfect news."

"I'm scared for you, Scarlet," he told me, nudging closer. "Those bruises aren't all from Rob that night, are they?"

"No." I slung a grin his way. "When were I ever afraid of a little bit of purple?"

"I'll find a way to help," he promised. "I'll find a way to make sure you're not alone."

"I'm well enough, Much. Needn't fret," I told him. "Are the menfolk well?"

He nodded. "Yes. Hugh Morgan's trying to make one of the knights wed Aggie after some improprieties, which is entertaining, but the food is almost gone. We won't last till Christmas, much less the rest of the winter."

"You should see the feasts they have here. It's enough to make you sick."

He smiled at me. "It doesn't take much to make you sick, Scar."

It were meant to be funny, so I laughed.

"What's it like, being one of them?"

"A noble?" I asked. He nodded. "I'm not, I don't think. I don't talk right. I for certain don't look right. They all think I'm off and mad and contrary."

His grin sloped sideways in a silly way. "You are all of that."

"Are we talking about me?" John asked, coming up my other side and wrapping his arm round my back. "Look at the little lady we have here," he laughed, looking at my clothes. "Where's your knife?" he asked.

I frowned, shrugging him off, but I showed him the one I hid along my back.

Much laughed. "But where's your second knife?" he asked.

Leaning on the rail again, I said, "My boot. But ladies ain't supposed to show their ankles."

John guffawed at this, leaning beside me and tucking his

hat down low, and Much did to match. I wouldn't never tell them as much, but with them on either side were the closest I felt to right in the past days.

Thoresby were next up, and getting himself onto the horse he looked frail and old. He weren't—he were bare older than my father, and I remembered my father strong and young. But his armor were too big and his face were too grave, and my chest were strapped tight with fear for him.

The herald blew his horn and called out Thoresby's name, and Wendeval's came up behind it. I sucked in a breath.

"Not good?" John asked, raising his brow to me.

"If you knew how to joust, he would be a fair likeness to you," I told him. "I saw Wendeval last night. He's a big bruiser."

John scowled. "I'm not *just* a bruiser," he muttered.

The horn blew again and the horses launched forward. Thoresby didn't sit well, didn't hold the lance well, didn't move well. "Christ," I hissed. "It's a damn wonder he's riding in a straight line."

"And this is our champion," John said.

I hit him.

They crossed lances, and Thoresby's lance glanced off Wendeval's shoulder, shooting up and launching from his hand.

Wendeval's lance struck Thoresby's ribs, ringing with the impact but glancing rather than holding. His lance dropped, and pages ran out to get the fallen weapons.

The riders trotted back to their places and were handed up another lance.

"He's going to lose," John said.

"Shut it," Much snapped at him as the horn blew.

John shrugged, and my fingers curled into the wooden fence as the horses' strides shook the ground. Wendeval's form were stronger, better, his arm high and lined to his shoulder, his body balanced over the horse.

Thoresby, if anything, looked worse.

Several more pounding hoofbeats and they met on the field. Wendeval leaned out and struck, his body like a strange, stretched version of John throwing a punch. Thoresby moved late, the lance hurtling toward him overfast, like he were fixed and couldn't much move.

The ball head of the lance struck dead in the center of Thoresby's armor, not with the clangs that the glancing blows made but with a low, hard boom.

The horse thundered on, but Thoresby were still, hanging in the air for breath after breath as his horse charged forward without him. Then his body twisted, light flashed from his silly, useless armor, and in a spinning mess he clattered to the ground, a still, twisted heap.

I ducked under the fence and ran.

Thoresby weren't moving when I got out there, a healer a breath behind me. Thoresby's arm were tucked under him at an ugly angle, and he uttered a groan.

My heart lurched to life in my chest. *Jesus.* He were alive.

The healer rolled him over and started checking him, and I sat by, kneeling on the frozen ground as more people clustered round. The crowds parted for Lady Thoresby, and I stood to meet her.

She were looking at her husband. "It's done, Scarlet," she whispered to me. "He can't fight with his arm like that." She glanced at me, her blue eyes full of water. "And I won't ask him to."

A cold, empty chill snaked round my spine to pool in my belly. I gripped her hand. "I know. I know. I'm sorry."

She gripped back. "Find some other way, Scarlet. You always do."

Her hand fell from mine, and she went forward with her husband. The crowd shifted and moved as my chest went tighter. Gisbourne would be sheriff, and all these people . . . all these people would suffer for it.

There wouldn't never be no relief, for none of them. Certain not for me.

"Scar?" John said low, catching my arm. "You all right?" He pulled me over to the side, and I went, leaning on the fence as the people started to clear from the field and Thoresby were carried off it.

"He's done," I told them. "*We're* done."

"You'll find another way, Scar," Much said.

My hands trembled with the damned desperate need to push him till he lost his feet. "*Me*," I growled, but I were dangerous close to wanting to cry. "It can't always be *me*. I can't figure it out."

"Scar—" Much said soft, touching my arm.

"Scar," John grunted, raising his chin. I looked past Much and frowned.

"I don't think Gisbourne would appreciate his wife mixing with the common element," de Clare said, walking close, his armor clattering and making me jump, though it looked fair foolish on him. "It doesn't look good for a man of his, well, *uncertain* stature." De Clare were inches away, and with my back against the fence the space felt oversmall.

I slid my sore hand behind me, keeping it from him, but even though every muscled bit of me were screaming to step away from him, I wouldn't do it. I wouldn't never run from a bully.

"His wife's fair common herself," I said. "And between the two of us, you're the only one looking foolish."

De Clare's lip curled. "You brazen little animal—" he started, but John laughed. John were leaning on the fence with me and Much, looking easy enough, but his jaw were bunched with muscle and his neck looked like a sailor's rig with all the lines running to and fro. "Something amuses you?" de Clare asked John.

"Begging your pardon, my lord," John said with a dash of his head. "By all means, keep talking. I would dearly love to see your face when you see how I—and all these menfolk behind me—take to you insulting her."

De Clare smiled at John. "Yes, I'm sure you're quite interesting to tangle with." He sneered. "Quite the brawler. Don't worry, you lowborn churl, she may be safe out here with your kind of rabble. But I can find her in the castle, alone, vulnerable. I can do whatever I want to her, and you won't—"

He stopped yapping, most because there were John's fist crashing into his mug—the one bit of him that weren't covered in shiny metal. And, like a toy, he spun a mite bit and fell back, dropping onto the ground.

"John, go," I told him as everyone began to look over. "Well put, but go."

He smiled and grabbed Much, and the townfolk stood and covered them as they went. The nobles were all looking over and staring at me.

"Marian?" someone said, and it took a breath to realize it were meant for me. I turned and Gisbourne were there, in only a bright chestplate, his black hair wild and wet. He reached over the fence and pulled me to him, and even with a giant beam between us, it were surprisingly close in a way I didn't much like. "Did he touch you again?" he snarled.

"Why, he threatened her life!" someone said. "Her life and all her future progeny! Awful!"

I turned to the voice and saw Allan there, looking overbright in a red cape. I frowned at him.

"And one of the townsfolk stood up for her, he did. The beloved jewel of Nottinghamshire. Never fear, my lord Leaford, for no true harm would come to her while these good people can prevent it."

Gisbourne glowered at him. "You sound Irish, minstrel."

He gave an elaborate bow. "Well spotted, my lord Leaford."

"Then how have you any idea what these people will do?"

Allan sprang up, unruffled. "Tis clear, my lord. Your wife—and for certain yourself, by your nearness to her—is adored by these people." He bowed again.

Gisbourne grunted an oath under his breath. Other men were helping de Clare up, and he were muttering without making much sense. Gisbourne shook his head and ducked under the fencing.

"What are you doing?" I breathed, stepping back from him.

Muscles in his jaw rolled like wagon wheels, and he stepped forward, taking my arm. "Come, Marian. I'll see you back to the dais."

"Gisbourne," Winchester called, coming from the noble's side. "You're up in the lists. I'll escort your wife, if you wish."

Gisbourne swept down his head so beads of sweat flew off. "Your Grace."

Winchester ducked under the fence. He had no armor on, and his arm were warm as it held mine. "Not tilting today, your Grace?" I asked.

He shrugged. "I have all the favor, money, and glory I require. I don't see the point in it. Besides, then how could I rescue young ladies?"

I looked back at de Clare, who had just bare found his feet. "Who or what were you rescuing me from?"

"A treacherous walk back to the dais, clearly. And myself,

from boredom. I did so enjoy seeing de Clare flat on his back. Your friend has excellent aim."

"You have no idea," I told him. "It is fair strange that I've found myself unable to do my own defending."

"You have a broken hand," he told me. "And yet I'm sure, without so many men eager to prove themselves around you, that knife you have along the small of your back would have been marvelously well employed. Your seat, my lady."

We had reached the dais and my empty chair. He held my hand until I were settled into it, and I stared up at him, fair shocked.

He bowed over my hand. "My lady. Your Highness," he said, and I turned.

Eleanor inclined her regal head to him. "Winchester."

Winchester left, and I drew a breath. I didn't much know what to say to a queen.

"You have many friends," she noted. "It seems they are a more common equivalent of my loyal knights."

Looking at Isabel's seat, I sighed. "I reckon I have more enemies than would-be knights."

"You know," the queen said, her voice thoughtful and quiet. I went fair still, listening. "When I was made Louis' wife and queen of France at fifteen, my husband's court thought me ... wild," she said slow. "I spoke my mind, and I loved to dance more than they thought entirely appropriate. They called me such names." Her cool, austere face curved with a regal smile. "I won them over, in time. They shouted my name and threw roses at my feet."

I stared at her. "I always heard you were unhappy in France."

She nodded, not looking at me. "Yes. Well, becoming an English queen after being a French one does call for some revision in history, doesn't it? And in the end, Louis' betrayal was perhaps the worst I have suffered." She lifted her shoulder. "But it led me here, to England, to my children." She chuckled. "Louis and I never fought quite so viciously as Henry and I did, though. Marriage is complicated."

I looked out over the field at Gisbourne's black-clad form. "Quite." I looked at her. "Is it true you fought in the first Crusade?"

She laughed and stared out over the field with a glow like a moonbeam. "A queen cannot reveal all her secrets, my dear." She tapped her lip with her finger, then continued to watch the jousts without saying another word.

My husband tilted in that round and won after a series of broken lances. His next contest were against de Clare, and he rode again, slamming a blow to the middle of de Clare's chest and unseating him with the first ride. When de Clare's helmet rolled loose, Gisbourne scooped it up with his lance and brought it to me on the platform like a trophy.

I took it. I stared at it, wondering if, without Thoresby in the race, Gisbourne had just won the whole of Nottinghamshire and didn't much know it yet.

CHAPTER

TWELVE

—o—

I stayed out on the grounds till all the other ladies had long gone to fires, and my bones were ice even 'neath the furs and the softness. Gisbourne did well, but my eyes weren't for him. I'd seen John and Much, Godfrey and even Tuck, but never once Rob.

I wanted to see him, to touch him again, to tell him my heart were near to bursting for him having slept a night. Even if it had to be without me, I wanted him well. A thousand times I started, seeing his height or his shape or his sand-fair hair, but it weren't never him, and by the end of the day my heartstrings were plucked as raw as the rest of me stood cold.

Even making my slow way back to the keep, I waited for the crunch of snow, the flash of dark against the white. He weren't there. He weren't with me. And hoping for it each moment were fair awful.

Though it weren't nothing close to hot, inside the walls of
the castle were warm and heavy, like the truth of things cast
about my shoulders thicker than a cloak. Outside, it were a
glimmer of hope to see Rob, but I wouldn't never catch him
inside the walls. Least, not without him being in trouble.

Sneaking about weren't as easy in noble's things, but I still
managed, hanging about enough servants' quarters to hear them
speak of Lord Thoresby, his arm broken three times over. He
wouldn't never hold a sword again, and never ever could he
fight for the role of sheriff.

I wanted to go to Lady Thoresby, but I couldn't. I couldn't
face her.

I went back to the chambers slow, dragging my slippered
toes along the stone. I'd wanted boots, but all the ladies wore
the flimsy things, made sillier still by the servants dropping car-
pets over the snow to keep the ladies' toes dry. I'd muddied mine
up a bit and the things were ruined, the whole of my feet ice-cold.

The chambers were empty, until my being there signaled
my lady's maid to come in. I waved her off, dragging one of
the furs from the bed to the fire, sitting on the hot stone by the
hearth. I pulled my soaked, foolish stockings off and pressed
my feet to the brick as close to the fire as I dared. I leaned
against the stone, half inside the fireplace itself, trying to curl
tight into the fire.

My eyes shut, and a vision of last Christmas, spent huddled
in Tuck's with his girls and my boys and a roaring fire. There'd
been dancing—I never danced, even when John asked me, even

when Rob stood and looked at me for a long breath. It had burned me then, thinking he looked at me and saw me and wouldn't choose me, but I knew better now. I knew he hadn't asked me for the same reason I hadn't asked him.

The door opened—in the chambers, in the castle, though for a breath I didn't know where I were—and my eyes dragged opened with it. Gisbourne walked in with his chamberlain clucking behind him, and he looked at me and I looked at him. His shirt were off, and his skin were red and raw like it were holding all the cold in Nottinghamshire. There were patches of darker red too, and I wondered, for the first time, if he'd been hurt during the joust.

"The snow prevents swelling," he said, and his eyes broke from mine.

I lifted a shoulder, looking back into the fire. "Cold is fair good for you, I reckon."

He grunted. I weren't sure if that were meant to be an agreement or not, but I didn't look over to decide. I shut my eyes, wishing for the dream again, but it didn't rise in the dark of my eyelids.

"Come along, Marian," he said after a while. "Supper is soon."

Supper weren't the torture it had been the night before. Men were tired and quiet. Isabel led much of the talk and didn't steer none of it toward me. For once I didn't raise my husband's ire, and when the meal ended, he offered his arm and led me out of the hall civil-like.

When we changed for bed and his shirt came off, I saw his body had taken hits; there were dark bruises on his shoulder and chest. For a joust, though, he had taken impressive little punishment. His eyes caught mine, his face dark and closed like a door.

I looked to the fire. "You'll do well tomorrow," I told him. "Might even win the joust."

"It doesn't matter," he said. "The archery is the only thing that matters."

"And bruising your competition, it seems."

His teeth bared. "Battering them, if I can."

I pulled a fur blanket around the loose dress for bed and climbed into the chair, curling tight.

There were a knock on the door, and my lady's maid went to answer it. She spoke in hushed tones and then shut the door, coming back into the room.

"My lady, the princess requests you attend her on a purview of the market in the morning."

"What does she need my attention for?" I grumbled.

"You know very well that a princess cannot be waited upon by commoners," Gisbourne said. "It is an honor to be asked."

"A backhanded honor," I said.

"Yes."

"Tell her no." The order were for Mary, but I were looking to Gisbourne.

"The princess did not wait for a response, my lady," Mary said.

"You can't tell her no; that's why she didn't wait. Mary, Eadric, you're dismissed," Gisbourne said.

The servants left with the milords and miladies and such, and then I couldn't hear naught but the fire crackling before me.

"It's cold," he said, looking at me.

That were as close as he'd ever come to asking for my wellness, and I looked away. "I like the cold."

"It wasn't always so," he said, and I heard him creak into the bed. "I was hard pressed to get you out of the sun in the summer gardens when we first met."

My chest went tight and my pipes stopped up as I thought of that, chasing Joanna's streaming blond hair through the garden, watching as it caught the light and glittered. I thought maybe if I could just catch her, I could become her, all blond hair and light and happiness. But it weren't never to be; the summer ended and Joanna died, and I were left in the dark-haired winter that I were born for. "Things changed."

He grunted. "Quite."

"Why did you bring me here?" I asked. "You knew they would hate me. You knew you'd be ridiculed for me. Why do it to yourself?"

"You are my wife."

"But it don't help you none."

"You are the only reason I have a claim here. It doesn't matter if I speak like a lord, they'll always treat me like a dog until I have the lands and titles for their damned respect. You were born a lady and these adventures of yours are nothing but a passing fancy. You should know that by now—you can run from it, but you can never unmake your birth, and they know that. For both of us."

"But—" I started.

"Besides," he continued, routing me off. "Prince John demands, and I answer."

"*He* wanted to see us as man and wife?"

"He doesn't like people subverting his control. Did you think your follies would go unnoticed?"

I frowned. "Well, it ain't like it were all my fault."

"You are more dangerous than a few peasants and a fallen earl, Marian."

"Why? Just because I'm a noble?"

"Good night, Marian."

"Gisbourne—"

"Please let one night pass where I don't need to be furious with you."

It weren't my fault he had the temper of a bear. It weren't my fault that he made me come here, made me stay in this god-awful place. None of it were my fault.

Still, I stayed quiet.

CHAPTER
THIRTEEN

***

The morning dawned cold and clear, and my husband were up as early as me, dressing for the second day of the joust. Mary fussed over me to make me ready to walk beside the princess, and I ain't never felt so foolish.

"Here," Gisbourne said as I were done. He tossed a purse of coin my way and I snatched it. "The princess will expect you to spend."

I peeked inside. "You won't see any of this back, you know."

His lip curled up like a dog. "So be it. You've already been stealing from me anyway, haven't you?"

Tying the purse inside my skirts, I didn't cop to it none.

"Marian," he said.

"Fine, I nicked the coins," I said, rolling my eyes. "You married a thief, you should hide things better."

"*Marian,*" he said, and I looked up. "Impress her."

I wanted to ask why, but I knew he were sweet on Isabel. Or I reckoned I knew—but that would be part and parcel with my husband having sweetness, or even a heart, which I weren't sure were so.

"I'll try to be less your wild wife," I told him. He nodded like it were some solemn thing I promised, and then he left.

Mary heaped me with a furry cloak and fancy gloves and ladylike boots that were fair useless, little more than fur-lined fabric in the shape of a boot with nothing to make it sturdy or stalwart in any measure. If I were to so much as run to the gates, they'd be naught but a heap of fur-lined shreds.

But for walking slow and making pretty, they were just fine.

I were shown to the princess's chambers and made to wait outside until she were ready, with the higher-ranking ladies flocked about her. When she emerged, the few others standing there dropped to curtsies, and it took me a breath to remember I were meant to do it too.

"Come along," she said, and we all stood and followed her out.

It were a messy business, so many puffed-up ladies walking down a single hallway, but the overly layered parade made it to the courtyard intact. It seemed we were meant to follow along behind the princess in a half circle, which one lady—who hadn't introduced herself to me—waved her hands and swatted at me to make sure I'd do.

My hands curled to fists—I left my damn knives in the

chambers. Which were probably a blessing, considering what notions ran through my head just then.

"Lady Leaford," Isabel called, not turning her head to me. She did crook a finger, though, and I took that as a summons. I stepped on the swatter's foot as I went and stood beside Isabel.

"Your Highness," I murmured.

"You shall be our guide," she said. "Come. This is your city, is it not? I wish to see it."

"It isn't truly," I denied, careful to say it straight.

"But you know it well. Don't be difficult. Show me," she said, meeting my eyes and still keeping her nose up. She weren't hard to look at, that were sure. Her skin were pale and her eyes brown and dark lashed; she were a fair English rose.

My mouth went tight. "Yes, your Highness."

We walked side by side down through the castle to the gate. I couldn't help but watch her dress drag through the dirt and mud and snow. Course that happened to most common folk too, but they tried to avoid it. The princess's dress were meant for it, and yet it might see a washing or two before the thing was cast aside. It were a miserable practice to flaunt to those that were oft born and buried in the same clothes.

The guards opened the gate, and like the skirt collecting dirt, two guards followed behind us as we went out.

I counted in my head. I were used to moving fast and quick—it didn't help to be a still target when you were a thief—and these ladies were slower than changing seasons. I took a step and counted, then took another.

"So," Isabel said to me, "you must tell me how you know Eleanor."

My mouth opened to question it when I realized who she were thinking of. "Of *Aquitaine?* You mean the queen?"

"Queen Mother," she corrected. "Yes, of course."

I made a fair unladylike sound that one of the women jumped at. "I never met her before yesterday." I shrugged. "Well, she near run me down in a carriage the day before."

"My dear, you are not well skilled at such games. You see, I know there is something between you two. Eleanor of Aquitaine approves of no one and she's publicly lauded you. Beyond that, she requested to sit next to you at the joust."

My fingers pressed light to the bruises on my face. "I fair think she only defended me, not approved overmuch," I said. "And I can't speak to the rest. If Eleanor has some sort of interest in me, I don't know of it."

She waved her hand. "Fine. Keep your secrets; I'll discover them in time anyway." She sniffed, raising her chin. "It was curious that my husband and I didn't see you with Guy while he's been at court," Isabel said, her voice fair quiet, like she wanted it to be kept secret.

"Not so curious," I said with a shrug.

"No? A dutiful wife should always travel with her husband."

Were this where he got the notion? "I'm not the most dutiful of wives."

She looked at me and her eyes caught on the bruises. "No," she said, "but you are lucky. Guy is a fine gentleman."

I frowned at her, but caught the disbelieving words that were like to fly out of my mouth. Like it or not, I told him I'd behave and I never liked to cross out a promise. "You must know him . . . better than most."

She smiled. Beautiful girls shouldn't smile half as much as they do; it weren't nearly fair to the rest of us. "I do; I've known him since I was a child. He was always such a kind friend."

My mouth twisted up to keep words in. Kind? *Kind?* "I watched him kill a child without any cause," I said, my voice quiet and low, the proper words not hard to find when my blood ran hot. "An innocent child. Such a man can never be called kind."

Her shoulders went back and her chin went up higher. "You may be married to him, but you don't know him. And you have no right to judge. You glorify that thief Robin Hood, but he's killed as well. You, a *lady*, I can well imagine has killed. A despicable thing. And yet, you don't even pause to consider what a man Guy was before you ran from him, before he scoured the earth to hunt you down. *You* created his cruelty."

"No," I said, vicious and fast. "He had a black pall on his soul before ever I met him. I could feel it from the first. And Rob and I never harmed a living thing for profit or sport. You know nothing of this."

"Scarlet!" someone yelled, and I turned. It were Ben Clarke, the oldest of Mistress Clarke's three boys and Will's older brother. He were tall and long, like someone had stretched him before his body knew to do it. He were standing before a stall in the beginning of the market lane, with armor plates and such.

"Morning, Ben," I said with a smile, trying to cool my rushing blood. It were a strange thing, how much the use of my name soothed me.

The ladies behind me were tittering though, and it took me a long moment to remember that in London, the night girls were called scarlets.

"You look awful fine," Ben said to me with a laugh. "Passing strange, but very fine."

"Ain't no way to compliment a lady," I told him, smacking him up the head with a touch of effort for his height.

Isabel made a noise, and Ben looked past me, losing his color and bowing, then dropping his rear down to kneel. Then he thought better of his knees in the cold mud and sort of crouched.

"Get up, Ben," I said.

"No," Isabel corrected. "Good morning, young man. And who might you be?"

"Milady. Ben Clarke, milady. Of the Clarkes. Of Edwinstowe. Milady."

"Blathering idiot," I muttered, crossing my arms. Tucking my hand in hurt, though, so the crossing didn't last long.

"Please rise, Master Clarke," she said. He did, awkwardly. "And what wares have you brought here?"

"My master's. He's a blacksmith in Worksop."

"Scrawny for a blacksmith," one lady said. Ben set to blushing and I glared at her.

"Ben's learning," I spat back. "He's a good lad. Been providing for his family for years."

Isabel held her hand out toward the ladies behind her, and one placed coins in her gloves. "I think my husband should like some new armor, Master Clarke. Please come to the castle when you're finished for the day to fit him." She pressed the coins into his hands. "Something to reward you for being such an excellent salesman."

He bowed clumsily over the coins, looking fair awed and bloodless. "Thank you, your Highness. Milady Highness."

Isabel nodded and turned away, and Ben threw his arms around me. "Thank you, Scarlet. Thank you so much."

He let me go quick as he started, and immediately set to closing up his cart, I imagine to run back to his master and give the good news.

Isabel crooked her fingers at me, beckoning me along like a pup. Less than a pup, really. Least you called out for a pup.

I went. Most because in spite of her beauty and terrible sense of men, I liked what she'd done for Ben. "That will mean a great deal for him," I told her. It were the closest I could come to thanking her for it.

She lifted a shoulder. "My husband's reputation needs improvement, Lady Marian." Her eyes met mine sharp. "It may be expensive to buy a loyal sword, but peasant loyalty is bought rather cheap, don't you think? They will talk of it for years. The kindness of the prince and princess—and when Richard returns, he will hear of it and reinstate John as his heir."

As much as I wanted to stomp about and tell her the hearts

of the people weren't just open and eager for purchase, I didn't. I wanted them to have her coin, even if it meant damn little in the end.

She weren't shy about it neither. At the next booth she told one of the other women that the lady needed to buy new gloves; she told another lady to buy several new combs. On and on she went through the market, spending all our money for us and giving it to the vendors. The guards were piled with the parcels, including a lamb on a tether that the princess thought were the dearest thing.

Halfway through the market, people were well aware of the princess. I caught Allan sulking about and he gave me a wink before he lifted a purse from one of the ladies. Vendors were crowding closer, shouting at the princess, begging for her coin. And they weren't the only ones begging—Nottingham's hungry had come as well, calling to her. The ladies crowded closer together, but the princess pretended not to hear the voices of the poor.

More guards filled in behind us, pushing the people aside and crushing into the narrow space to put themselves between the ladies and the common folk.

Someone tugged on my coin purse, an inept thief, and I caught him by the throat with my good hand as I whipped round to press my elbow against his chest, keeping my hurt hand away from him. It were a young boy I didn't know. He couldn't have been more than ten. Even caught, he stared me down with the fiercest look, and I stared back. He were so young.

He moved, striking like a snake to spit in my face and try

to wrench free. I had him tight though, and I shook him. "Stop," I grunted. "I ain't trying to hurt you."

"Oh!" someone cried behind me. I let him go to turn and see, and the princess had her arms up. There were a girl clinging to her skirts, round the same age as the boy, and I wondered if they were partners. Or siblings. Which I reckoned were much the same thing.

A guard rushed forward at the same time I did, only he raised his sheathed sword to hit the young girl back with his hilt. The angle were such that I couldn't get full between them, but I pulled the girl back and by instinct blocked with my other hand. Which were broke.

I fell back and choked on a yell, holding the girl to me still as stars shot through my eyes.

It were a bit of a mess then. The guard tried to help me and several of the vendors what knew me hurried forward to help. I stood and kept the girl close in the crush of people, trying to wave them away. The princess were talking to the guards it seemed, and slowly eyes went back to her, and despite all the people around I weren't the focus.

"Are you all right?" I felt a body press close to mine like the crowd pushing too close, the whisper right into my ear, the brim of Rob's hood skidding over my cheek.

"Get her out of here," I said to him, pushing the girl against him. She looked up at me, eyes wide. "I think she has a brother. Feed them." I pushed Gisbourne's coin into his hand, and his lips pressed my cold cheek, setting the whole thing to flames.

"The shadows aren't the same without you, love," he murmured soft.

Then he were gone, and the girl were gone with him, and the crush of people, like they had been there just to hide Rob, started to fade.

Isabel were staring at me like she had seen the whole thing, like I were betraying Gisbourne, like all the power of her beauty were meant for hating me.

—⚭—

My hand had started to bleed again from the blow, and as we were shepherded back to the castle by guards, one of the ladies fussed over it so until I finally agreed to let a runner go for the monks. It would be a fair long while before the runner made it out there and the monks made it back, and I prayed the ladies wouldn't be clucking near so much. As soon as I agreed, though, the ladies ceased to bother me, and Isabel went out to watch the joust. I headed for Gisbourne's chambers and stopped at a window, looking out over the grounds. They were far enough that they looked like toys, knights on runners set to lance each other.

I couldn't see the royals under their tent, but I wondered if Eleanor were there. What had Isabel meant, making so much of her interest in me? She had been kind, but I didn't know enough to reckon if it were a special thing.

What other notice would she have of me? Unless she had a softness for half-wild girls with a penchant for thieving. She had been her own brand of wild when she were young—she fought wars! Incited her children to rebellion! Taught her sons how to be kings and married her daughters to some of the most powerful monarchs in Europe.

I shook my head and went back to the room. Without Gisbourne there, it were quiet and calm, and I locked the door and took the chance to lay on the bed for once. It were a fair fine thing, and before I knew better, I were fast asleep.

—⚍—

I woke to a pounding on the door. Startling awake, I stood from the bed and frowned at it like it had betrayed me. Going quick to the door, I opened it to see Brother Ignatius and a figure a bit taller than him in a hood. It were too short to be Rob, too slight to be John—

"Much?" I asked.

He pushed me gentle-like into the room, dashing the hood off. "Hush," he said. "Still an outlaw, you know, even if I'm not the most recognizable one."

"He insisted," Brother Ignatius said, bringing me to the heavy, carved chairs. He were one of the older monks, but by far the best at healing arts. He unwrapped my hand and I hissed as the cloth tore free from the blood and muck that weren't quite skin. Much were bent over my chair, peering over my shoulder to glare down at it.

"Hmm," Much said.

"You see," Ignatius said, extending a finger over the cut on my knuckles and looking to Much. "It isn't so much the cut, but the worry that the bones aren't setting straight. And won't be able to." He turned his gaze to me. "My lady, you seem to so treasure your hands and yet you are impeding their healing."

I grit my teeth as he pressed the bones. "I ain't meaning to."

"Aren't," Much said. "Come on, Scar, you have to try harder to speak right."

That made my heart thud heavy and I looked down at my hand.

"That's why they keep hurting you," he plowed on. "Isn't it?"

"No," I snapped, not looking up at him. "They keep hurting me because they like to hurt people. Same as the old sheriff. It *ain't* nothing I've done wrong."

He eased off my shoulder, coming round front. He crouched in front of me, his stump near to my wounded hand. "Scar, that isn't what I meant. I just thought that you started talking like this for a purpose, didn't you? You must have, being noble to start with. But why don't you adapt back? Change again and prove them all wrong."

Ignatius set to wrapping my hand again and I turned into my shoulder 'gainst the pain. "It isn't that easy," I hissed after a moment that stung at my eyes. "And I don't see why I should. I don't want to be here. I don't want this."

"Scar," he said soft. "Didn't you see how the people looked at you today? Same way they look at Rob. You *are* nobility and they all know it. If you want, you can live up to that. Embrace that. *Use* that."

I thought of Isabel and Prince John, and damned Gisbourne. "I never want to live up to that. I never want to be part
of that, Much. That's why I ran away in the first place."

"Was it?" he asked.

I lifted my shoulder, hindered by the Brother tugging on
my hand. "Somewhat. I knew I weren't never going to be the
lady my mother wanted me for. I knew I didn't want to marry
Gisbourne. And that were enough to make me run."

"You can't run now," he reminded me soft.

"I can always run," I growled at him. "But running won't
never change that these are my people. Running won't give me
an annulment and let me be with Rob, proper and right."

"Then fight," he told me. He grinned at me, slow and
bright like the sun, holding my hurt hand gently as the Brother
tied it off. "And try and use your words."

CHAPTER

FOURTEEN

$\sim$o$\sim$

The Brother gave me a cloth sling to keep my arm tucked away, and I fidgeted with it on the way to supper.

"Will you stop that," Gisbourne grunted.

"The damn monk tied me up," I grumbled back. "I can bare move my arm."

"I believe that's the point."

"I don't like it."

"That doesn't really matter, does it?" Gisbourne snarled. "Be still."

I frowned.

"I won the joust, since you're so concerned."

Were I meant to have been outside, watching him get his prize? "What did you win?" I asked.

"A gold figurine of a jousting knight."

"Fitting."

"Quite. I've had it melted down."

I snorted. "So much for symbols of glory and the like."

"I won't need symbols when I'm sheriff. I'll need money, and a lot of it."

My belly twisted up at the reminder. It weren't the archery tournament yet, but what had I been doing to see that he would lose? Not much. Mooning after Rob, without any hope for a replacement in the contest.

The smell broke my thoughts, long before we turned into the hall. The halls were filled with scents of food, like fat roasting, and something sweeter too. We turned into the Great Hall, and I saw the cause of it.

Three great spits had been built over giant copper bowls of fire in the center of the hall, three giant pigs skewered on the spits and pages slowly turning their round, heavy bodies over the fire, basting them with honey that dripped onto the flames. They must have been doing it all day.

Around the spits were huge tables filled with lavish food-stuffs. There were woven breads several feet long, geese that were in their full feathered glory but still and clear dead—one even had a tiny crown on his head. I had no idea how they could do such a thing, or if it were even meant for eating—the creature looked like it were about to leap into flight, but it never flinched.

There were pies with such decorated crusts, slathered and buttered and baked brown, and I could only guess what were in them. The tables were studded with finery, velvets, and gems, like even the furniture needed jewelry.

I frowned, and my stomach turned. There weren't enough people here to eat a third of this food.

We took our seats, and the prince and princess entered. All the men stood for them, and the ladies just looked solemnly to them. Prince John helped Isabel to sit, and then took the wine glass that were already filled and waiting for his touch. He held it aloft.

"To Guy of Gisbourne, Lord of Leaford," Prince John bellowed out. "Our brave champion this day and the guest of honor for our feast this night!"

The hall cheered and minstrels struck up, and I saw Isabel clapping hard, gazing upon my husband. Christ, but she were daft.

I drank to him, wishing there were more of the drink to let me forget that I were married to the beast.

Far across the hall, past the fire of the spits, I saw people coming in the back of the hall. They looked to be servants of the castle, maybe folk from Nottingham. They came closer, the fire playing in their wide, wanting eyes and making their faces look brighter and warm.

He had invited common folk to the feast? Were this Prince John's idea, or my husband's?

I looked to Gisbourne, and he frowned at me. Doubtful. I looked to Prince John, who were listening to a whispered word from his wife. He wrinkled his nose a touch and drank deeply, waving a hand for the food to be served.

Then his eyes caught across the way, same as mine had.

He stood, violent, so his heavy chair rocked back on its legs before settling. "What is the meaning of this?" he bellowed over the minstrels. They stopped, scared straight out of their instruments. "Guards!" he roared, using his arm like a lance of earlier in the day to doom their fate. "Remove the rabble!"

I put my arm on my chair to stand, but Gisbourne grabbed it, steel in his eyes. "Our deal is off if you say a word," he said.

"My lord prince," said Isabel. I whipped my head round to her, but she were only looking at the prince, beautiful and calm like the moon, staring at him, her head tilted back and exposing her throat like a lamb. "My lord, they are hungry. Surely you cannot ignore the plight of your people—they turn to you for every sustenance, both human and spiritual. You are their bread."

The court were rapt, her pretty lies captivating them all.

He put his hand over her cheek, and she closed her eyes like it were God Himself touching her. "My princess is as beautiful as she is wise," he told the court. "And so close to Christ's own birth, we shall not be the only ones to feast tonight. Hertford! Where is de Clare?" he shouted, looking round.

De Clare stood and came forward, kneeling hastily before the prince's table. "My lord prince."

"See to it that the people of Nottingham feast tonight as well."

Isabel swept her head down like she were to cry. "My lord prince is generous and kind," she cried, overloud for talking to her lap, and the hall cheered. De Clare came up and whispered in Prince John's ear, and the prince whispered back. De Clare nodded and left.

"Will he really feed them?" I asked quiet of Winchester.

"He will," Winchester said. "The prince is capable of great generosity; I wouldn't say it's natural to him, but he is capable."

They began carving the pigs and soon a plate were heaped in front of me with a trencher of bread beside it. I took some of the roasted pig and though I half expected the whole thing to taste like the cuts of bacon Tuck sometimes made, it were more like crisp-skinned ham. It were hot, which weren't an everyday luxury, and rich beyond measure. I took a few bites and ate some of the bread, watching those around me.

Men were filthy things. They bit until the juice ran into their beards, and they swiped at their maws and wiped it wherever they could land their hands. They let bits of food drop into the rushes on the floor and the dogs had a grand time of it. They ate and ate and ate.

The wine flowed overmuch, and by the end of the meal, the minstrels were kicking up a fine tune, and Prince John clapped his hands and called for dancing. He took his wife's hand and led her closer to the minstrels, to the bit of room between the eating tables and the ones laden with food.

I didn't ever remember seeing dancing much at Leaford, but I were shocked by how common it seemed. Granted, the village folk held each other close and tight when they started to dance wild and fast to music, and Prince John left a much more respectable distance between him and his wife, but they were hopping and kicking and turning about, clasped at the hand, like anyone were wont to do round a fire.

Other nobles joined in, and Winchester asked me quiet if I should like to dance.

"I don't much know how," I said to him. "Another night, when I've watched a fair bit." I smiled. "Or perhaps when they all think me less wild. Though if you could help me with the chair, your Grace, I wouldn't mind making a slip of it," I said.

He chuckled. "Of course, my lady," he said, and graciously stood. "Lord Leaford, permit me?" he asked of Gisbourne.

Gisbourne waved his hand. Hawk-eyed, he watched as I stood, but Winchester offered me his hand like we were to dance and led me off until Gisbourne looked away.

Winchester kissed my hand. "You're free, little bird. Fly as you will."

I bobbed a curtsy to him and quit the hall.

—◊◊◊—

The door I had chosen led out to the upper bailey, and the night were warmer than some, with a crisp smell to it that probably meant snow. There were a page at the door that called me "milady," and I sent him to fetch my cloak from my chambers. And he went.

Seemed there were loads of useful tricks for noble folks.

I weren't halfway across the bailey when the page brought it to me, settling the warm weight on my shoulders. "Thank you," I told him.

"Milady."

I walked closer to the gaps in the bailey wall—meant for archers and the like—that looked out onto the town. I heard the snow crunch a bit and looked back toward the boy. He were just standing there, watching me.

"Are you from round here, or do you travel with the prince?" I asked him.

"I'm in the earl's household, milady," he said, showing me his tunic. As if that meant something to me. I knew most lords branded their servants, but I knew little of the colors and he didn't have a coat of arms on it.

"Sorry, lad. Winchester, yes?"

He nodded.

"An excellent man. Is he a good master?"

"Excellent in all things that I've seen, milady."

"Are you training to be a knight in his household?"

"Yes, milady."

I rested my arms on the smooth stone ledge, imagining the months before when all the nobles, gussied up like I were now, rushed over to see smoke in the village below. I turned back to where the entrance to the prison stood, half hoping to see Gisbourne towering over me and Rob fighting him back, but it were silent and empty. So much had changed that night. Rob gave himself up to save me, gave me the first hope for his heart, and started me down a road that led to the cursed ring on my hand.

"Milady?" the page asked me.

"Hmm?" I looked to him, but he weren't looking at me.

"Milady, do you hear that?"

Shaking free of the past, I listened. There were shouts and clanking, heavy clangs.

Fair awkward, I jumped up into the narrow, tilted window and leaned out, holding careful with my good arm. I leaned till I could feel the wind whip me and see the fuss.

"The gates," I said, jumping down before he could help me or protest. "Come on, lad, the gates!"

Picking up my skirts with my one hand, I set to running, and he yelped and followed. We slid down the snow-slicked gauntlet to the second bailey, running over that yard to the next gauntlet.

Breaking onto the lower bailey, the gates were in full view, and it were mad. The gates were half lowered and the people were heaving against the guards with torches and twisted faces, screaming and crying and throwing food.

The castle guards were yelling to each other, barking to push the people back, keep them out of the castle, protect the prince. A layer of guards with drawn swords were setting up behind those with their armored hands on the people of Nottingham.

The food that were sailing over their heads were splattering in the snow. Bits, scraps, black-spotted potatoes, and other things I couldn't quite name that smelled of rot without so much as a hot wind to carry it, and I knew what it were in an instant—the prince's gift, his mighty bounty. Spoiled food and leftovers.

The gates lowered another notch.

My place weren't never inside the castle, not while the people were being pushed back and abused.

My place weren't never behind a line of men with their swords drawn who knew not what they were meant to protect.

My place were on the other side of the gates.

I took off running.

The guards may have called to me; they weren't ready to hold back someone from behind them, and I broke through the armed guards with ease. I ran for the seam where common folk and guards were pushed together, and saw them heave their fists and elbows like arrows through the faces of the hungry and the poor. I saw blood and brutal injustice.

The gates slammed down not moments after I made it out, and the crowd surged against the portcullis, carrying me with it in the flicker of torches and dark.

I fought my way back until the crowd let me go, and behind the throng were other souls standing about, watching, clutching their children and keeping back.

"What happened?" I asked a full-cheeked woman, going to her three young girls and pulling my cloak off my shoulders and round them.

She showed me a bit of bread, crawling with mealworms. "They gave us food," she said, sniffling. "And it was rotten. A few of the children took sick fast, and then the men started for the castle."

It dawned on me, sick and awful. "Because you ate the food anyway."

A fresh wash of tears went down her cheeks, but her little ones didn't notice, giggling and playing inside the cloak. "We're hungry," she whispered.

I looked at her, straight in the eyes, and I wanted to wipe her tears off her face but I couldn't rob her of them, like for me to say it weren't so would unmake her pain. It would be a mock of it. "I'll get you food," I said. "Before the night is over, I'll get you food."

She cried more, but I didn't think it were much because she were grateful. I think it were because she didn't believe me and feared for her babies.

"Go get warm," I told her.

She nodded, taking the cloak from her daughters.

"No," I said quick, stepping back. "It's for them."

"You'll freeze," she said, confused.

I shook my head. "Keep it. Please."

I went from her before she could give it back, and I set to running, down to the closest inn I knew. I didn't bother going inside. I went to their stables and filched a horse before any could tell me no, hauling atop it and tearing my skirt to sit astride the beast. I set off for Edwinstowe, praying Rob were awake and I wouldn't have to venture into hell to pull him back. I rode into the dark, snow-silenced countryside, for the first time in months feeling like my feet were carrying me toward something and not away.

—m—

It were long enough into the night that the lads might have been at the monastery already, but not enough that it were a certainty. I didn't think, at least. My blood roaring were the only thing keeping my body in motion; my skin were thick and clumsy and I'd long since stopped feeling for the wet and cold.

I went to Tuck's, sure I'd at least find John there. Not even bothering to peep in the window, I dropped from the horse and burst into the place. It felt like my body caught up to my blood, and it were a violent coming together, more like stabbing pain than heat. There were a fair amount of men there, and I could bare look upon them before I bent over, wheezing and shivering as the warmth broke through.

Someone were calling my name, and I straightened in time for Rob to pull me into a hug, dragging me off the ground and hugging me so hard I feared I might shatter, and my hand slung against my ribs protested.

"Scar, you're like ice," he said, pulling me over to the huge fireplace and kicking other folk out of their seats. Much appeared with a blanket and John were a moment behind him, and in a breath, even half-frozen, I felt like no time had passed, and all were like it used to be.

Rob tugged off my silly shoes and wrapped his hands around my feet even as I winced away, the heat hurting. "Jesus, Scar," he murmured, looking at my face in full. "What, did you run here from Nottingham?"

"There are riots," I said, trying to suck in a deep breath against the cold.

"Riots?" Much asked. "What for?"

"The prince gave the people rotten food from the feast," I said. "A few of the little ones took sick, and the people just . . . fought."

Much looked at John, who frowned back at him, but Rob just rubbed my feet more and smiled. "I take it you came up with a plan on your way."

I nodded. "I know where the castle food stores are. Most of it collected from Nottinghamshire."

John shook his head. "No," he said.

We all looked to him.

"No," he repeated, fair shocked, like it were a crime we didn't know what he were about. "I'm not doing it."

"You heard her," Rob said. "Children are dying. What would you have us do? Nothing?"

"Yes!" he snapped. "Because that's all it ever is. Nothing but sticking our necks out. Changing nothing, *fixing* nothing."

"John—" Much said.

"Actions have punishments," he said. "We steal the food, hand it out, then what? You think Prince John will just let us off about our way? We almost died fighting the sheriff and this is the prince. He will kill us," he said.

"He won't kill me," I said, scowling at John.

He jumped forward and grabbed my chin, tilting my bruises to the light. "No, he has his own ways of punishing you, Scar, and I'm not putting that on you. Rob may be fine with turning your face purple but I'm not."

Rob let go of my feet to stand to John's challenge, but I didn't bother. "Oh for Heaven's sake, Rob, sit," I said.

"Are you questioning my honor, Little? You, who is acting like a damn coward right now?"

"I'm questioning all of it! You think you're ready to fight the damn prince? You've barely slept in a month! You'll get us all pinched covering your worthless hide."

Much stood too. "Are you two really going to brawl in Tuck's? Again?"

"Again?" I snapped, and they both looked fair sheep-like 'bout it.

"If you want out of the band, just say so, John. That's all there is to it," Robin spat, sitting back down and grabbing my feet.

I kicked him, dangerous close to a part of him he prized. He grunted and held my foot up, scowling, but I scowled back. "Don't threaten him," I said. "Honestly, you like to throw that about a fair bit. 'Out of the band this, out of the band that.' We're barely a band right now so don't go kicking people out. It ain't nice."

Much frowned, and I sighed.

"Isn't nice," I corrected.

Much smiled.

"I want out of the band," John said, quiet and serious.

"John," I said soft, looking to him.

Much looked betrayed and Rob just gaped, rage-filled.

"Bess is carrying my child," he said, quieter still, glancing 'bout the room to see who heard. "And she has finally agreed to marry me. I have a family now, and I'm not risking that so some other family can eat. It may be selfish, but what the hell are we doing this for if not to protect our own?" He looked at me, just at me, and I knew it hurt him to say it. "I'll help where I can. I'll go hunting tonight if you want me to. But I can't do anything that's going to get me thrown in prison and leave her alone."

"It *is* selfish!" Rob railed. "What do you think will happen to Bess if we can't feed the people of Nottinghamshire? If we can't have a sheriff that will care for us?"

"Then I will hunt and feed her myself. And if they come to our door with swords and knives I will kill every one that tries to step over the threshold." This stare were for Rob now, and Rob looked ready to step up and counter that too.

I stood, going over to John and hugging him tight. "You may be an overprotective lout, John, but if for that and nothing else you'll make the best father. And husband." I squeezed tighter with my one good arm.

He hugged me straight off my feet. "Thank you, Scar."

"When will you marry?"

"Soon," he said, putting me down. "After the new year."

"Congratulations," Much said, shaking John's hand. "A baby. That's . . . that's . . . well, I suppose it's not surprising, given how often you—"

"Much!" I snapped.

Much smiled and nodded. "She's right, you know. You'll be a good father."

We all turned to make room for Rob to come over and give his congratulations, but he were still sitting at the hearth, scowling. He stood. "I won't congratulate you, John, on deserting us. We've been your family for years and you're abandoning *us*."

My heart dropped. "Rob, you don't mean—"

"I do," he told me, harsh. He stared at John. "You bedded enough tavern wenches to have gotten one of them with child, and now—"

He didn't get to finish the thought; John flattened him.

CHAPTER
FIFTEEN

Yˮou can't just not talk to me," Rob said.

We stole across the lower bailey in a quick line; me, then Rob, then Much, then Godfrey. Rob stayed close, his hand grazing against mine as he whispered to me.

I glared at him and slapped his hand away.

Coming round behind the food store, I looked up at the highest bailey, the lights bright in the bit of the residences that I could see. I wondered if this were breaking my deal with Gisbourne.

We came to the window. It needed a jump up and a much longer jump down. "I can make it in," I said, "but the unlocked way out is a narrow stair to the kitchen. If we want to bring all the food out fast, we'll need to open up the front. Which is locked."

"Don't worry about it," Much said, nodding to me.

I frowned. "What does that mean, Much?"

He smiled, nodded again, and said, "It's taken care of."

Godfrey looked to me. "I don't understand."

Much sighed, shaking his head. "Why do you lot get to say things like that and I can't? All blustery bravado, you are, but no one trusts me to handle anything."

"We trust you, Much." Rob's head tilted a bit. "You just have to explain a little," he told him.

"You never make Scar explain." He crossed his arms. "I learned how to open locks."

I gaped. "You learned that in a book?"

He shrugged. "More from a blacksmith who makes the locks, but yes, you can learn that from a book."

"Can you teach me?" I asked.

"You're supposed to be a proper lady," he told me, turning up his nose. "But after you're done with that, yes."

"Well, let's have at it," Godfrey said. "Right? Time's wasting."

Much nodded, and he went round the front of the store room while we watched. Much pulled two thin, short metal pins from his pocket and set them to the hole in the lock. He held one with his hand and leaned down to catch the other in his mouth. In my eyes, it looked like all he did were jiggle a bit and the whole thing sprang open like he'd set a key to it.

He waved us forward and spat the second stake into his hand with a broad grin.

"Well done, Much," I praised, clapping his arm.

He beamed.

We ducked inside and shut the doors again, keeping the lock with us just in case a wandering guard passed by.

I settled my free hand on my hip. "We need something to carry the lot of it, don't we?"

Godfrey went to a sack of flour and could bare heft the thing. "I reckon so," he said.

A frown came to my face. John could have taken two of the sacks at a time without a worry.

I shook John free from my head. "There should be a cart by the stables. Godfrey, why don't you help me nick it and we'll get it over here."

"I'll come with you," Rob volunteered.

"*Godfrey,*" I snapped, glaring at Rob.

Rob strode forward anyway. "I'm coming with you," he said. "Godfrey, stay with Much."

Godfrey looked at both of us and didn't move forward.

Which made me miss John again.

The stables were on the same bailey, right near the barracks. While they weren't so much guarded, they were lousy with armor and the men what wore it. We went the long way to the back, peeking round the building to see three men drinking and laughing. I pushed Rob back from the corner.

"We have to wait," I told him.

"There. You spoke to me."

I glared at him. "You want me to speak? How the hell could you be so cruel, to deny him his happiness? What are you thinking? You *know* what a family would mean to John after his whole family were taken from him. John, more than any of us."

"You think me cruel?" he asked, angry and sad both, stepping from the wall to look at me full. "I can't *stand* this. He runs around dishonoring as many women as he can get his goddamn hands on, doing whatever the hell he wishes, and he gets a child, a wife, a reason to stop fighting and think of himself for once. Whereas *I*—"

He stopped sharp, looking away from me.

My heart cracked. "Oh, Rob."

He looked at me. "I've been playing by all the rules, Scar, and I don't think I'll ever have any of that. Maybe he deserves it more than I do. Maybe he does. Because even if you were to get an annulment, even if"—his throat worked—"even if I get to marry you, I'll never be able to stop fighting. I will never be free of this burden, and I hate him that he can lay it down."

I stared at him, drinking him in till I felt tipsy with the sight of him, and pulled him closer to me, wanting to touch him. His arms came round me and I pressed my face to the crook of his neck. "We'd never be happy without adventure," I murmured to him. "But we'll be happy with each other. We will have that chance. I promise."

His arms shifted, wrapping round my shoulders and head, and it felt like he were shielding me from the world. "I hope so, Scar," he said in my ear.

Sighing, I pressed closer to him. "We should look...," I reminded him.

He moved over a bit, tugging me with him, to peek. "They're gone."

His arms began to loosen, but I fast whispered, "Kiss me, Rob."

Like any good gentleman, he didn't deny me. He picked me up a bit and held me against the wall, kissing me and making heat and courage flow from my toes to my hair.

He let me down and his mouth left mine. His forehead touched mine, and I couldn't bring my eyes to open just yet.

"These schemes may benefit the people, Scarlet, but I fight for you." His hands squeezed my waist a little bit, and it made my blood run fast. "I will always fight for you."

I opened my eyes, pressing my hand to his face, making him look me in the eye. "Rob," I murmured. "I will do everything I can so that you don't have to fight anymore. For me or anyone else."

He pressed his lips to my forehead. "Come on, my love."

—⁓—

It were short work to get the cart over to the food store. It were terrible hard work to load the thing up, especially where only one of my hands worked and I got shouted at when I tried to use the bad one, and Much had a stump for only a bit more use than me.

We couldn't close the doors, neither, so it were a fair messy business, and it weren't long before a guard came over, shouting at Rob and Godfrey.

"Stop! What are you two doing? Guards!" he roared.

I heard quite a clatter and put the cheese wheel wedged under one arm on the cart.

I just hoped that being a noblewoman had as many nice bits as it were meant to.

"What is taking you so very long?" I asked, stepping out of the food store. "Guard. Perfect. Where are the rest of your men, you were meant to be here ages ago."

"M-my lady?" he asked, looking at my coat that Rob had given me, made of peasant's felt.

I raised my chin. "Lady *Leaford*," I snapped. "Perhaps I should send one of these men to tell the prince his orders are being ignored."

"The prince didn't give no orders," he said.

"He most certainly did. Were you aware that the food dispensed earlier to the people was rotten?" I asked.

"No, my—"

"Well, the prince caught wind of that in more ways than one, sir. And he isn't pleased. His Highness has ordered this food to be brought to the people at once."

"It's the dead of night—"

I fought to draw myself up higher. "The same time of night that our Lord Jesus Christ *overcame* death, sir." I sniffed. "Now will you and your men do as you're told or must I wake the prince?"

The man grumbled but turned his back and shouted to several guards for help, and I watched, breathless, as they looked to me for instruction on what to take. They wheeled the cart to the gates and called to their fellows to open it while I followed behind with my friends.

There were still some of the rioters outside the gates who rallied when they saw them open, and some people ran fast from the square, though I weren't sure if it were for fear or to spread word. I saw Allan doing tricks for some children, and he turned to me with a solemn nod. The guards hung back, and I walked forward, looking back to Rob and the others. Rob nodded me forward.

"This food isn't spoilt," I told them. "I promise. It's safe for you and your children. We won't let you starve, and monks have already been sent for the ones that took sick. Please. Take the food."

"Who are you?" one man said, spitting at my feet. "Why the hell should we believe anyone from that godforsaken castle?"

"I'm not from the castle," I said.

"That's Lady Scarlet," said Allan, coming beside him with a smile. "And that's Robin Hood," he said, pointing to Rob.

I went back to Rob's arms as the people trusted his name enough to come forward, and soon the square were filled with folk taking their share of flour and grain and cheese and dried meat.

Hidden amongst the crowd, I pressed a dangerous kiss to Rob's mouth. "You should go. The prince will figure this out soon."

"Come with me," he said. "They'll punish you for this, Scar."

I shook my head. "I won't break my bargain. Go."

His hand slipped from mine, and he faded in the crowd.

I caught Godfrey's arm before he passed. "Godfrey, you may not have the stomach to fight Rob the way John does, but you damn well keep him away from here when the trouble starts, you understand?"

His nod were lost on me as the crowd started to move, and Much yelled, "Scarlet!"

I turned toward the castle; Gisbourne were coming out of the castle on horses, with a force of knights and lords alike. "What the hell is going on?" he roared.

The crowd were flung into chaos as everyone grabbed fast for the food and Gisbourne spurred his horse to them. I ran out, ducking as he reined in his horse hard so not to trample me. Before I could even straighten, he were off his horse and charging toward me. "Goddamn you, Marian! You're behind this? You!" he bellowed, drawing his sword and running for me.

I ducked under his swinging sword to grab the knife in his boot, angling it at him.

"Really!" he laughed at me. "You want to fight me with naught but a knife in your hand?"

I glanced at the cart, where the food were almost all gone. "I don't need long."

Gisbourne swung and I ducked. He lunged and I twisted

away, trying to figure out where to stab him that it would get through his thick leathers and chest plate.

I weren't doing much to capture their attention. De Clare and several knights were going for the cart with children and adults alike still scrambling for food, his sword outstretched.

"Gisbourne, de Clare's going to kill them!" I shouted.

Gisbourne's eyes never left me. "He will end what you started, Marian."

He swung his sword again, and I ducked, but he tamped his foot down on my bedraggled skirts. With a cry I fell to the ground, and in a swift breath he caught me up, forcing the knife from my hand and pinning me to his chest. He clutched my one good arm and turned me toward the cart.

I struggled hard as I could as the knights and de Clare grabbed as many people as they had hands. De Clare grabbed a little girl by the arm. I yelled and yelled, and Gisbourne ducked his head to my ear. "This is what you have done, Marian."

"Thief!" de Clare cried at her. The little girl sobbed and tried to jerk and twist from his hold, but he paid no attention as he dragged her to a short stone wall. "Do you know what the punishment is for those who steal from the prince?"

"Leave her alone, you bastard!" I screamed. I knew what he were about as he called a knight over to him.

"Hold her hand out, sir," he said, showing the knight how to stretch it over the stone wall so that the wrist were flat and bare.

"No!" I screamed, fighting against Gisbourne as hard as I could. "Stop it!"

The little girl understood as de Clare raised his sword to hack at her arm, and she screamed too.

So did Much. He ran down the wall to barrel into de Clare, knocking him over. Rob took the knight and Godfrey took the little girl and ran.

Gisbourne's chest pounded and rolled with deep, hearty laughter. "Robin Hood," he said, not loud enough for Rob to hear. "Seize him. No one else matters," he said, and turned to drag me into the castle as the guards and knights flooded past us.

I slammed my foot into his knee as he tried to walk, and he dropped me, still holding to one arm so I fell and jerked, twisted and hurt. He gathered me up again. "Behave or I will make you still," he said.

I did it again, and he dropped me in full, throwing me on my rump so I winced.

"Damn you!" he growled. "Won't you stop? Don't you see what you do, how you hurt these people? That girl would have lost her hand because of you."

"No," I snarled. "That girl will eat because of me. You cannot do your violence and blame it on me. If she lost her hand it would have been because you sat idly by and watched de Clare hurt an unarmed child. It would have been because de Clare is a bully. If anything the only thing I see is how god-damn powerless a noble lady is meant to be, and I am *not* powerless."

He dragged me up. "You're bruised all to hell, your hand is broken, and can you even imagine how much more pain waits for you tonight?" he asked. "Why won't you just learn? Why must you make me keep hurting you?"

"I'm not *making* you do anything, Gisbourne. Hurt me if you want, but I've felt pain. I know what pain is. And it's less than love, than loyalty, than hope. You can make me cry, or scream, or whatever else. All that will mean is that I feel the pain, that I'm still alive. And as long as I'm living I can promise I'm not afraid of you, Gisbourne. I'm afraid of sitting quiet while the people that are meant to protect others do their best to hurt them. I'm afraid of people like you and Prince John going by unchecked. That's what I'm afraid of. I'm stronger than your damn pain, and I do *not* give up."

His eyes met mine, his terror-dark brown ones bearing into me. "Neither do I, Marian."

My breath caught and I just hung there, staring at him, both of us too damn stubborn to look away.

I weren't sure I liked the notion of sharing something with my husband.

He shook his head and started marching me, holding my arm and walking me on my own two feet, and we stopped and turned to hear a clatter behind us.

It took about seven knights with their hands on him, but they held Rob fast, dragging him into the castle and sealing the gate behind them. All the brave words I'd just spoke drained out of me as I met Rob's eyes for a moment. In the dark and the distance, I couldn't even see the ocean blue of them.

The last time he were in this castle he were tortured. He

had come back to me broken, and my mind tumbled now with all the new horrors they could inflict. All the things his hurt heart couldn't withstand and should never have to.

Gisbourne dragged me out of his sight, and I prayed with everything I knew that I would see the ocean blue again.

CHAPTER
SIXTEEN

—o—

Gisbourne didn't bring me to the chambers we shared. He went up, straight to the prince's chambers. Gisbourne entered without being announced; the prince were awake, in a heavy brocade mantle, the princess in a chair facing away from me. Gisbourne pushed me in front of him and I stumbled, catching her chair to stand. The girl jumped out of the chair and stared at me, but it weren't the princess; it were one of the young ladies that had attended the princess in the market, in nothing but her underdress and a mantle.

"Out," Prince John ordered her. She looked at him, pale and wide eyed.

"My lord?" she questioned.

"Out," he repeated, glaring at her.

She looked at all of us and ducked her head and scurried.

"Sit," Gisbourne said, pointing to the chair under my hand.

"No," I said, standing straight.

"She can stand if she wishes," the prince said, looking at me. "It makes little difference."

I stared at him. It weren't so simple as saying it were his evil heart what made him ugly—Gisbourne had the same such heart and I still knew he looked well. The prince were different, like gazing into the eyes of a snake; there were a beauty there, but the only thing it had ever been used for were terrible things, and it made the prettiness terrible too.

"Do you have any idea the ways you have vexed me?" he asked, turning away from me to the window. He opened it, and I could see him watching something. "You and your lover."

"What have you done with Robin?" I asked, my voice rushing higher than I wanted. I stepped forward but Gisbourne grabbed me back and pushed me into the chair. I cast about; there were a knife by a tray of cheese on a small table too far from me. There were heavy cups in my reach. Gisbourne's knife were tucked into his belt now, not far from me.

"He's simply in the stocks. If he doesn't freeze to death by morning, I'll deal with him then." Something caught his eye outside and he sniffed, then looked back at me. "But you. You are a problem."

He ran his eyes over me, then looked at my face. I didn't move none.

"Do you have any idea what's going on here?" he asked, spreading his arms. "Do you?"

"You're feeding my people rotten food. That's all I need to know."

He looked fair worried. "No, my dear. No. We are on the brink of civil unrest; with Richard away and England splintering at the helm, they need someone strong to lead them. Someone beloved. Someone to unite everyone. Someone to bring them back to the faith of the Crown."

"Faith of the Crown? You make yourself a false idol," I spat.

"No. They will make me into an idol, Marian. They will *worship* me." He sighed. "But only if you stop telling people that I'm doing very bad things. It's my turn to be the hero, not yours." He waved a hand, not even looking at me as he said, "Gisbourne. Kill her."

I leapt from the chair, grabbing a cup and sliding sideways, making myself less to aim at. "Oh you can try, *love*," I growled at him.

Gisbourne just stood there like a lump. His jaw were awful tight, like every muscle had been twanged like a bowstring. "No. My lord prince."

"No?" Prince John snarled.

Gisbourne pulled the knife from his belt and handed it to Prince John. "No. I'm not killing her."

Prince John looked at the knife handle like it were poison. "You know why I cannot spill her blood," he sneered.

"I will not dishonor my name, your Highness. And I will not take *that* curse upon me, even to spare you from it."

Prince John's chest began to rise and fall faster and faster. "You disloyal scum," he growled. "I do not fear God," he said, snatching the knife and turning to me.

"Like *hell*," I snapped. "Come at me with that and I'll break your pretty face, your Highness."

"Gisbourne, hold her at least, would you?"

The door opened rough and fast, and Eleanor strode in with fair surprising speed for such a woman. I thought I saw the pretty girl that were half dressed in the hall behind her, but I couldn't be sure. "John."

Prince John looked to his mother, his lip curling. He didn't lower the knife. "Mother."

"Put the knife down."

"Mother—"

"If I wanted a discussion, I would have asked you a question. Put the knife *down*."

"I will punish her for what she's done!" he roared.

Eleanor folded her hands calmly in front of her. "You will not kill her. If I have prevented you and your brothers from killing each other for the past twenty years, I will prevent you from doing this. Royal blood is sacrosanct, John. I will not allow you to kill the girl in cold blood."

The knife lowered marginally. "You never seemed to mind murder and bloodshed when my dear brothers raised war against Father."

She lifted her chin. "Oh, I suppose hurting her will win you a kingdom?" she asked.

His sneer folded slowly into a frown. "She must be punished. Severely."

"Go to the window," Eleanor said, still standing calm in

the center of the room, like all the energy and life in the place were coming from her alone.

Prince John rolled his eyes like a willful child but he went. "What am I meant to be looking at, Mother?"

"Tell me what you see."

"I see a criminal in the stocks."

Robin.

"And?" she questioned.

He huffed out a sigh. "And a considerable amount of people around him. Servants. Lesser nobles."

"And what are they doing?"

"I'm not a child!" he snapped at his mother, whipping his head round. "Don't make the mistake of treating me as such."

"You are a child," Eleanor said, stepping forward, her voice like steel and fire. "You are a pouting bully and in danger of being held in my esteem as the stupidest of my sons. Isabel gave you such a grand opportunity tonight. A *coup d'etat.* An idea, by the way, that your wife stole from her." Her long, elegant hand thrust out like a bowstaff to point at me. "Feed the people and they will love you. Helplessly and eternally. And what do you do, my stupid, stupid son? You squander the opportunity and make them hate you."

"How dare you speak to me—"

"Silence." She paused a moment, but he stayed quiet. "Who else do you see out there?" she asked. "Who of the highest ranking nobles beneath you—a man just beneath the shades of royalty—do you see standing beside him?"

He looked out again, resting his hands on the window ledge. His chest began to rise and fall again, and he turned from the window with a wail fit for the tantrum of a five-year-old. He grabbed the nearest table and threw it toward me, and Gisbourne grabbed my arm, pulling me out of the way. It hit the stone fireplace and shattered, and soon cloths and coins and cups followed behind, a storm of small things smashed to bits.

Gisbourne pressed me to the wall, his big body over mine as the prince raged. He didn't look at me, his head over my shoulder, his chest breathing against mine. Soon the screams turned to words, and Prince John swore profusely, mentioning Winchester's name several times.

Gisbourne jerked and grunted, and I knew something hit him in the back. I didn't dare look at him. I couldn't much confess to know anything of what was going on, but I knew he defied the prince for my life, and I didn't want to know why. I didn't much have space in my heart to care for another tortured man.

For a few breaths, things stopped flying cross the room and the cursing ceased. "Are you quite finished?" Eleanor asked.

Gisbourne eased up on me, and no sooner did he step away than the prince pointed to me and yelled, "You stupid bitch! You did this!"

"You will fix this," Eleanor said. "John. *John*. You will fix this."

"I will kill *all of them*," he snarled.

Eleanor slapped him. "John. You will go out there and say

that your orders have been wildly misinterpreted. You will say you have come to thank Robin Hood for championing the people and protecting them from the gross misconduct of those serving you. You will say he is cleared of any wrongdoings tonight or any night past; you will invite him to participate in the tournament as the people's representative."

I couldn't much help myself; I gasped.

Prince John scowled. "Why would I ever do that?"

"Why would he do that, Marian?" Eleanor asked, fixing me with her stare, sharper than my knives.

"I-I don't know, my lady."

"Then why did you so sharply inhale?"

I looked to Gisbourne, but his face held nothing for me. "Because Rob would stand for the people, fair and true. None of these other men care a whit about the people, but Rob—he does. It would change everything." I looked fast from the prince to Eleanor.

"Precisely. You must give the people what they want, John," Eleanor said. "If you ever hope to be your brother's heir."

Prince John looked out over the crowd again, his shoulders rolling with muscle and anger. "Fine," he grunted. "But I still get to punish her."

Eleanor let out a breath. "You cannot kill her."

"I won't kill her." He glared at me. "She fancies herself a thief. I will punish her as one."

His eyes drifted to my hands.

I jerked back, but Gisbourne caught me, and a scream

tripped and caught in my throat. He dragged me forward and I fought him hard as horror dawned sick and dark in my stomach. Gisbourne caught up some rope from the bed that had been a victim of the prince's wrath and lashed my good arm to the chair before forcing me into it. I kicked and kicked, but he tied me to the chair, gripping my good wrist and not looking at me.

"You are certainly within your rights to punish her," Eleanor said, raising her chin a little and folding her hands in front of her. "But you will not."

The prince laughed. "I will, Mother."

"Really?" she asked. "You are a prince, and you are so undone by the actions of one small girl that you will punish her severely? Richard would have been too busy to notice, much less make a spectacle of such a small crime."

The prince rolled his eyes. "Fine, Mother. I won't hurt her."

She nodded and stepped toward the door, and my blood rushed fast and cooling like summer rain. My breath came again.

The door shut and I looked to the prince, who hadn't unlashed me from the chair.

He were studying me close, looking at me in a way I didn't much like.

"Let me see her broken hand," the prince said, and Gisbourne looked at him.

"My lord?" he asked.

"Let me see her hand," the prince repeated, and Gisbourne took my hand, unwrapping the bandages, tearing it off where he needed. Gisbourne showed it to him and stretched it out painful. I screwed my eyes shut, desperate not to make a noise.

"Mother's right," he said. "Taking the whole hand would be too noticeable." He chuckled. "How many times has she run from you, Gisbourne?"

He hesitated.

"Gisbourne?" Prince John asked.

"Too many," Gisbourne said.

"Yes, but twice she made promises, yes? Once to be trothed to you, and then to be your wife, and she ran from you." Prince John said it like it were a delicious secret, something he loved. "Two fingers, then."

Prince John went and got the knife, and my heart ran fast and slipshod in my chest. He went to the fire and put it in the low, hot part of the flames and my feet scraped on the ground, trying to find a foothold to push, to kick, to fight.

I didn't move an inch.

Breath rushing faster, I looked to Gisbourne, but he wouldn't look at me. I jerked at my bonds until my skin tore and bled, and Gisbourne clamped his hands down on me.

I knew Rob were out in the courtyard below the window. I knew if I cried out he'd hear me, and he'd know, and he'd fight and he'd hurt to try and help me when he couldn't.

The prince turned toward me, holding the knife, hot and glowing dull. "I can't stop you," I told him, trying to keep the tremble from my voice at how fast my breath were coming. He smiled at me. "But I swear, if you do this, I will visit this back upon you tenfold. Christ may well have turned the other cheek, but I won't. Remember this act, because you'll be cursing it for a damn long time to come. I will make you pay for what you do, *your Highness.*"

"*Rruff,*" he barked at me. "Your pup has quite the mouth on her, Gisbourne. Hold her hand flat."

"Not her ring finger," Gisbourne said harsh and low as the prince gripped the two smallest of my fingers. "That ring will stay in place."

The prince chuckled and moved to my pointing and middle finger, and I shuddered.

With one last look out the window, I shut my eyes again and curled my lips over my teeth.

Water washed down my face, but I never once cried out. It were some sort of judgment from God, for I felt every cut and crack as they did it, but when it were done, and Prince John pressed a knife hot from the fire to sear the wound shut, only then did my world go black.

CHAPTER

SEVENTEEN

—o—

I watched the fire die, shaking with cold and pain in the chair, the lot of which made me feel thin like worn-out rags, like wind would pass through me and not notice me there.

Gisbourne hadn't moved in the bed. I didn't much think he were asleep, for something still crackled in the air like he were watching me.

I wanted to push open the shutters and let the cold in and wait for the sun to rise—it couldn't be much longer—but I couldn't move. I could bare think. Words and notions crossed my mind like whispers.

Robin were to compete.

Thoresby.

Sacrosanct.

Eleanor.

They'd never let Rob win.

This last bit made me shut my eyes against it every time. He were the best archer in England, I fair thought, and it were an archery contest. They wouldn't never let him compete without a way to keep him from winning.

I couldn't turn my thoughts to my hand.

I hadn't changed clothes from the day before. Gisbourne must have dragged me here after I passed out; I had woken up in the bed in the middle of the night. I woke to pain, brutal and awful, and I cried out before I knew better of it. Gisbourne were awake, watching me in the bed beside me, and he just stayed there as I struggled to get up, staggered like a drunk, and collapsed into the chair. He didn't say a word.

Tears stopped and started and I weren't much aware of either part. I crushed my head into my knees and struggled to think of anything that were light and lovely and safe. I tried to think of the first kiss Rob had ever given to me, at the edge of Nottingham when everything felt, for a moment, like glittering light and sun.

It twisted dark, and all I could see were flames flickering into demons and frost stealing over to freeze the world, and Rob withering and dying like crops in winter.

Moments and decades passed all at once till the sun rose and Gisbourne rose with it. His eyes were dark and his face worn as he stared at me.

"I didn't intend for this," he said. That were all, and then he turned to his manservant and readied for the melee.

I wouldn't let Mary touch me when she came. Pain were

spreading through me like a spider's web and I didn't want to move, much less to change and dress. Gisbourne told her to just bring me a heavy cloak, and she obeyed.

It took me several moments to stand on my feet, but I weren't never going to miss this day.

Gisbourne strode off to the fields, and I followed slow behind, pulling myself tighter with every step.

I would get to the tourney grounds.

I would sit there and stare at the prince.

I wouldn't never be defeated by such a coward.

I would cheer for Rob with my heart and soul.

My whole body were shaking by the time I made it outside, and the cold rushed around me like a bear hug. It made it easier to breathe, to think beyond the pain, and I loved it.

Even walking toward the grounds, I could see what difference a day had made. The place were overrun, packed with common folk everywhere you could look. Children were hoisted on shoulders and people pressed together in a crush, wedged together to get a glimpse of the people's champion.

Guards appeared to escort me into the nobles' dais. One reached out to cup my elbow and help me along the path, and I wondered how rough I looked. My hand, still tucked safe in the sling, weren't bleeding through; save for any sign of it that showed on my face, no one should be able to tell what had passed, and I were glad for it.

It were the first time I wanted to hide their cruelty. I didn't want them to use me to hurt Rob; I didn't want him for one moment to take my pain and make it his. And I hated that in so doing, it seemed like I were ashamed they'd done it.

I slid into a chair, feeling more like the washing run over a washboard than a whole girl. A trumpet sounded and the contestants were led into the arena—it had been rearranged from the day before into one wide space, the grounds for the melee, a mock battle where all the men fought in chaotic hand-to-hand combat.

A mock battle they were placing Rob dead in the center of.

Robin were one of the last to enter, and the whole place broke open with cheers and noise and sound. He were tired, that were fair clear, his face shadowed and dark. He walked cross the arena and his eyes set to searching the nobles.

He were looking for me.

His eyes moved past me, then roved back, his face folding into a frown, looking me over like a mother searching her cub for scratches. I met his eyes and smiled at him, but it felt weak and sad on my mouth.

His eyebrows wove together like knitting and he looked more worried 'stead of less.

The prince stood and spoke, but I didn't hear it. I weren't sure if it were the wind and where he stood that carried his voice off, or if it were the awful pounding in my hand that rang back through my skull what made it hard to hear. Didn't matter none; I knew he were saying something about fight, fight, fight, someone will win when you are all mock dead.

The fight didn't start just then. The players vanished from

the field like smoke, and I shut my eyes for a moment, trying
to breathe as pain rushed over me in a wave. Time dipped and
swung, and I weren't sure how long they'd been shut when
someone called to me and touched my arm.

It were close enough to my hand that it felt like a knife, not
a finger, and I fought back a howl as I turned to the source.

Eleanor's blue eyes, made fierce and cool by the white,
white skin around them, stared at me from her seat beside me.

"What did he do to you?" she said soft. She blinked, and it
felt like whatever tether had bound us in her eyes were broke.
My eyes slipped back and her next question sounded far off.
"Marian, what happened?"

I heard her voice, murmured to her ladies near her, and
soon I opened my eyes into leaping fire.

For a breath, I thought I were back at the monastery and the
pain had come from Rob, but then the threads of reality braided
back together and I saw a brazier fire had been brought on the
dais before us, the guards banking the coals to lower the flames.
Were I too cold? Were that what were wrong?

"Marian," she said quiet, only to me, and her hand slipped
along mine, fishing into the sling. I hissed; it felt like it were a
hundred times too big, too sore, too everything.

She saw the red starting to bloom on the bandage, and she
fixed my cloak to lay over it. I twisted as my blood pulsed
double-hard in my hand.

"Hush," she said to me, and her hands were gentle on me.
"You are strong, Marian. You are well and strong."

Something cold fell on the bandage and I wrenched at

the weight, but didn't yell. I tried to look past the fire to the field, to Rob, to see if he noticed, but I couldn't see past the flames.

The cold sank through the cloth and began to ease the pain, and I were only just aware of myself. My chest were heaving like iron bellows and I were half out of my chair. I straightened, raising my head up to look out on the field.

The melee were on in full. Most were mounted; I reckoned that losing your horse were probably the first round of elimination. I saw Gisbourne, all in black on his huge white destrier, slashing with his broadsword. He looked like a demon.

Rob were half swallowed. He were on a farm horse, a head and hands shorter than the rest of them, but he were charging through more men than Gisbourne. And every hit he made were followed by cheers like an echo.

Watching him made everything hurt less. He were handsome beyond measure, his face carved stone and living all at once. His body moved with a grace that made me admire every bit of the fighter in him. He were trained for this, the act and practice of war; built for it, honed by it.

And haunted by it.

Part of me cheered with every strike of his sword; part of me mourned.

The main battle line broke as victors like Robin, Gisbourne, and more crossed through to the other side where the infantry would have lain in wait if it were a battle in true. Their horses galloped free and were wheeled back by their riders, ready to clash again.

A great horn sounded, and the horses slowed, halting and turning toward the ends of the arena.

The first round were done.

Nobles stood from their chairs quick, drawing close to the huge braziers as servants hurried to fill wine glasses and offer food, like a moving banquet set in the snow.

Eleanor waved her fingers and her ladies drifted in front of us, blocking out everyone else with carefully turned backs and angled bodies. She handed me a cup of wine and I drank it fast, eager to put off the shivers and pain both.

"Your husband did this, or my son?" she asked.

There were dregs of something in the wine and I spat it out, not caring a whit if I looked like an ill-mannered heathen. "You really thought he'd let me go?" I asked her. I looked to her, to her face like white stone and her eyes of cold water, and I stared down the great Eleanor of Aquitaine. "You left him full of fury and me lashed to a chair. If you didn't know how that would end, you didn't want to know."

She looked away from me, and the white cliff of her throat worked. "This was not what I wanted," she whispered. "Not for you."

"You let him do it."

Her eyes shut and her fist opened, like she were letting a secret out into the air. "No. He must grow; he must be a stronger leader and he cannot do that if I do not give him the trust to make the best decisions for his people. I must not be his puppeteer."

"He deserves no trust."

Her eyes opened and looked to the back of his chair, ahead of us on the dais. "He will. He must."

I were tempted to lift my hand, but I didn't dare. I couldn't feel much of anything of it now, and I weren't ready for the pain to start again. "Why bother for me?" I asked her. "Why bother about any of this for me?" Isabel's words drifted back to me— what interest did Eleanor have in me that I didn't know?

She looked to me, warm and sad now. "You've had a difficult journey, Marian. I feel for you, very keenly. And I don't like to see any woman harmed."

My gaze ran back to the empty mock battlefield. She may care for my harm, but few others did. And they cared for Rob's life even less. How many noble sons had been sent to war? And for each of those, how many tens of common sons? Live or die, their lives were nothing more than this battle: a game.

"Can I see him?" I asked her. My voice bare croaked out; it were a strange thing. For all the times I spoke when I shouldn't, when it came to speaking words that my whole heart were bound up in, it were a difficult thing.

"Not yet. Perhaps after the second round; there should be a longer break then."

She clicked her fingers and one of the ladies turned. Eleanor ordered for more snow to fill the cloth on my hand, and I shut my eyes and waited for the tournament to continue.

—m—

It weren't long before the next round; this time all the remaining competitors—roughly ten in all—were on foot, and for the close combat, the weapons had been replaced with blunted versions, scattered around the outside of the arena. They were all clustered in the center, shoulder to shoulder, their backs to one another, shields touching like a chain to keep them in.

The horn sounded, and everyone ran for the weapons— except Rob, who immediately swiped his leg down to take out the competitor on his right. Not near expecting it, the man launched into the air like a hound trying for a scrap and Rob stood straight, the sole person still while all others raced for the weapons.

He retreated back to the center, and my heart beat fast as he watched them all. They chose weapons and turned to him, and the grounds held a breath.

Gisbourne turned and swung his heavy, blunted broadsword at the competitor nearest him, and the man howled as the rest of the fighters leapt into action.

It were a large field, and ten men across it left space by spades. The men started to form clusters of activity, mostly fighting round the edge as they started to challenge each other. Only one man went straight for Rob, and it were Wendeval, the big hulking fighter that trounced Thoresby. As he ran across the open field in full armor, I knew the brilliance of Rob's plan— Rob were as fresh as he could be and Wendeval were half to exhausted already.

He swung at Rob with his blunted sword, and Rob ducked

easily and cut up with the shield so that Wendeval dropped
his sword and fell backward. I expected him to go for the
sword straight, but Rob waited as Wendeval staggered up, and
slammed him again with his shield so Wendeval fell back, out
cold and disqualified.

Rob took up the sword and waited.

A cluster of men were to the far left of the field, and Gisbourne finished dispatching two men before turning to Rob
with a wicked smile. He stalked out to him slow, and without
a helmet on his head, I could see him turn to me, staring at me
as he went to fight Rob. Even across the field, his cruel laugh
made me shiver.

Rob saw him coming and stood ready. If he were tired, it
didn't show a lick. He were fierce and still and calm, waiting
for his opponent. His opponent in the truest sense.

Gisbourne closed the gap and Rob made the first move,
a hard strike with his sword that Gisbourne parried, with a
smooth follow by Rob's shield that cuffed Gisbourne hard.
Rob snapped back to the ready.

I had never seen him fight with a shield. It had to be something he learned at war; he used the defense as another weapon
like he'd been doing it all his life.

Gisbourne charged him with flashing swordplay, their heavy
swords clashing and spitting light in the winter sun.

"He's impressive," Eleanor murmured to me.

I turned my head; I had forgotten her. In the same look I
saw Isabel, gripping her chair, staring at Gisbourne.

"Which one?" I asked. It were a fair question; they were both beyond all comparison.

"Yours," she said. Before I could ask more, she ducked her head a little and said, "The one who should be yours, at least."

"He's beyond compare," I whispered, sinking back in my chair. With the pain numbed I felt so tired I could bare move. It felt wrong, to be confessing how I admired Rob to Eleanor, but I didn't have the strength to care.

Each sound their blows made rocked me, and they were fast and steady both. They turned slow, a foot with each hit, moving with each other, locked. Endless and eternal. They were too well matched; it was just a matter of how long they could stay moving.

Across the field another man took a knee rather than face down another blow, and it seemed the needed count was reached. A horn blared, and Rob and Gisbourne fought a few moments more before breaking free of each other.

I waited for them to leave the field, but no one did. Pages ran out onto the field with short fences and made a small ring in the middle of the field. The final players were herded in there—five in all.

Only moments had passed, and the fighters were still heaving with breath. Another horn sounded, and their weapons raised. I wanted to turn to Eleanor and accuse her—there was no space between these rounds, no time to see Rob at all.

But I couldn't. I just watched.

No one rushed forward. Gisbourne were talking—I could

see his mouth moving—but I couldn't much hear his words. Then the four moved closer to each other, and all set on Robin.

My nails dug into the wood of the chair.

Gisbourne were the first to strike, and Rob blocked it with his sword and swiveled to take another blow on his shield. He ducked another and struck at Gisbourne, hitting his shoulder.

Rob moved fast, his feet trained for the forest where you could never trust the ground for long. I could hear their shouts of anger, bare loud over the shouts and cheers of the people.

The four were starting to get their timing better, and de Lacy struck a hard blow to Rob's shield and Gisbourne swung hard for Rob's arm.

It were hard enough to make him stumble and drop his sword.

Prince John laughed.

Water pricked at my eyes as they set upon him in true. He were good at using his shield like a weapon, slamming them with it, twisting this way and that, but without his sword he couldn't survive. I wanted to shout at him to take a knee, take a knee, but if he ever heard, he wouldn't have done it. Surrender weren't in him.

Gisbourne swept out his feet, and he fell. They all managed to get a sickening blow in to his body before Gisbourne took the opening and heaved a blow at de Lacy, and they left Rob on the field.

It were Winchester who strode out to the ring and shifted

one of the fences to pull Rob out. I watched him help Rob hobble off the field and wiped the tears off my face.

"Do you know where they'll go?" I asked Eleanor.

She gave a careful, queen-like sigh. "I imagine the earl took him back to Robin's quarters. Robin was situated in a low room in the residences, in the small building," she told me.

"Right next to the prison," I realized.

"Yes," she said. "It was all I could do to talk my son out of that."

I stood, tucking my hand and the half-melted snow purse inside my sling. My heart beat thick and heavy like it didn't have many beats left, but I turned from the nobles and the Queen Mother didn't stop me none.

CHAPTER
EIGHTEEN

The walk were a hundred times longer than it had been the day before. I stayed outside for as long as I could, but as soon as I stepped into the warmth I felt like I melted with it. I fell against the wall, breathing hard.

Sucking in a deep breath, I pushed off the wall and walked quick through, desperate to get to him. When I came to his hallway, I knew his room by the guards outside it.

But they weren't there to keep me out, only keep him in, and they didn't even look at me as I opened the door and entered.

I shut the door and slumped against it. It were a small room, and Winchester's wide, tall body were brimming it over. Rob sat on the bed. His shirt were stripped off in a sweaty heap on the floor with leathers and a tunic besides. His body were glowing red, his mouth drooling with blood, and he held a balled-up cloth to his face.

His eyes met mine, and the ball in his throat ran up and down. "Scarlet," he said, soft and rough.

Winchester turned, ducking his head to me. "My lady," he said. He glanced back to Rob. "I shall leave him in your care—my own healer should be along shortly."

Winchester came closer, blocking my body from Rob's view. "Perhaps," he whispered, "you should allow him to look at you as well." His jaw worked. "I regret that I feel I was protecting the wrong party last night."

Without much knowing why, I were dangerous close to crying. I shook my head.

He nodded and opened the door. I could hear him telling the guards—his guards, I realized—to allow no one but his healer in.

"Rob," I whispered. "Are you . . . are you all right?"

He walked over to me slow, his eyes never leaving mine, and he stood just before me, holding his breath before he touched me. His fingertips touched the side of my mouth and slid back along my cheek, first one, then three, then four grazing along my skin. His thumb skidded over my lips, dragging my breath away with it.

My one hand slid up, doing the work for two as it ran slow over his chest, ridges and dips and smooth planes like the forest itself, beckoning me and tricking me and drawing me in deeper. The bit of hair furring over his chest licked at my fingers as I ran over it, phantom touches along my skin. I hit smooth skin again and pushed my fingers wide to curl over his shoulder and round his neck, drawing him closer to me.

"Scarlet," he whispered, staring at me, his eyes checking my face. "What happened last night? You look . . . you scared the hell out of me when I saw you. You're wearing the same dress."

"You first," I said, shutting my eyes. I pulled him closer still, waiting until our faces touched, his forehead resting on mine.

"Scarlet," he said. "You know what happened to me. They're letting me compete. And by some miracle, they haven't been cruel to me. Which makes me think that cruelty has gone elsewhere."

"I don't know, Rob. I see you out there, fighting like that, and I don't know anything about you at all."

"Scarlet." His eyes were steady, not thrown off. "You're shaking."

I were?

He leaned away a bit. "I frightened you," he said, and his voice were more low and dark than a well.

"No." My hand on him turned to a grip as the floor tilted.

He frowned and moved quick, taking me about the waist and pulling me down upon the bed, sitting beside me. His hands on me changed, running through my hair to check for lumps on my head, pressing my skin to check what were broken. Soon enough he went still, and after a breath gentle fingers went about the wrist in the sling. Even that touch sent pain like shards of glass through me, and I shook my head, moaning.

"What did they do."

It weren't a question. It were dark and angry.

"Rob."

"No more, Scarlet. Tell me. Now."

"They punished me," I said soft. "The prince. He . . ." I had felt the point of the knife before it touched my skin. Watching it, waiting for it, knowing the pain were about to come, it were like I made it happen before it really started. How did I tell him that? "Nothing," I ground out, meeting his eyes. "He did nothing that I can't take, nothing that makes me wish I'd done different. And nothing for you to hurt over."

But Rob kept on, taking my hand and seeing the way it were bandaged, two small fingers and a flat stretch before my thumb with blood starting to seep through.

His chest started rising and dropping fast, like he couldn't breathe swift enough and none of it were doing no good. His hands went to fists, pressed hard on his knees, and then he struck his knees, hard and fast. He bent forward, then sprang up and drove his fist into the wooden post with a cry.

I tried to stand, but my legs couldn't hold it. "Rob," I sighed. "Rob, come to me."

He growled low, kicking the post once, twice, three times in sharp succession.

"Rob," I said again. "I can't come to you."

He turned and came forward, dropping to his knees in

front of me. I pulled him closer, feeling the world rock a little less with my hand on him.

He went still, his face a scowl and his eyes on mine. "They did this to you because of me. All of this is because of me."

I stared into his eyes, unwilling to look away, unable to let him go. "No. The prince did this because he is cruel and jealous and Gisbourne allowed it because he's weak. They just gave you the best chance to fight this, Robin Hood. To prevent this from happening to anyone else."

His big hands spread like fans on my back, tight but gentle. "I can't do it. I won't win—not in the shape that I'm in, Scarlet." His eyes shut and his forehead pushed against my stomach. "Every hit—every time—it feels like I'm back there. It feels like it's all starting again."

"What is?" I whispered. I ran my fingers over his hair, slow and kind. "What is?"

"How much do you know about the Crusades?" he asked. "What I did there?"

"You left after the siege of Acre, didn't you?" I said.

He didn't answer me. He swallowed. "The siege was long. It was the first real battle, and Richard couldn't afford to give up. It took us more than a month before we first broke Acre," he said. "For so long a wall had been between us, but then the wall broke, and they flooded out. And we ran."

I shivered at the picture in my mind—it were all too like the melee, the sudden and unleashed clash of two lines. Chaos.

"I was so afraid of that day—of the crush of war. I didn't know how I would tell my men from the infidels. Then they ran at us, and I was relieved—there would be no mistaking one of us for one of them. They looked so very different, they didn't wear armor of any kind. With the sun glinting off our metal, it was like God had sent an angel to each of us to shine a light on us, keep us safe. And I found I could fight. I found all my training meant something; I could fight and never tire, never break."

One of us were shaking, and I didn't know who, but it didn't matter. If one person shook, the other's body took it in.

"And then the wind rose, and the sand rose with it. They continued to come at us. We were blind, and more than that, the ease was gone. I couldn't see who was right in front of my face, much less what they wore."

His body leaned tighter against mine, careful not to lean on my arm.

"I can't take this back, Scarlet, once I've told you," he breathed.

"You won't have to, Rob." I stroked his head, his neck, his rough cheek.

"The sand cleared," he said, "as quick as it had come. And at my feet were three men I'd fought beside for months. Three men I knew. One was even younger than I was. And I had killed them. You all think I'm so noble and goddamn righteous, but I don't even know who the enemy is. I don't know who the enemy is if not the demon that's within me.

Those men, the hostage children I was made to kill—Scar, they haunt me. They haunt my nights and they remind me daily that even if by some miracle I can win this, I should never be sheriff. I know the weak and evil parts of myself too well."

It were him what were trembling, and I tugged on his shoulder until he drew up, guiding him to the bed and making him lie in it. He were sweating hard, and I feared for a fever. I stroked his hair back as it slicked over with sweat. He were staring at me, waiting for what I would say.

Slow, I shook my head. "That isn't evil, Rob. That isn't weak. It's horrible and unfair. But it's not your fault." He tried to pull away from me but I stroked his cheek. "There is so much more in your heart than your ghosts," I told him. "And in mine too. I don't care how many sleepless nights it takes. I don't care for bruises or fire. I won't let them take your soul."

He gave me a tiny hint of a smile and it felt like sunlight breaking on me. "I don't know if you have much of a say over it."

"You gave your heart into my keeping, Rob, and I protect what's mine. Because I know what is in there true, and it has naught to do with demons." I bent down, coming closer to his face and letting our lips bare touch. His hand ran into my hair and he pulled me closer for a proper kiss. I felt him breathe deeper, slower, into me, calming, our souls rushing out to meet.

I broke off, then ducked again for one more touch. "They can't have you," I whispered to him. "You're mine." I kissed the corner of his mouth. "And I look at Gisbourne and he don't know he's weak. The prince don't know he's cruel. But you know your most dangerous parts and you act like a hero anyway. That's what will make you a wonderful sheriff, Rob." I stroked his face. "But if you ever wanted to run, I would run with you. This will be brutal and punishing, Rob, and if you ever think you can't fight in true, I will run with you in a breath."

"I can't run," he said. "But I fear I can't win, either."

The guards outside spoke to someone, and I sat up straight as the healer came in. He came with a tray of jars and knives, and my lip curled. The monks disliked the practice because of its weakening effects, but I forgot how common it were for these noble healers.

"No," I said as he crossed the threshold. "No bloodletting."

The man's mouth dropped. "My—my lady, his humours must be brought into balance."

"Poultices, tinctures are fine. No bloodletting."

Rob squeezed my hand tight.

The healer's chest puffed. "With respect, my lady, his Grace instructed me to bring the young man to full health."

"You bring a knife near his skin and I will have it at your throat," I snapped.

He went red and started sputtering, but Rob managed a weak chuckle. "Please, my lord, denying her wishes would be much more hazardous to my health."

"If the lady would remove herself," the healer said, "I must examine his lordship."

"I'm no lord," Rob said. "And I would like you to look at her hand first."

The man's eyebrows what were thicker than the feathers of a ruffled chicken rose up, but he didn't say anything as I drew the hand slow out of the sling. He unwrapped the wet bandages careful, and when he were done he looked at my face in a way full different than he had before.

He handed me the pain tincture. "Several drops of this should help, my lady," he said grave.

I shook my head, but Rob sat up, sliding one arm around my waist and taking a dropper full with the other hand. He held it up and I opened my mouth as he tapped it in. I shut my eyes against the taste and turned full against him as the healer put a salve to the wounds that looked sick already.

It were so raw and sore that his touches hurt more than the cut what did it. To my horror I started to sob, but Rob held me tight, squeezed against him.

When it were done, I were shaking violently and Rob held me, kissing my cheek and temple and hair. "Go on," he said after a moment. "Rest. You need it."

"I'll come back," I promised him.

He nodded, kissing my cheek once more.

Careful to walk proper out of the room so Rob wouldn't worry, I near collapsed outside the door, and one of the guards caught me in his arms. "My lady," he said. "His Grace asked me to see you back to your chambers."

I nodded, fair grateful. It seemed miles back to my room. We started walking and I were more grateful for the earl's care when I fainted dead in the hall.

—⚓—

When I woke, it were to a soft, metal noise and the cracking of fire. I were in the bed I didn't like, and my whole body felt like a sack of flour. I struggled to sit up in the bed; the day-old dress had been taken off me and I was just in the long, loose gown, deep under blankets and warm.

Gisbourne were near the fire, and I could see the glint of steel as his whetstone passed over the sword, sharpening the blade careful and slow.

"Do you care to tell me where you were this afternoon?" he asked, not turning to me.

"A healer checked my hand." Which did feel much duller, now.

"The earl's healer."

"Yes."

"And how did you come by that?"

I sighed. "I reckon you know just where I were, Gisbourne."

The whetstone stopped. "Yes."

Pushing from the bed were awkward with one hand, but I struggled free of it and went for the other chair by the fire. "Did you win the melee?"

He tossed his sword down so it clattered loud. It were

meant to intimidate me, I think, but I were far beyond such.
"Does this marriage mean nothing to you, Marian?"

I frowned at him. "Of course it doesn't. You knew that
from the first."

"Then why come here at all?" he growled.

"Did you hit your head?" I demanded. "The annulment.
All I've ever wanted were the annulment."

"And to make a *fool* of me!" he roared, throwing himself
back in the chair.

"I never lied about what and who I am. You knew that.
You brought me here. If I make you a fool, it ain't my fault." I
tucked my legs up, cold and simmering with anger. "Fool
indeed. But what the hell is wrong with you, that you defy the
prince to protect me in one moment—what, so your *honor*
remains intact?—and then help him cut off my damn fingers
the next?"

He stood, scooping up the sword and slamming it into its
scabbard and throwing it on the bed. "Because there is one line
I won't cross—and that's the whole reason I agreed to this
exercise in idiocy to start with. You think you were my first
choice, Marian? You think I was desperate to marry Leaford's
younger, uppity daughter? With an unmarried, beautiful older
sister hanging about?"

This stole my breath. "You wanted Joanna?"

"*Wanted?* No. Hell no. But why would I take you over her,
hmm? She was stunning, graceful, sweet—she would have
bent very well to my hand. So why you?"

My lip curled at the thought of him raising a hand to Joanna. "You never wanted either of us from the start. You wanted Isabel. It's obvious every time you look at her, Gisbourne—"

"Use my given name!" he screamed. He stepped over to me, catching my throat, but not squeezing, not hurting me. "Say it," he said. "Say my given name. You are my wife, Marian. Use my given name."

With unblinking eyes, I stared at him. I had lost fingers to his master; his threats seemed hollow and idle now.

He shook his head with a sad, helpless laugh. His hand left my throat to catch my cheek, looking at the fading bruises there. His rough, calloused thumb ran over the cut by my lip. "You won't, will you? I can beg you and break you and you won't do a damn thing I ask."

It seemed wise not to answer that.

His thumb went to the scar, testing it, feeling its depth and the odd jumble of skin and scar under the surface. "You are the most unnatural, vexing woman, Marian." He tilted my chin farther up. "You didn't scream once last night."

"I told you," I said quiet. "I'm not afraid of your pain. Or his."

His thumb ran over my mouth, and I went tense. "I am," he admitted. "But it's his bribes that are so much darker and alluring."

"Is that why you married me, Gisbourne?" I asked. "He bribed you?"

He nodded, and my breath left me.

"Why?" I asked. "Why would he ever? How would he know of me at all?"

His hand left my face. "You're like a wild horse, Marian. Utterly untamable, unassailably noble. No—not a horse." He chuckled and looked at me. "A *lion*," he said. "And you are the fool in truth if you don't know what that means. Why it is the one thing that means the prince can't kill you and the one reason he will always want to. Why you are dangerous to him."

"Eleanor said he can't kill me because he has royal blood. Godly blood."

His grin was wicked and dark. "I can't kill you, Marian, and I have no royal blood. Hell, I barely count as noble. But to kill you would be to defy God himself—not to mention Eleanor."

"I don't understand."

He laughed, and I stood.

"Tell me! I don't know what you're talking about!" My voice raised dangerous close to a shriek.

He began stripping off his clothing, not answering me.

"Gisbourne!" I yelled again.

"Your parents have come to the castle," he said after a moment, stripping off his tunic. "They expect an audience with you tomorrow morning."

"My . . ." I dropped into the chair. My parents. I had been so long gone from them it seemed easy not to think of them at all. A thousand thoughts twisted through my mind. Did they hate me? Were it all forgotten and forgiven now I had done what they first asked? How would I explain leaving them at the first?

Christ, how would I explain Joanna?

He chuckled. "I thought that might shut you up."

CHAPTER

NINETEEN

$\sim$o$\sim$

When I woke up, Gisbourne were sleeping and there were early, gray sun in the room. I called for Mary and when she set about pulling fabric round the bandaged hand, she stopped but didn't say nothing. Gisbourne grunted and sat up in bed, watching me and yelling for Eadric.

My head were running fast, thinking on my parents. What would I say? How could I possibly say anything? What if my parents wanted to know—anything. Everything.

"You're quiet," Gisbourne said.

How much time had passed? I weren't sure. He were dressed. I realized Mary weren't flitting about, and I were dressed too. "Thinking," I said.

He went to his coffers, shuffling through until he found something. It were a long, black-sheathed boot knife. He drew it half out and showed me a wicked-looking blade. He pushed

it back in the sheath and tossed it to me. I caught it and looked
at it; I couldn't even draw it out of the sheath the way my hand
were bandaged, so I just stared at him.

"Does that help?" he said.

Silent, I nodded slow.

He nodded once, sharp. "Good."

And then he left.

I wedged it into the edge of my kirtle in the back, hoping it
would hold snug enough that I could pull just the blade with one
hand. Not that I expected to draw a knife on my parents; having
it near me, a reminder of who I really were, helped in true.

It were strange both that Gisbourne knew it and allowed it.

I went out behind him, starting for my parents' chamber.
Sucking in a breath, I changed my mind.

I went to Rob's room, and the guards let me in without a
word or a harsh look. He were awake, lying in bed, and he half
sat up, looking at me.

"Scarlet," he murmured.

I came forward without a word, tucking myself into the
bed beside him. I laid on his chest and shut my eyes, trying to
wish the world away. His heartbeat were leaping out at me,
beating into my skin till my heart beat back, matching the
tune.

"I slept," he marveled to me. His lips touched my forehead.
"All night, as far as I know."

I pressed my face to his chest and let my eyes close. "The
sword fights are today," I said. "Individual matches."

His neck bobbed a bit as I felt him nod. "And I'll fight," he told me soft. "There's no running." His hand dragged along my back. "Or, rather, I could always run—but I want to fight for you more than I want to run."

Inching up, I raised my face to kiss him. I shut my eyes into it, trying to forget what would happen today, for him and me both. "Just lose in the sword, Rob," I told him. "You don't need the prizes or the money. You only need to win the archery for sheriff. Anything more ain't worth the bruises, the punishment."

He sighed. "Maybe. Will you be there?" he asked. His nose nudged my cheek. "You should probably stay warm and rest."

I took a breath like could draw his strength into me. "My parents are here. They want to see me."

"Your parents?" he asked, looking at me.

Lying on his chest felt like home. "I don't know what to say to them."

"I visited them," he said soft.

I pushed up off him. "What?"

"After you married Gisbourne. He became the landholder, and I wanted to make sure he wasn't hurting them. You would have never forgiven yourself if he had, and my father always liked your parents. I spoke to them. I never told them I knew you."

Blinking, I stared at him. "And?"

"They were lovely people. They've kept their lands well and protected their tenants from the worst of the taxes. They were very kind to me." He swallowed and touched my cheek. "I had this fantasy that I could return to ask them for your hand in marriage and explain I'd been protecting you from harm when they hadn't been able to. They would hug me and tell me that if they weren't there to love you, they were glad I had been."

My chest felt tight to bursting, and before I could stop it, tears ran down to kiss his hand. "I love you, Rob," I told him, swooping in to kiss him.

"I love you too," he told me. "Go, before anyone discovers you here."

I kissed him once more, the kind of kiss that burned through me and made my whole heart fill with him.

Leaving Rob, I went to the room the servants told me were my parents', and I stood outside. Then I paced. Then I stopped, for pacing made me dizzy, and stood there still.

I left. I had no idea what to say to them.

—◊—

I had missed the first several sword fights, but Isabel informed me that Gisbourne destroyed his first opponent. Eleanor quietly let me know that Rob won his first contest as well. My heart were still pounding at the idea of talking to my parents, and it took long for it to quiet.

Gisbourne came up again and turned to the prince to bow. He caught my eye and frowned.

His partner were de Lacy, and I found that I were hoping

my husband crushed the man who called me a wild animal the first night at court.

Gisbourne came at him hard. He were all power, my husband; fierce and overwhelming, but no speed and little finesse. He had footwork when he needed it, but it weren't his skill. He knocked the sword out of de Lacy's hand and gave him a moment to reach for it when he brought the heel of his boot down hard on de Lacy's other hand, stretched flat on the ground.

Despite the pain, it gave de Lacy the space to grab his sword and bring it up to Gisbourne's neck. The match was over; de Lacy had won.

"Quite cunning," the queen mother murmured to me.

"My husband?" I asked. "He lost." I looked back to the field where de Lacy nursed his hand and sucked in a breath. Gisbourne had sacrificed the fight to take out de Lacy's hand—because de Lacy were favored in the archery, from what I heard. While he could still use a sword with his right hand, he could never hold a bow without them both. "Cunning indeed," I muttered.

De Clare were next, fighting a man named Doncaster who I didn't recognize. Doncaster were a heavy brute, and he were beating de Clare quite roundly when someone stepped in front of me. "My lady wife," Gisbourne grunted. "Don't you have somewhere to be?"

"Where is that, my lord Gisbourne?" Eleanor asked.

"Her parents have arrived, and she has yet to greet them."

I looked to Eleanor for some excuse, but she gave none, save for losing a precious little bit of her color. Her mouth fell into a thin line. "Yes. You must speak to them, my dear. They must have . . . missed you, after so long." Her voice had fallen quiet and low.

"My lady?" I asked soft. "Are you all right?"

Her chin raised. "Just cold. I think I shall retire." She waved her hands for her ladies, and they set about readying a sled that would take her back up to her rooms.

Gisbourne took my hand and pulled me up. He put my hand in his arm and escorted me back to the castle, not saying a word the whole way there. I didn't say nothing on his loss, neither.

He brought me to their door, knocked, and let go of me only when the servant answered the door and ushered me into their chamber.

They were sitting by the fire in two chairs, and they stood up the moment the servant announced me. My eyes went to my mother first. Tall and long with hair like wheat on willows, she looked so painful like Joanna my eyes sprang with tears. I blinked it back. My father were there, his handsome face older, his strong body softer by a hair.

He came to me first, cupping my face in his hands and looking at the bruises, my hair, judging me. His eyes closed with a sigh. "Marian," he said.

I wanted to tear away from him and run, run from his judgment and whatever he thought of my strange looks. My mother came over, covering her mouth as she started to cry. "Oh, my darling girl. I had hoped—I thought maybe, when you ran, you would learn to obey. I didn't want—I didn't want—" She shook her head. "My sweet!"

My father grunted. "I will speak to him, Marian. He must have patience with you, if you are to learn to be a good wife." He rubbed my mother's back. "Dear, it's all right. Come, there is much more to talk about."

My father reached forward, taking my good hand like he'd done when I was a little girl. He patted it and brought me over to the fireplace, letting me sit in the chair while he sat on the hearth before me. "There is much to hear, Marian."

I nodded slow, my mouth dry like week-old bread. "I-I know," I said.

"Where have you *been*?" my mother wailed. "Why didn't you write? Didn't you ever think—" She started crying again.

My father ignored her. "Start at the beginning," he said. "Why did you leave us? Was it Joanna's idea?"

"It was my idea," I admitted, shame making my words slow but proper. "Neither one of us wanted to marry, but she would have done as you asked. When I said I wanted to run away, she wouldn't let me go alone."

My mother bent. "She has always loved you so very much," she moaned.

"Where did you go?" my father asked. "How on earth did you manage, two girls on your own?"

"We went to London. Joanna took some coin she had saved, and we used that at first."

"Who took you in London?" my father demanded, his face folding into a scowl. "What blackguard sheltered you and didn't tell me of it?"

"We rented a room," I told him, my voice tiny.

"A room?" my mother repeated.

"Like a—" My father didn't dare finish the sentence.

"We managed," I said quick, trying to keep my mind from wheeling into those days. "We managed."

"*How* did you manage?" he snapped. "Did you sell yourselves? Is that what my daughters have become? Scarlet women?"

I flushed at the name. "We stole," I said. I would never tell them what Joanna did at night to manage. I would never tell no one that.

He jumped to his feet. "Stole! Like criminals!"

My mother's wail distracted him, and he stood by her, rubbing her back.

"I was an exceptional thief," I told him, squaring my shoulders. "So good that Robin Hood asked me to join his band. And I've been doing that ever since. Helping people. Saving people."

"There is nothing exceptional about a woman of noble birth embracing a criminal life," he told me. "Nothing! And just how long have you been here? How long have you lived half a day's ride from us and we never knew?"

"Years," I breathed.

"Years!" he roared, stepping forward. My mother looked up, though, and caught his arm.

"Wait. When can we see Joanna?" she asked. "She's here, isn't she? We thought she'd come with you."

I stood from the chair, needing to feel my knife, needing to be able to move if my father lunged for me. "No," I said soft.

"So she married after all," my father said. "Where? In London?"

"No," I said, and my face twisted, my eyes filling.

"Where is she?" my father demanded.

"She died," I whispered. I felt like crying but the tears didn't come. I had cried so much for Joanna; it didn't seem right to cry now when it were their turn to mourn her. I turned and looked at my parents, shamed. "In London. Three years ago."

My father roared and came toward me, but I ducked away from him as my mother wailed in pain. "Where is she!" my father bellowed.

"My girl—" my mother cried, sobs stabbing in the middle of her words. "My only—girl is—dead—"

"What?" I asked, but I weren't sure if I even really said it over their hollering. My father continued to rant at me, yelling and coming after me, making me shift round the room. "Mother! What did you just say?" I demanded.

"You killed our daughter!" my father screamed. "You killed our daughter! You took everything we ever had and never gave a damn about us! We never would have taken you in if we knew you would kill Joanna!"

This stopped me dead in my tracks. "Taken me . . ."

He grabbed me by the shoulders and shook me hard enough that I thought my head would wrench straight off. I couldn't stop him, couldn't much think. *Taken you in.*

My hand jerked and hit my chest, and searing pain made me gasp, jerking to life. I drew the knife and angled it at his throat. He let me go, madness in his eyes.

"One of the other things I'm good at," I told him. "Knives."

His face twisted and he spat at me. "You are not my daughter. You never were."

"Marian."

My head twisted to look at Gisbourne, standing in the doorway. "I believe you are needed elsewhere at the moment."

He folded his arms, looking at my father, and even if the kindness came from Gisbourne, I took my chance and left.

But I didn't run.

I were done running.

—ɷ—

I went to the tourney grounds, but not the the dais where I were meant to sit. I went into the crowd and found Much. "Rob told me what happened," he told me.

My face dropped. How did Rob know? *Did everyone know?*

He were looking at my hand, though, and suddenly the world spun into sense.

"I'm sorry," he told me.

"It won't change a damn thing," I spat, waving him off. "You taught me that."

His shoulder touched mine. "Still."

"No John?"

He shook his head.

"Will you do something for me, Much?" I asked.

He nodded. "Of course, Scar."

"You can't yap about it," I told him, looking toward him but not at him.

"Even to Rob?" he asked.

"Sort of. It has to be me what tells him, not you, Much."

"All right. What is it?"

I scratched at the velvet on my gown, trying to push blood into my cold fingers. "Find out if anyone knows of someone who gave their baby to the Leafords."

He stared at me. "You mean . . . ?"

I nodded. "I think. I don't know."

"You, or your sister?"

"Me," I said soft. "And fast as you can."

He nodded. "The monks might know. They would have cared for your mother in childbirth—or noticed the lack thereof."

"Or Lady Thoresby. Her mother were a midwife too."

He nodded. "I'll find out, Scar."

A grunt rang out and we turned back to the field. It weren't Rob fighting. "How has he been doing?" I asked.

"Fought twice. He's winning, but my guess is they've been ordered to hurt him more than beat him. He's taking punishment."

I pushed my shoulders back. "One more day, Much, and it all changes. Forever."

He squeezed my good hand. "I'll go and find out, Scar."

"Thank you."

Much left, and I went to find my next quarry. He were there, in an overloud red felt hat, selling a crowd on some story. I moved into his sight and motioned to him, and it took him a moment to end the story with a flourish and collect some coin before coming over to me.

He flipped me a coin. "For the lovely lady," he said with a bow.

I caught it, then tossed it back to him. "I don't want your coin, Allan."

He raised a charming eyebrow. "Then there's something the lady does want?"

I met his eyes dark and true. "Confidence."

He straightened, and the playman fell away. He looked at me. "I am a confidence man, Lady Scar. And at your faithful service, if you wish it."

"I do," I said soft. "I need information."

"On what?"

"Lord Leaford's daughters."

He squinted. "It would seem you have the natural advantage to that information."

My pipes were thick. "I don't. And I don't know if this was said to wound me or if it's true, but they—my parents—rather, the Leafords let me think I'm not their natural daughter."

His eyebrows rose. "Then to whom does the fair thief belong?"

"That's your bit to find out."

He bowed and kissed my hand. "It shall be done."

"Thank you, Allan."

—⟋⟍—

I went back to the castle, and I walked past Rob's room. I wanted to wait for him to return, to tell him everything, but it felt too raw, too new, too strange. And tomorrow would decide it all—he needed rest.

I continued on, praying my night would be the only sleepless one.

Gisbourne were waiting in the chambers. He raised his eyebrows. "I was not sure that you'd return."

I raised my chin. "My parents can say what they want, but that don't change that I'm married to you, and that don't change that I want that annulment. So I'm here."

He nodded slow. "All right."

"But I ain't faking this anymore, Gisbourne. I'm not talking in the fancy way you want, I'm not wearing these damned skirts, I'm not going to supper tonight, and I'm not smiling and scraping to your princess. None of it."

He shrugged. "Fine." He sat before the fire. "Though I

would recommend at least wearing the dresses. I haven't any men's clothing that would fit you."

I crossed my arms. That were worth thinking over, but I weren't going to say such to him.

He nodded and didn't speak no more.

Gisbourne ordered the servants to bring an early supper to our chambers, and we ate in silence. He retired early and I stayed up, watching the fire, my stomach a knot.

CHAPTER
TWENTY

~o~

The morning came in hard. Shadowed skies blew out over Nottinghamshire, hailing the castle and grounds with snowy breath. I watched it through the window, and it did nothing to ease my heart. The cold and the damp would change the tension of the bows and arrows. But Rob wouldn't never shoot without testing his arrows first. I wondered if they would let him use his own bow.

No. Why would the prince ever give Rob any such gift?

Rob would be fine—he knew any bow well enough and were no stranger to such weather. He were leaps and bounds better than Gisbourne if he had his own weapon, his own arrows, his own target. With such things taken from him, they'd still be a fair match. Rob would win. Rob *had* to win.

Or, at least, I prayed it were so.

With de Lacy out of the way, it were truly a contest between

Gisbourne and Rob. Gisbourne slept sound as I watched and worried and ached. Gisbourne were in the best condition he could be. What if Rob hadn't slept a lick? He were good with his weapon, but would he win?

I looked at my husband and thought of de Lacy's hand. What would they do to Rob to keep him from winning? It seemed they were trying to beat him down yesterday, and it had been close to working. But he were still in for the archery, and I knew the prince wouldn't never let it be won so easy.

My hand burned and I wondered what price Rob would have to pay for being the people's favorite.

Gisbourne stirred and I tucked the blanket tighter round me. "Close the damn window, you crazy woman," he grunted from the bed.

I didn't. I stared outside, watching the swirls of snow like it were meant to sweep me into it, steal me away into its silence. Snow were a thief of noise, of sun, of darkness. No day would ever be bright and no night would ever be truly black under its curtain, and all that were under it fell silent and still.

It were a fair perfect thing for the archery competition.

Gisbourne cursed and threw off his blankets, bellowing for Eadric to come and dress him.

I felt Gisbourne's eyes on me, and I looked to him. "Do you fear for your beloved?" he asked me, smiling dark.

"Always," I told him. There didn't seem any need to lie or bluster about now. "I think that's the nature of loving someone. I fear for him with every breath." I met Gisbourne's eyes.

"But I also trust with every bit of my heart that he can trounce you."

Gisbourne's smile twisted. "Don't think for a second, my dear wife, that Prince John will ever let a vagabond be named sheriff."

"And your honor can stand that?" I asked. "To win, knowing it were all false?"

"False?" he asked, chuckling. "No. The prince promised this seat to me long ago and he damn well better deliver. The winner isn't the falsity; it's the entire game. It's been nothing but a farce from the start."

"And what of me? What did he promise you to marry me? You say it were a bribe, but I don't understand why he would ever do it."

"You'll figure it out."

"I think you're lying. Most because if the prince bribed you to marry me you'd never grant me an annulment. You'd never even think of it."

His eyes met mine, dark and level. "He's toyed with me for long enough. I have followed the letter of his orders. I don't give a damn if he doesn't like it."

Staring at him, I almost believed it. I shook my head, looking out at the snow. "That ain't the way of it at all, is it? You will always fear the prince and his wrath." I laid my head on my knees as winter wind blew over my face. "You're just his dog. That's all you ever were."

He made a grunting sort of noise but didn't answer. Eadric

came and began to dress him, and after a while, Mary came for me, in what I hoped would be the last day I ever sat in noble dress.

—∿—

The nobles' dais were bigger and fancier than before. The prince, Eleanor, Isabel, and Winchester were all on a platform higher still, the rest of us flanked out more careful than before. I were closer to the edge now, displayed, and I felt like some weak thing they had trussed up to remind Rob to keep his place.

A horn sounded and the contestants took the field. They high-stepped over the falling snow—which, in fair amusing fashion, pages were sweeping idiot-like from the field of play— and came to the cleared space several feet from the nobles' dais, full across from the heaving, cheering, wild throng of common folk.

The men looked different now. Free from the metal of armor, it weren't a game of defense now. Each man were bare of all but his skill.

Rob glowed. He were red-cheeked from the cold, but more than that, his eyes were bright, a lush blue like fall sky that every flake of snow seemed to make brighter, bolder, more beautiful. His shoulders were square and strong, standing firm against the world.

His eyes met mine and his smile were quick and sly, a slip of the old Rob I knew before the nightmares had begun. The

Rob that were every inch the hero of the people. My blood ran hot and I smiled back at him.

It would stand. Whatever strange and awful tricks Gisbourne and Prince John had devised, whatever the outcome, I felt it in my heart that the world would be right again. Even if it weren't Rob, a lawful sheriff would take the seat and the people would eat, and live, and be free from such tyranny as they had known. Good would stand, and evil wouldn't win out this day.

Their names were called, and Prince John welcomed them. He explained the game—four rounds with a target that would be more removed with each round, and anyone that missed the inner circle were eliminated. Best shot would win the game, the prize of the golden arrow, and the seat of sheriff. Him what won were to take his oath as soon as the game were done.

There were five targets; the first distance were twenty paces from the mark. It were a shot a child could make, but it were meant to be easy. The men took several minutes to practice, testing the spine of the foreign arrows, testing their bend. How supple the spine of an arrow were changed everything in the way it flew, and it weren't something you could know without flying them first.

The horn blew for the start of the first round. Fifteen men were competing, and the first five stepped up. Gisbourne were in them.

Edward Marshal were overseeing the competition, and he stood to the side, half between the target and the archers.

He raised his arm, and they pulled arrows from the quivers staked into the ground, and five creaks sounded as the archers drew the strings back, fixing their bows with that lovely tension that set an itch in my hands.

I looked at Gisbourne. His stance were perfect, balanced, easy, and sure, his arms filled with strength and power that the bow didn't bother with. All a bow cared for were the beat of your heart, that tiny space between beats, between breaths, when your mind were clear and clean and the arrow could slice right down the center of it.

Marshal's hand dropped, and four arrows flew. Gisbourne's took a moment to fly, and I could feel it, him waiting for that perfect half-breath.

His were the only one to hit the center ring, and as the others gaped at him, he turned around and smiled at me, wide and brash. I nodded to him. It weren't within me to try and say he weren't an epic marksman.

Five more stepped up, and Robin were in that wave. He rolled his shoulders and smiled at the crowd, and they cheered for him. He could make this shot blind, and they all knew it.

His arrow hit center. Of the other four, three more hit the inner ring.

Robin turned to me and winked as they left the marks. The last five moved to the marks, notched, drew, and let fly. Three more arrows hit the inner ring.

It were a fair paltry showing, to be true. Even with a broke hand I could have made that shot.

Eight archers moved to the next round, and the herald sounded the horn, causing four small pages and one overtall page to run hell for leather over the snow, churning up flakes behind them and even kicking snow onto their own backs. They grabbed the targets and hefted them up.

"One!" Edward Marshal bellowed to them. They all took a pace. "Two!" he cried, and they moved again. He did it eighteen more times till they had moved twenty paces.

Isabel were the first to titter. The lanky lad's target were the full length of a man farther than the other four, and Marshal yelled and waved his hands till the red-faced boy brought it back in line. The whole court and stands laughed at the show, but I were silent.

Five men stepped up to the marks, Gisbourne and Robin at opposite ends of the line. This time their brash and boastful looks weren't for me. They looked down the row to each other, and I watched as Gisbourne grinned and nodded, and Robin just inclined his head with a touch of a smile.

Marshal's arm fell, and only two arrows flew; the third, a smaller man, waited a breath, same as Gisbourne and Robin. I watched as Rob's eyes drifted shut right before he let the tail of the arrow go.

Rob, Gisbourne, and the short one advanced.

—⁓—

In the next wave, two more advanced to the next round. It seemed silly, really; already, their lack of skill were showing and their arrows were just in the bounds of the inner circle, where Gisbourne and Robin's were true and hard to the center.

The horn blew again, and this time the sweeping pages set to the fields and the players withdrew. Eleanor and Isabel stood, handed off the dais by Winchester and the prince. I stood too, swaying toward Eleanor like I were naturally drawn to her, but Isabel stepped quick to me. "Come, Lady Leaford. My legs want for walking." She hooked her arm through my good one like a man might, and drew me off with a wave to her ladies to leave us.

"I don't care if you tell anyone, you know."

I looked to her. She raised her chin, and her pale skin against the snow seemed bright like oyster shells. "Your Highness?" I asked.

"That Lady Essex was attending my husband so late. Gisbourne was quite upset about it, but if you think I will waste breath trying to convince you not to tell the court, you are mistaken."

There weren't much like getting fingers hacked off to make you forget an adultery or two. "It's not my place to say such or judge," I told her honestly. "But I don't hold no thoughts of your husband being a great man."

Her head whipped to me in such a way what sent her dark curls flying, lush like suede and making me miss my hair, my only bit of vain. "He *is* a great man. All great men cannot be held accountable to the standards of peasant marriages."

"It ain't about nobility," I snapped back. "Faithfulness is

God's own law. It's a commandment. Break it or don't but don't say that nobles aren't accountable."

"Royalty is picked by God," she told me. "They rule by the right of God. That's why it's a mortal sin to spill their blood, to dishonor them. And John is no different." She tossed her hair again. "Besides, I hold no illusions that he ever loved me for more than the gold I brought him. I know him better than he thinks I do, you know. I see him looking at that French tart *Isabelle*—like two more letters without sound makes her name so much more elegant than mine—and he doesn't care for her beauty. He sees French armies, French power. French gold. When he wants beauty he'll turn to Lady Essex."

Who were the French Isabelle? I wanted to know, but it didn't seem wise to ask.

"You see, you think you're so very special for your marriage without love. So tortured and martyred. But we all marry without love, Marian. You aren't special at all."

I frowned. "Did I ever say different?"

Isabel stopped. "Just tell me. I don't like not knowing, and even Guy clearly knows *something* and won't tell me. I won't have it."

"I don't know what you're about, Isabel," I told her.

"Eleanor!" she near shouted, and looked around like it might summon the white lady. "What interest does Eleanor have in you, your parents, the lot of it?"

"My parents?"

She folded her arms. "Eleanor of Aquitaine saw the lord

and lady Leaford off from the courtyard this morning. In the snow. Alone. I saw her *embrace* Lady Leaford," she told me, her nose raised higher than ever. "Tell me what that is about this moment."

My face folded into a scowl. "Your Highness, you should ask Eleanor. Or my husband, it seems, but I don't know a damn thing about it." She started to speak again and I shook my head. "I intend to find a fire," I told her.

She crossed her arms and frowned at me, but she let me go.

I skirted round the edge of things, looking for Eleanor. I saw her standing near one of the great bonfires built on the edge of the nobles' area—I reckoned much to keep the common sort out. Whether or not she were wearing one, she always looked like she should have a great crown upon her head. Her skin were wrinkled over again and again, in a way that made her look lived-in and world-wise. She were small, but she had brought England and France to their knees, with every man in between begging for her. She had crumbled old kings and raised up new ones.

She were everything a woman could ever dare to be, and my heart felt such a kinship for her. Yet I didn't move much forward, staying back, knowing if I went to her I couldn't help but ask all my questions.

Like she felt me watching her, she turned and looked to me, folding her hands in front of her. She met my eyes and nodded once.

I stepped forward.

The horn blew, calling out for the next round, and we went back to the dais.

—⚬—

The next round seemed awful slow. Now the archers had to shoot three arrows from the increased distance, one in each of the three different circles. It were a feat of skill what would narrow the field down sharp, but rather than understand this and allow themselves to be picked off, the louts went about it slow and deliberate, like waiting and licking their lips would help them strike a target.

My hand set to aching besides. It hadn't been bad; I kept it out from the blankets so it never got too warm, and that had worked for the first two rounds. By the end of the third, I were breathing harder and could bare sit still as the pain mounted.

The third round narrowed to Rob and Gisbourne, and as the crowd cheered and jumped and waved, there were only one still body in the lot, and he were looking at me. Allan nodded slowly and my heart jumped.

The horn sounded, and I leapt from my chair. Skirting wide around the bonfires, I moved quick to get to the stands and through the crowd. The people swallowed me up, bodies pressing and pushing on every side, and I yelped as someone knocked into my hurt hand. The fellow turned and gave me a dirty look.

A big body stepped in front of my path, and a warm arm came around my shoulders. "Need a hand?" Much asked, keeping me behind the shield of John's back.

He raised his stump with a grin and I frowned. "Terrible humor, Much."

He shrugged, his grin fixed still. "Nobody thinks I'm very funny."

John started moving, forcing people out of the way like a wave. "I need to find Allan," I told Much.

"I know. He was asking for you."

"Did you find anything?" I asked him. "Did he?"

"Find anything about what?" John asked.

"I asked the monks," Much said. "They remember when Leaford announced his second child, but they didn't attend lady Leaford."

"Had they for Joanna?" I asked.

He nodded.

"What's this about?" John asked. "What about your parents?"

I sighed and shook my head, and John craned round to glimpse me do it. "I'll tell you later, John," Much said.

John scowled. "Just because I'm out doesn't mean I want to be *kept* out," he grumbled.

"Allan!" I yelled, seeing the red of his hat. It ducked and bobbed and reappeared a moment later by me.

"My lady thief," he said, taking my good hand and kissing it. His eyes fell on my arm, tucked in the sling, and his head lowered. "Yesterday—I didn't know what had happened."

John looked at me, fury clouding over his mug.

"John, it's done," I said quick. "You don't need to fuss."

"What *happened*, Scar?"

My shoulders lifted. "The prince punished me," I said, trying to say it like it were nothing. "He cut off two of my fingers."

"Your—" His nostrils flared and he turned away from me, crossing his arms and glaring at the ground.

I stared at his back for a long moment before looking to Allan. "What word, Allan?"

"About your parents, none."

"Allan! Why—" I started, but he shook his head.

"They switched the arrows."

CHAPTER

TWENTY-ONE

―o―

W ho switched them?"

"Rob's arrows?"

"For this round?" John, Much, and I all spoke at once.

"The prince's men." Allan looked at me, answering my question. "I don't know what they did, but Gisbourne has the same arrows he did for the last three rounds. Robin's are different."

"So?" John asked. I scowled at him, but he shrugged. "Bow's not really my weapon, is it?"

"If the spine is even slightly different, it will be damn near impossible for Rob to get a perfect shot, which he'll need. And Gisbourne will win, and it will be very hard to prove they cheated," Much explained.

"Like the prince would do anything about a cheat he helped with," John grunted, half turning back to us. His eyes fell on my hand and his shoulders rolled.

The horn sounded and I whipped my head over to see pages walking onto the field with the arrows, filling two of the standing quivers. Rob and Gisbourne set out onto the field, walking toward the marks.

"Allan, please tell me you're better at sneaking than wagging your chin," I said, nodding him forward and pushing through the crowd to the edge.

"Scarlet, what are you doing?" John yelled.

"John," I said, turning to him. "Stay here—we have to switch the arrows back." He stepped forward, but I shook my head. "You're one of the people we protect now. And that's a good thing."

He looked at me, and he looked less sure and cocky than I'd ever known him. He nodded once, and I took off.

The first steps jangled pain through my hand and stole my breath, but I kept moving, desperate to get to them before a shot were flown. My dress and cloak dragged over the snow like a horse's harness, hauling me backward, but I kept going, Allan keeping pace at my side. We weren't close. We weren't going to make it.

The herald raised his horn and I cut onto the field, running through the snow.

My head and hand were pulsing. My feet were awful heavy to lift and I were going slower.

Slower still. I twisted my arm out from the sling—I couldn't much run like that, hobbled by the awkward weight on my chest.

"Scarlet!" Allan yelled. Had he stopped running with me?

I turned and Winchester were there, catching me about the waist and bodily pulling me off the field. "Let me go!" I howled. "I have to warn him! The prince switched the arrows!"

Winchester gripped me, holding me still to watch from the fencing. "The only thing you will accomplish is getting yourself—or possibly Robin—hurt," he told me. "Robin knew he was always going to cheat somehow, Lady Marian."

I pushed him off. "You don't know what you've done," I told him, slumping against the fencing. My heart felt heavier than any of my injuries or snow-soaked clothing. My chest were trembling for breath. "If he loses—this is the only chance for the people." *For Rob.*

"Have a little faith, my lady."

Marshal strode out onto the field. "Three shots," he yelled, and I could bare hear him from where I were—I doubted the common folk could hear him at all. "Best single shot of the three is the winner."

With this he raised his arm, and lowered it. Gisbourne and Robin both let their arrows fly at the same moment.

From the second it left his fingers, I saw Rob could tell something were wrong. The arrow flew wide, lodging in the outermost ring. The stands went silent, and I heard chuckles and laughs from the nobles.

Gisbourne's arrow were within the innermost black circle, but it weren't dead on. His shot drew cheers from the nobles, and quiet from the stands as the people looked to each other, wondering what had happened, wondering how they were being cheated of their hero.

Rob's chest were rising hard and fast, pluming white steam into the air from his breath like magic were circling him, giving him power. Rob's feet drew together, and he raised his chin. He were staring down the target, running his fingers over the arrow.

He were the best shot I'd ever seen. He could do this. He could do this.

Marshal's arm raised again, and they notched their arrows and drew. Gisbourne let his arrow fly first, singing in a careful line. It bit deep into the target. It were to the other edge of the inner black circle.

A good shot. An excellent shot, to any other archer. But it still left that small circle of hope, the size of my fist. A chance.

Rob's stance were wide and comfortable, and he shook the tension out of his shoulders. His elegant, long arms raised again with the bow and arrow, and he let the arrow fly after a moment more.

It struck the outside of the second ring, and though it weren't enough even to compete with Gisbourne's strikes, the common folk leapt to their feet, cheering and shouting.

Gisbourne glared at Robin, but Rob paid no mind. He were in his world, speaking to his bow like it were his heart. My skin ran over with gooseflesh.

Marshal raised his arm again.

I shut my eyes. I had done as much as I could, and this bit

weren't for my heart to decide. I shut my eyes and I made the sign of the cross and I prayed. I prayed for hope, for fortitude, for something that could defend my heart from breaking if Rob lost this. Something that could find a way to help him forgive himself if he couldn't do it. Something that could stem the tide of blood that would flood out onto the people if we had to suffer another cruel sheriff. Something to keep warm the feeble hope that fluttered in me, that awful cruelty of hope that would never go out, no matter what I did.

No matter if Gisbourne won and I had to spend the rest of my life suffering and watching as those I loved suffered, I would still hope. I would hope for another chance like this, another day like this one.

Please, God. Defend my heart. Defend my hope.

A low gasp ran through the crowd, and I opened my eyes. Rob still had his arrow notched and ready; Gisbourne's bow were lowered. Gisbourne's shot were in the black, a thumb closer to center than his other shots. Rob's target had narrowed to the size of a peach at eighty paces.

Shivers ran over my skin. I knew too well that the world were meant for cheaters to prosper in, that those who took advantage of the weak and defenseless sat comfy and warm in guarded castles. There weren't no natural justice. There weren't no way for Rob to win this, to scrape back from the switch of the arrows.

I didn't shut my eyes again. I raised my chin and watched as Rob's arm went tense and then loose as the arrow shot out from his bow, making its graceful arch over the snow-covered field. I lost it for a moment, a thin shot of black against the backdrop of trees, and then the *thunk* of it hitting the target drew my eye.

The first arrow wide. The next in the second ring.

And the last so close to center there were no question that it had to be the winning shot.

I ran, and Winchester didn't stop me this time. I picked up my skirts with my one hand and flew over the snow, the Archangel's own wings carrying me forward. People were breaking through the fencing and flooding the field, but I made it to Rob before any of them.

He dropped his bow and picked me up as I threw my arms around him. I were careful to keep my hurt arm up, but it hurt anyway and I couldn't much care. Tears were overrunning my face and I buried it in his neck, my whole body shaking, though I weren't sure if it were tears or joy or running what caused it.

"I love you," he murmured. "I love you."

"You did it," I told him. "You won. You did it, my love."

He rubbed his face into my neck too, and I felt him shudder.

"Guards!" the prince roared, and we broke apart to see him flinging his arm this way and that. "Stop the rabble!"

Guards flooded forward, but Rob turned and spread his hands wide, and the people stopped running but started cheering. Rob raised his hands and lowered them, and the people grew quiet slow. "Please retake your seats," Rob yelled when they were quiet enough. "I believe I have an oath to take!"

This drew cheers and whoops and unending clapping, but the people, with the prodding of the guards, took their seats again. Turning back to the nobles, I realized Gisbourne were gone from the field.

"Your champion!" the prince yelled.

I laughed, unable to keep it in as the happiness bubbled up in me. The people were cheering themselves hoarse.

"Kneel!" the prince called.

Robin knelt.

"Repeat this oath," the prince said. The people went silent.

"By the Lord, I will to King Richard and the office of sheriff be faithful and true, and love all that he loves, and shun all that he shuns, according to God's law, and according to the world's principles, and never, by will nor by force, by word nor by work, do ought of what is loathful to him; on condition that he keep me as I am willing to deserve when I to him submitted and chose his will."

Robin repeated it, his voice strong and powerful in the quiet. Snow drifted down on him, crowning his head and anointing his shoulders like holy blessings.

"Stand," the prince commanded. Isabel came forward and presented a golden arrow on a velvet cushion, and Robin bowed low to her.

"Sheriff," she greeted, nodding her head. "Collect your prize."

Rob straightened up. His eyes met mine, hungry and wanting

in a way that made my skin rush over with red. He took the
arrow but looked the whole time at me. I could see it, then—
our future together. That it could happen. That one day soon
he might be able to look at me like that and I could kiss it right
off his face, in front of all these people, the wife of Robin
Hood—a true wife. A loved wife.

Rob broke our gaze and turned to the crowd, holding up
his prize. The prince said something further about congratulations or some such, but it were lost.

Nottingham had its hero.

—⁂—

The prince announced that there were to be a feast that night,
and the whole castle and courtyard would be open to the
common folk. They had their sheriff, and he didn't want there
to be any more mistakes with his orders and generosity. I saw
Eleanor nod slow while he said it, and I suspected his true
motive were pleasing his mother.

The sun began to set, and I fair floated back up to the castle
proper, going to the chambers I shared with Gisbourne eager,
for once, to wear a dress. I wanted to try and look well for Rob
that night; I wanted to dance with him and bask in the strange-
ness of this single happy moment.

The first of many happy moments, perhaps.

I opened the door and much of my mood changed. Gisbourne were there, bent over in a chair by the fire, his shirt off,
looking broken. I stopped in the doorway and didn't move
farther in.

"Marian, close the door," he grunted.

I nudged it shut with my foot, coming closer to him. I sat in the other chair, drawing up my feet, resting the hand that had set to aching.

"How did you do it?" he asked, his voice low and rumbling like a dog's.

Scowling, I asked, "Do what?"

"Switch the arrows back. How did you even figure it out?"

"I didn't switch anything."

"I don't believe you."

My shoulders lifted. "As a rule, you shouldn't."

He sneered. "Of course. Thief, liar, all that. Only you aren't any of those things, are you? You're honest, and honorable. Good." He stood and never looked to me, leaning over the fireplace instead. His body were bruised from the days of abuse. "You knew I'd cheat. And you still believed in him. Believed he'd win."

"I thought the prince would cheat for you," I said. "But yes."

"This isn't how it was supposed to be," he said to the fire. "You were mine, Marian, long before you even knew he existed. Your unassailable loyalty and unshakeable belief should have been for me."

That stole my breath, and I stared at him as he turned, his face broken open and wide, like a hurt little boy instead of the evil warrior of a man I knew. He came closer to me and knelt before my chair, pulling me closer to the edge of it. "What are you—" I started.

"Hush," he said, and he leaned forward and kissed me. Even if I saw a hurt soul, it weren't in his kiss; it were forceful and hard and strong, overpowering. I tried to pull away and he held me still.

My breath started rushing faster and my heart fluttered with fear. I curled my nails into his face, digging at the flesh as I tried to cry out.

With more speed than I thought he had in him, he grabbed my arms and hauled me up before him. He let my mouth go but held me still. "Get on the bed," he told me.

"Are you *daft?*" I wailed. "No!"

His fingers pinched my arms, squeezing overtight. His face turned into a sneer. "Tell me, my dear, what did you think my reaction would be to losing this competition? Just hand you over to your hero with a smile on my face? Let you live as lord and lady of the manor?"

"The annulment—"

"Getting rid of you seems quite thrilling provided I have something left. But I don't, and you, Eleanor's favorite, will buy me something more. So get on the bed, Marian, because I will never annul this marriage, and in a few minutes, it won't even be possible."

He let me go, which seemed a fool thing to do. I ran for the door but he were too close, and he slammed against my back, trapping my hand between me and the door.

I wailed in pain.

His hands caught my waist, running up to squeeze my bits.

"Since when did I ever mind chasing you, love?" he growled in my ear.

I smashed my head back against his and got an inch of space, running to the window, trying to get my knife on the shutter. He caught up and pinned me to the ledge so I bent forward, straining for the knife.

"I'm not Eleanor's favorite," I grunted through my teeth. "What would she ever give you for me?"

His hands ran up my back and caught the back of my gown. He jerked hard and the thing tore. I pulled back from the shutter to try and hit him, but his giant paw on my neck heaved me forward. "Stay," he snapped. "Foolish little thief. You know nothing of who you really are. Why, Eleanor and Richard will do anything to keep you safe."

His hands were on my naked back, and he pressed a kiss to the long scar that ran from my shoulder to my spine that his sword had given me months ago.

"Lovely," he murmured as my skin crawled over my bones.

The extra weight had pushed me forward, and my hand closed on the hilt of the knife. I couldn't push up—he were too heavy on my back and my good hand had the knife in it. I pulled it under me. "Eleanor wouldn't give you anything for me. And what the hell does Richard have to do with it?"

"You don't think?" he mused. "You haven't figured this out, clever thief?"

"What the hell are you talking about?"

"Your father, Marian."

"My father?" I asked.

He were pulling at my skirts and trying to drag them up while he were still pushing me down. I kicked out vicious, trying to hit him. Gisbourne laughed. "You know. Don't you? *Coeur de Leon*," he said to me.

Lionheart.

My blood started to drain from my skin. "What?" I asked.

"I know your parents said something about it. Didn't they?" His voice were taunting me now.

"N-no."

"I heard them say you're not their daughter. Whose daughter are you, Marian?" he asked, chuckling. "Who do you think could place you in a noble household? Who would?"

My good hand curled into a fist around the knife, shaking and waiting for the right moment even as I felt his hands on my legs. "What do you know, Guy?"

"I know who you are." I were still and he leaned close to whisper in my ear. "I know who you've always been. Whose blood is really in your veins. I know why it would be the most mortal of sins to spill your blood. Why Eleanor won't allow her son to harm you."

"Say it," I snapped.

He laughed. "Who hid you, Marian?"

"Eleanor," I guessed.

He nodded. "Why?"

"Do you think I know that! Tell me, Gisbourne!"

"Because you're a *bastard*," he told me, pulling my skirts higher.

"Whose?"

"I already told you that."

My head swam, and my knees went soft. *Coeur de Leon.* "That's not true."

"Of course it is."

"No."

"Yes."

"I would have heard of it!" I said. "Everyone would have heard of it!"

"Eleanor's not that foolish. You would never be allowed to rule, of course, but a bastard princess—that's still a considerable power. Eleanor knows better than anyone how to wield a child. She uses her own like chess pieces."

"But he weren't—he weren't even king—" I were struggling to breathe right.

Gisbourne chuckled, and he lifted his hips off me to pull my skirt up. It were a tiny bit of space, but it were the moment I needed.

I sucked in a breath and twisted hard, slashing out with the knife.

It hit him in the shoulder, sliding a red ribbon of blood across his collarbone, and he jumped back with a howl. I ran to the door and opened it, angling the knife at him as he came closer. He scowled and stopped.

"Mary," I snapped. She appeared.

"Fetch the earl. Quick. And I will be needing a new dress for dinner."

"Y-yes, my lady," she said, looking between me and my husband. She went.

Gisbourne stayed where he were, looking at the knife. "You call me a fool so often," I snapped. "But you just gave me your best bit of information. If I mean as much to Eleanor or the king as you say, she won't never let you force me, Gisbourne. I thought I'd have to run far but all I have to do is go down the hall, isn't that right?"

"Oh, I'm sure she'd protect you. But if you go to Eleanor, if you aren't in my bed by morning light, ready to do your willing duty as my wife, I will raze Leaford to the ground with everyone inside it. And that will only be my first action."

My courage faltered.

"Everything has been stolen from me, Marian, since I was a boy. You are my only chance of having Richard pay me any mind at all, and I won't let anyone, least of all your mewling pup of an outlaw, take another damn thing from me. Besides, you really think Prince John is finished with you, Marian? With your dashing hero? He will crush you both. He will make you wish you never won this so-called victory. He will have his underhanded, vindictive way, and if you ever forget that, look to your hand."

He were silent for a moment.

"He will make you pay for this, Marian."

"My lady?" the earl asked, appearing slightly breathless in the doorway. He looked me over and frowned.

"Your Grace," I said. "It seems I am in need of your assistance. Would you mind detaining my husband so I may change for dinner?"

He folded his arms. "With pleasure."

"Just remember, Marian," Gisbourne told me, sitting in a chair by the fire. "You have till morning."

CHAPTER
TWENTY-TWO

~o~

The earl insisted on escorting me to dinner. I wore the grandest piece I had—a blue velvet dress sewn with scrolling silver thread over a silvery kirtle so thin it were near sheer. Mary brushed my hair and left the pieces free and loose around my face. It were useless to try and keep them back.

"May I ask what happened?" Winchester whispered to me.

I were shivering. "I was very grateful for your help, your Grace."

He nodded. "My pleasure. I am assuming, then, that our new sheriff should not know of this?"

"As much as I would like for him to kill my husband, murder doesn't speak well for a sheriff."

Winchester nodded. "I'm glad you called for me."

My hand tightened on his arm at his kindness. "Thank you, your Grace."

"May I ask what happens in the morning?" he said. "He was clearly threatening you."

I shivered, and his jaw worked. I couldn't say the words.

He cleared his throat. "I will post a guard at your chamber, my lady. Whatever he's threatened you with will not happen tomorrow. Beyond that I cannot make promises, but from what I've heard it doesn't take you long to figure out a plan, does it?"

My chest drew a shaky breath. "No, my lord. It doesn't. Can your guard see that he doesn't leave the castle grounds tomorrow?" I asked. I weren't sure if having the earl's guard there would be the same as telling Eleanor, but I wouldn't risk his ire.

The earl gave a sharp nod.

I felt quiet, my heart and head at odds. Had I achieved anything? I had purchased a few hours, perhaps—but I didn't doubt Gisbourne. If I asked Eleanor to intercede, Leaford and all the innocent people there would burn. I couldn't run. I couldn't stay.

And what of Gisbourne's other words, claiming I were the daughter of the king of England? It couldn't bare be true. And yet, I were someone's child, and it didn't seem I were the Leafords'. It were possible, then, that all of the mysteries I'd seen at court would be answered with this one thing, but it didn't feel like the truth in my bones.

Then again, nothing much did feel right anymore. In the flimsy shoes and floating dress, walking through Nottingham Castle like I were meant to be there, I didn't know myself much at all. Rob were sheriff. I were Gisbourne's wife, and not in a small way, but in a forever way. He'd never let me go, no matter what I threatened. I didn't much doubt that he never meant to annul the marriage at all, and I were a fool to have ever thought he would.

I thought of every moment of pain, every threat, every leer he had brought upon me. I had borne it all—for what? For the ashes of his promise at my feet. I were a fool to have ever believed him. I were a fool in every way.

My life had become something I couldn't fair recognize.

I walked into the hall, and people were everywhere. The seats were gone, save for a single table to make the royals untouchable. The rest of the food were heaped on the tables, and people thronged around it, a feast in true. Music were playing, a lovely tune with laughter and chatter twining through it.

"Your pardon, your Grace, but may I steal the lady?"

I turned and a short, small laugh came out of me. It were Much, clean and kitted up and looking older and stronger than I'd ever known him.

Winchester bowed and relinquished me. Much bent his arm to me, and I grinned and wrapped my arm around his, trying to forget what Gisbourne could do to my friends to make me do his bidding. "You look very handsome," I told him, and he beamed.

"Come along, everyone's here," he told me. He pointed to John and Bess and Godfrey, and I'd never been so happy to see the inside of the hall.

John hugged my waist, pulling me off my feet and careful

not to crush my hand. When he put me down I went to Bess, looking about unsure and shy. She had one hand on her stomach. She met my eye and frowned a little. "Am I meant to curtsy?" she asked. "I don't know much about curtsies."

I rushed forward and hugged her. "You're family," I whispered in her ear. "You're one of us now."

She hugged me back, tight. "Thank you," she whispered back.

Godfrey were next, and he bowed over my hand and kissed it. John made a face. "See, you can't do things like that if you're meant to replace me," John said. "Scar's head gets much too big."

"Then maybe you should learn a thing or two about manners from me," Godfrey told him with a grin. "Lady Scar, you look beautiful."

"Only I'm allowed to tell her that," said a voice in my ear. My heart broke painful open and I spun around as Rob's arms circled my waist, hugging tight against him, desperate to hold on to him. He hugged me, rubbing my back, dragging his fingers over every silver swirl.

"Is it over?" he murmured to me. "Is it really over?"

Tears rose up and my throat went tight. I pulled back to look him in the eye. "You're sheriff. The people have nothing to fear."

Our faces swayed closer, and I shivered again. I would never have this, the right to kiss him in public.

We didn't kiss, but a faster tune began, and Rob took my good hand. "Please dance with me."

"I never learned the fancy dances," I told him, frowning.

"I don't care how we do it," he said with a grin. "I just want you in my arms."

He tugged me along to where a throng of common folk were dancing, and, careful to tuck my hurt hand up on his shoulder, he pulled me in close. We danced along with them, jumping and stepping fast and foolish. My short, funny hair flew about my face, and my heart beat as fast as my laughter, all the while I stared into Rob's eyes.

He slowed down and pulled me out of the thick of the leaping throngs, dancing closer, rubbing his cheek along mine. "Marry me when the sun sets," he breathed.

I raised my head a little. "What?"

"If your marriage is annulled when the prince leaves tomorrow morning, marry me by sunset. I can't wait longer, Scarlet, I don't have it in me. I have missed you every minute, and I don't want to see another sunrise without you as my wife."

My heart broke, and water spilled out of my eyes. "What if it's not annulled?" I breathed.

"Then I'll wait. Every sunset, every day. I'll count them all until you're mine. My perfect wife. My only wife," he said. "The only heart that's meant for mine." His nose dragged on my face. "I only feel like a hero when you're with me, Scarlet. I feel like I have a destiny greater than pain and hurt when you're in my arms."

I tugged him closer, tucking my head into the bend of his neck to wipe my tears on him. "Me too," I said.

"Scarlet."

"Mmm."

"That was me asking you to marry me, you know."

My eyes pressed shut. "Yes," I whispered. "That's all I want."

"Oh, hell," someone said, and I looked up to see Winchester standing behind Rob. Rob turned and I wiped my face overquick. "I'm trying to wait, but I have to accuse Lady Leaford of hoarding you, *Sheriff*," he said.

Rob held me tucked under one arm, and bowed his head. "Your Grace," he greeted.

Winchester looked more like a boy than I'd ever seen him. He gripped Rob's shoulder and shook a little, laughing. "Your Grace! Do you know how odd it is to not be able to say that back to you? Though I'll much prefer it to the names you were calling me when the healer was working on you."

Rob winced. "He told you that?"

Winchester shrugged. "I've been called worse. You did very well today, Locksley. The master at arms would have been proud."

"Master at arms?" I questioned.

"That's how we know each other," Rob told me. "We were pages together for a time."

Glimpsing the regal tilt of Eleanor's head, I slipped out from Rob's arm. "Well, you two should talk." I smiled at Rob. "I'll find you."

He smiled back at me, fingers dragging along my hand as I

let him go. Winchester kissed my hand, and I went to find
Eleanor.

She weren't where I had seen her. Instead Isabel were there,
frowning at me. "Lady Leaford," she said.

"Your Highness," I said, nodding my head to her.

"Eleanor has called for you. She went to say good night to
my husband but asked you to escort her back to her rooms."

I looked to the royal table, where Eleanor stood beside
Prince John.

"That was a *disgusting* display this afternoon," she told me,
folding her arms. "You may as well have spat in Guy's face."

My eyes drifted shut and I shook my head. "Excuse me, your
Highness."

I went to the side of the royal table and waited. Eleanor
nodded to me and came closer, and I curtsied low to her. "Up,
up, my dear," she told me. I stood, and she twined our arms
together, clasping my hand. "Come," she said. "You shall walk
me to my rooms and ask me your many questions."

Dumb, I stared at her.

"You do have questions, don't you?"

"Most that I'm frightened to ask," I said.

She laughed. "Fear. Something I have yet to see from you,
Lady Leaford."

"That title's not mine, is it?"

She drew in a breath, and it made her look older as we
moved into the dark hallway, lit by torches and moon. "No.
The lord and lady Leaford are not your natural parents."

"Who are?"

"A very beautiful blacksmith's daughter, and my son. King Richard the Lionhearted."

I stared at her, her proud chin, her white neck, her clear, steady blue gaze. The moon made her pale skin look like she belonged to the other world. "I'm your granddaughter."

Her fingers squeezed mine. "You are."

"But Prince John—he hates me."

Her eyebrow arched high. "Well. My children cleave very close or hate very powerfully. It's only because Richard teased him so as a child. It isn't your fault."

"How does he know who I am, and I don't?"

She sighed. "He was near when it happened. Terrible penchant for eavesdropping, that boy. He knew it all from the start."

"Why did he send Gisbourne to marry me?"

"Because my John controlled Isabel, and since he was very young, Gisbourne loved Isabel. He never had the status to marry her, of course, and when she married, Gisbourne followed her. And John took full advantage of such a connection. You see, Richard was never meant to inherit the throne. He had two older brothers, but death befell them both. When Richard was crowned, John wasn't happy—he and Richard hardly got along. John knew about you—he wanted some way to control his brother, even a small one. So he ordered Gisbourne to marry you. John is many terrible things, but he is a master manipulator."

"That's no good thing," I told her.

Her head tilted. "It can be. A king must see not just the hills before him, but the length of the road at large. John can see many roads at once; he understands how long it can take to achieve a goal. When he has a good heart, he can be a master-ful ruler. But without it, impatience and selfishness cause him to use his gifts poorly."

A cold weight circled my heart. "He can never be king."

Eleanor frowned. "He will be king, Marian. I wish I could keep Richard as king forever, and I will keep him there as long as I can, but he is like his brothers—too good, proud, and brave for a long life. John is careful; he will outlive Richard, and he will take the throne. I just need to make sure that when he does, he becomes the extremely capable ruler he should be. And that he doesn't so alienate the common opinion in the meantime that they riot when he's crowned."

"You have such faith in him," I marveled.

"He is my son," she said, pushing her shoulders back. "He has my steel inside of him. And that steel must be tempered more carefully than any sword. Perhaps I spent too much time on his older siblings and not enough on him as a child, but his family will rule Europe. He will learn." She shook her head. "But it is not him I wish to speak of. Tell me why you ran from the Leafords. Were they unkind to you? I had many spies there, watching their treatment of you, but I confess I couldn't see you myself."

"No. They were loving and true. They raised me very well.

And my sister—my sister Joanna, she was everything I could have wanted for love." My voice went rough, and she squeezed my hand.

"You lost her."

I nodded. "We ran to London together. We both—we did things, to live. Different things. I stole."

"She fell ill?" Eleanor guessed.

"Yes."

"Why did you not go to a noble family for shelter? To court?" she asked. "A noblewoman—any woman—should never be refused such."

"They would have sent us back."

"So if it was not your family you feared, what was it?"

"Gisbourne," I whispered to her. "I were—I was so young, so unready to be married. And he terrified me. There was a darkness I saw in him, and I fled. And she came with me. He caught me, and cut me," I told her, covering my scar. "But Joanna hit him and we got away. We never let anyone find us again. And I learned to be a thief," I admitted to her.

"A very good one, from what I hear."

I looked to her. "You knew?"

"I heard of you, after you had left London. I made the necessary inquiries, but no one was sure where you went. Until Gisbourne found you here, and the famous Will Scarlet was discovered to be Lady Marian Leaford."

"Why didn't my mother keep me?" I asked quiet.

"I wouldn't let her," she admitted. "I wanted you raised a

noble, but I couldn't do it myself. Your mother—Lady Leaford, rather—was a friend."

My tongue ran over my lips, gone dry. "Where is she? My
natural mother?"

"She died," Eleanor said low. "A few years ago. In childbirth."

My heart froze in my chest. "I have a-a brother? A sister?"

She shook her head. "No. The child died with her."

Beats ran through my heart again, but they were heavy and
dark.

"Richard does have a son, though."

"What?"

She lifted a shoulder. "Illegitimate, like yourself. Philip.
He lives quite comfortably in France; Richard married him to
his ward, Amelia of Cognac. One day, perhaps, you and I can
visit him."

There were so many half promises in her words that I
couldn't much breathe. A brother—France—the faint idea
that I might have some kind of friendship with her. My head
went light and I gripped her hand.

"Come, my dear," Eleanor said, waving to a guarded door.
They opened the door for us and we entered. She showed me
to a chair near the fire and sat beside me. "Lady Leaford and
I would like some wine," she said to one of the ladies that
appeared to wait on the queen. They hadn't followed us from
the hall—had they waited in her room? "You look quite pale,
Marian."

"I don't . . . I just . . ." I shook my head, feeling a fool.

"You have royal blood in you, but that has not changed. Your heart is no more noble than it was before. Truly there is nothing to change."

"I'm . . ." I couldn't say the word.

"Royal," she finished. "Or do you mean a princess? The lovely part of all of this is that now you know, I can finally introduce you to Richard when he returns. He'll be pleased. He always likes to hear of you—of your welfare. He was quite distressed when you ran off—he accused Lord Leaford of having hurt you."

"Why did he never make himself known to me?"

"For the same reason I didn't, my dear. It wasn't wise." She waved her hand. "I should like to go to Aquitaine early next year; you shall come with me."

I pressed my unhurt hand to my heart. Hours ago I would have never thought to leave Nottinghamshire, but if Gisbourne wouldn't grant me the annulment, I would have to run. There were worse fates than getting to know my grandmother.

Grandmother.

Her eyes flicked down. "My dear, I may have considerable faith in my son, but I also know his faults very well."

"I do as well," I answered overquick, holding up my half hand.

She frowned. "Yes. You do. You must know this was not the way he wanted this tournament to end."

"He wanted Gisbourne as sheriff."

"He wanted to control one of the largest and most prosperous counties in England. A key point between the north
and south. He has lost that. He isn't pleased. And when he's
displeased, he can be rather . . . childish."

"So why does that mean I must go to France?"

She bristled, opening her mouth as the lady returned with
wine. She poured a cup for each of us, and Eleanor waved her
out. "Aquitaine is *not* France," Eleanor said sharp. "Not a bit.
Nor is it English. It is Aquitaine. Free from both countries and
the richest of all of them. But without you by my side, I don't
know if I can protect you from John's manipulations, his pet-
tiness. He could hurt you, and I won't allow it."

"He's hurt me," I said. "But I believe . . ." I halted, sucking
in a breath. "I believe I have more to fear from my husband."

"Ah," she said, understanding. She nodded slow. "Well,"
she said, "terrible husbands are a difficult problem indeed. But
a noble woman must learn her own ways of managing the men
that befall her."

"How?" I asked.

She lifted a shoulder. "It depends on the man, and the
crimes he commits against you. But there are ways. If you
embrace who you are, my dear, accept the fact that you are, in
a fashion, a princess of England—you might find a great many
tools at your disposal to soothe his male ego."

"I won't soothe any bit of him," I snapped. "And I won't
leave Nottingham for promise of pain. This is my home."
Were that even true anymore?

"And Aquitaine is mine, yet I had to leave."

"Hurt is a common thing. Scars, blood, none of it matters in true to me. It's a pebble beside love, and protecting the people what need it. My place is here, making sure he can't never hurt the people that can't protect themselves." I didn't have to run, did I? Rob were here. The band were here. I could run from Gisbourne and still do what I were meant—protect the people.

"Marian, you are royal. All of England is yours to protect, especially in your father's absence."

I drew myself up straighter. "Then I'll start with the well-placed, prosperous county between the north and south."

She drew in a breath and let it out slowly. "Do you love him, my dear?"

I looked at her. Were I meant to deny it?

"Robin," she said, as if my heart didn't know just who she meant.

"Yes," I said. "Yes."

She nodded. "And he very clearly loves you."

A thrill burned through my heart. "He does."

"Love and marriage are not easy bedfellows, my dear. It's rare that a woman gets to enjoy both with the same man. But I truly hope the future holds that for you."

Her words slid under my skin and circled around my heart. I held them tight there, like good wishes could shore up my courage and hope.

She patted my hand. "As for Aquitaine, it is not something that needs to be decided tonight. Or ever. You need not choose between them; perhaps we can still have a few adventures between protecting the people, yes? I should very much like to get to know you, now that I have you back."

I gripped her hand in return. "I want to know you too, my queen."

"Eleanor," she said. "You may call me Eleanor."

"Eleanor," I murmured slow, tasting it as it ran over my lips. My grandmother. *Eleanor.*

She loosed her hand from mine gentle. "I'm quite tired, now. I must retire, but promise you'll meet me in the morning. My carriage will be ready first thing to take me to London with the royal progress."

"I will," I vowed.

She stood and collected me into her arms in a tight hug. I drew in a deep breath; she smelt of lavender and snow.

"Go," she said. "If you happen to dance with a certain sheriff, I'm sure my minstrels will sing songs of it to me later."

I laughed. "Your minstrels are trouble."

She shrugged, but smiled. "Good night, Marian."

Her lady saw me out, and I drifted down the hallway, hanging in the dark, delaying the moment when I would have to tell Rob that there would be no sunset, no marriage, no life.

When I got to the hall, if many nobles were still there, I couldn't tell them from the common folk, laughing and sing-ing and dancing about. John found me first, catching me up and dancing with me with a broad, drunken grin. I yelped when he hurt my hand and he slowed, dancing more careful.

"She said you were the most kind!" he crowed. "Our mean, grumpy Scarlet—kind!"

"Bess did?" I asked.

He nodded. "I'm going to marry her, Scarlet! Rob's the sheriff; I'll marry her and live out the rest of my days as a father and a husband and a happy, foolish, fat, lazy man. A blacksmith! I'm going to open shop." His grin went wider and looked ready to crack his face.

I laughed at him. "As long as you fix my knives without my having to pay, I'll be happy for you."

He threw his head back for laughing. "You'd steal them anyway!"

"Where's Bess?" I asked.

"Winchester sent her home in his carriage. Good man, that. Much and I figured we'd sack out in the barn—by Christ, I don't think I'd make it halfway home!"

I laughed, but Rob caught my eye and I danced out of John's arms. John took up with Much, who frowned and pushed him off.

Rob pulled me to him, smiling with a fair amount of ale and cheer. "We need . . . I must talk to you before tomorrow morning," I told him soft.

His grin faded. "What's wrong?"

My nose touched his. "There's something to say. Many things."

The arms about me went loose but didn't let go. "Did Gisbourne do something to you? Did he touch you?"

I pet his cheek, flushing as a shiver ran through me. "No, no, nothing like that."

He nodded, kissing my forehead. "Go. I'll wait a moment and meet you in my chambers, all right?"

Blood pushed harder into my cheeks. My heart beat strange, like a drum played wrong and fast. Meeting him there, when he were whole and hale, under the cover of night—it felt different now. It were supposed to be the start of many nights alone in his chambers, and instead it were the last.

CHAPTER
TWENTY-THREE

~o~

There were no guards now. As soon as the prince left, Rob would move into the large chamber in the center of the residences. And he'd wait for me to be there with him, as his wife.

I shut my eyes. There were no way I could stay here, married to Gisbourne with Rob so close by.

Months ago there were so many places I could think of to run to; now there weren't any I could fathom.

I slipped quiet into his room and sat on his bed, thinking of the first I saw him. I'd been a girl, playing in the garden with Joanna, and he came out, his back straight, awful formal and awful old to my young eyes. I'd seen a man even then. Joanna blushed but I didn't have enough shame to, and I wound the chain of flowers I were making into a crown and put it on his head. He bowed to accept it, and when he stood, there were a smile on his mouth.

He stayed for dinner, but he didn't ever speak to me.

And then he left with his father, and not long after, for the Crusades.

The next time had been in a market in London, and his shadow-dark eyes looked like salvation for me. I knew him, I knew his station, I knew what would happen to the girl he couldn't recognize who stole his purse. I did it badly and he caught my wrist and stopped me. When he addressed me like a lad I went with it. I hadn't been trying to look so much like a boy before that, just not a girl, not a pretty thing like Joanna, that a man could hurt and think nothing of.

And then I'd looked on him every day since, each day my eyes a bit more open to his face, his heart, his soul. And then there were something else there, something quite like salvation but different still.

He opened the door, and I looked up. The moon were bright and the skies clear of snow, so I hadn't lit a candle. I liked the blue of midnight light. I liked it more when he stood in it, making him glow bright, the shadows that had haunted him leaving off for once.

I stood and walked over to him, holding up my palm and shivering as his slid into it, pushing my fingers apart and sliding his own between them, binding our hands together. He leaned his head down and kissed me, the first one cool and light like silver, then again, growing warmer, his mouth opening and his tongue speaking a strange new language into my mouth. His hands fell to my hips, and my body shook. All I wanted were to stop shivering, and I pressed tighter against him.

He made a sound that vibrated into my mouth, pulling my

waist tighter and up so I bent backward, leaning into him like a willow branch. I gripped his neck, not sure if I were on my feet or not, touching the ground or not. My name, my parents, my place—I weren't sure of a damn thing except his mouth, his kiss, his tongue touching mine and making me feel separate from my whole being. His hand came up and stroked my neck, so warm and hot on my bare skin that I gasped, and he pulled back, breathing hard.

"Good God, Scarlet," he moaned in my ear, pressing my cheek to his, his fingers on my neck, in my hair—I could feel their touches like he were plucking strings on an instrument, resonating on my skin like music. "We have to stop."

The shivery feeling changed fast. "I did something wrong." I pulled away. "Oh, Rob, I'm not very good at all *this*!" I told him.

He laughed and pulled me back against him. "Not the reason we have to stop, my love."

"Why?" I asked, my voice gone quiet.

His laugh went softer, and he kissed the corner of my mouth, my cheek, right below my ear. "I forget how innocent you are," he said, and I flushed, frowning. He kissed the hanging bit of my ear and my good hand curled into a fist on his neck, the frown forgotten. "If I kiss you once more, Scar, we certainly won't be talking for the rest of the night. And you can forget whatever you wanted to tell me before making you my wife, because whether or not the church agreed, you'd be *my* wife."

My blood ran thick and hot, rushing to my skin, everywhere. "Oh," I breathed. "But we were just kissing."

His lips were on my cheek. "Kissing you . . . ," he said, but he didn't finish the words. He kissed me again, and his lips and tongue and the wet slide of it all spun me. All I wanted were to touch him more. To touch his skin.

I pulled away with a sharp breath. "*Oh,*" I realized. A dizzy thought slipped through my mind—if I were meant to submit to Gisbourne, what were the harm in Robin's hands on me, blotting out the ink of Gisbourne's touch?

"Tomorrow," he promised, his voice low and rough, slipping into my blood. His eyes glittered. "Many, many kisses tomorrow."

No—if I were to keep touching Rob, I'd have to tell him, and if I told him, he would kill Gisbourne. He would lose everything for his love of me.

He leaned his head on mine, and my heart felt like a stone. "What do you need to tell me?" he asked. "You worried me."

"You don't seem worried," I murmured.

"Your kisses are very reassuring," he told me.

"I tried—yesterday, I wanted to tell you—but you needed sleep. I didn't want you not to sleep, not because of me," I started, and the shivering turned darker as I went. What if this changed everything? How could I say these things out loud when they had just bare started feeling true in my chest?

"What is it, Scar?" he asked, rubbing my back.

I shook my good hand out. "I saw my parents. You—you won't need their permission for anything."

"No? It didn't go well?"

The swamping wave of their hate hit me again, and the shaking stopped, covered with dark and shame. "They think I killed Joanna. Their real daughter. Their *only* daughter," I said, looking up at him.

"Only?" he repeated.

I nodded, feeling water draw up in my eyes. "They just kept saying it were my fault. My fault, and I weren't theirs."

"Love," he murmured, hugging me tight. "From all you've told me, Joanna lived for you. She didn't die because of you."

It seemed easier—less painful—to remember her when I were inside Rob's arms. Her smile. The way her long, elegant hands felt touching my face, tending to the scar Gisbourne put there. Rob stroked my hair, my neck, his hands on me melting everything away like butter in the sun.

"So they took you in?" he asked. "Did they tell you who from?"

"They didn't," I told him. "But Eleanor did."

He pulled me off his chest to look at my face. "Eleanor of Aquitaine?"

I nodded.

"Who?" he asked.

"Richard," I said, trying to find strength in my voice. "I am the daughter of Richard the Lionheart."

Robin's hands fell from me, and he staggered back a step. Then he stepped forward and kissed me.

I pushed him off. "What are you *doing?*" I snapped. "I just told you—"

"And I decided we're just going to have to do this the dishonorable way, because there's no way in hell I'm asking for *his* permission to marry you," he told me, stepping forward again with a grin. "I love the man, but he terrifies me."

I ducked his kiss. "Rob!"

He stopped, but caught me up anyway. "What?"

"This isn't a joke. Eleanor told me herself."

"Well, if you want me to, I'll ask for your hand from him. Maybe I can just ask Eleanor. She seems to like me."

"She does like you. But Rob! Please be serious."

"Why?" he asked, losing the grin. "What problem do you see that I'm missing?"

"It's why Prince John hates me. He'll keep coming after me. There's nothing to stop him."

His arms tightened. "I already knew that he hates both of us. *Why* answers a bit of a mystery but doesn't change anything. I'm sheriff now. I'll have guards and the means to protect us and our children. And beyond that, I'll protect you and you'll protect me. I was thinking I should give you new knives for a wedding gift."

My stomach twisted and my chest felt like stone. "Eleanor wants me to go to France. Or everywhere, with her, it seems."

"Well, she can borrow you from time to time—this seems to make her your grandmother, yes?—but she can't have you." He stopped. "Do you *want* to go everywhere with her?"

"No," I said. "I want to get to know her, but I told her I don't ever want to leave Nottinghamshire." I looked at him—how were it possible to feel so much love for a thing and feel so lost and hopeless at the same time?

"Then we'll figure out something that satisfies you both. I can share."

I blinked up at him. "This doesn't change anything for you, does it?" I realized.

"Of course not." He frowned. "Did you truly think it would?"

I nodded slow.

"Scarlet," he murmured. His hands squeezed my waist. "I've told you all along, I knew who you were from the first. I know your heart. Names, titles, hair, odd clothing choices, none of that changes who you are. And I am madly in love with who you are."

Staring at him seemed like the wisest thing to do.

"Do you know why I won today? How I won?" he asked.

I shook my head.

"I knew after the first shot they'd changed the arrows. I figured one more shot would never give me the feel of it enough to control the third. And then I imagined you, a tiny little ball of rage, berating me for ever doubting myself. Telling me that I'm the best damn archer you've ever seen and that there's only one thing the prince didn't count on—that I'm a better archer than he knows."

A smile crept over me. "I dressed you right down, it seems."

"You did. And you saw the effect it had on me." He sighed. "Besides, it isn't as if the nightmares are gone. It isn't as if I won't be dealing with this for a very, very long time, and if you can find it in you to love me despite all that, I don't think you can really find it unfair for me to love you back."

"How have they been?" I asked. I took his hand from my back and tugged him to the bed, sitting up against the wall, my feet tucked up. He sat beside me, jigsawing his body into mine and rubbing my knees.

"The first night I was here I didn't sleep—every time my eyes shut I was there again, and I couldn't breathe. After we spoke . . . it was better. I think I've been so scared of them— which makes them worse, I think—because every time I thought of it, I thought of the way you'd look at me. The way I was afraid you'd look at me. And when I told you, you didn't. They're not gone, but when I wake up, it's just awake, it's not blinded like I was before."

"What else happened in the Crusades?" I asked.

He sighed. "Is it strange to say that there was a lot of it I liked? The trip there—we were sailing for a year, and seeing so many strange, beautiful lands. The food we ate—my God, you should have these oranges that we just pulled down from trees. The juice was like nectar. And the colors—colors you never see in England. In the desert everything is tan, and white, with dangerous smudges of black. The buildings are all made from sand and stone the color of sand. And the Mediterranean is this changing teal blue, like a deep, faceted jewel, lined with olive trees on every bank, it seemed. I saw more things in those years than in all the rest combined. And the men I went with—there was something so strong there. We were fighting for more than England. We were fighting for God, for each other. I could ignore my own pain to protect the man beside me. It's a mentality of war, and yet when I came home, I found the same loyalty, and selflessness, in you."

My shoulder were near him and he kissed it, like he were worshiping a goddess. Blood crept through my face.

"Do you want to know about your father?" he asked soft. "Richard?"

A deep breath drew my chest up, but I nodded.

"He's a giant," Rob said with a grin. "Not truly, of course—maybe a head taller than me. But he always seems huge, and formidable. I was a young man when I first answered his call, a boy, really, and he was a hero. A titan. Seven feet tall, three across. The loudest voice I ever heard and the first to teach me that if you want to prove you're a leader, whisper, because everyone will listen to you no matter how loud you are. I think faith must run in the blood, because you're the only one I've ever met whose faith rivals his. He *knew*. Every battle, he knew we'd win, and he taught us to believe too. We believed in him." His face twitched with a frown. "Even the things I questioned, I trusted him that it was necessary. And it was. For the war, at least, if not for my soul."

I squeezed his hand.

"He had fire and temper too. I saw him lose at cards once and he beat the man—the *bigger* man—to a bloody mess because he cheated. It took a lot to get him angry, but Heaven help you if you did." He shook his head. "He taught me so much about strength and power. That the man who is truly powerful has the option to forgive, to pardon, to forgo vengeance and violence. It's the weak man that must prove himself through such." He looked at me. "I always thought my father was weak. He was a very tolerant man, very forgiving and kind. I thought it meant people took advantage of him. Richard made me think very differently of my father. Then he died, and I never got the chance to tell him just how much I loved him and respected him. And honored what he taught me."

I smiled at him, half for the softness of what he were saying, and half because I'd never heard him talk like this about war, and I loved it. Sliding my palm against his, he clasped mine gentle. "What are you smiling at?"

"My sheriff," I said. "So did you want to marry at sunset to beat John to matrimony?" I asked.

He brightened. "I didn't even think of that. Good! That's justice."

I laughed, and he pulled me against him. "He were so happy tonight."

A kiss landed in my hair. "We all were. In the castle, no less. Hard to imagine."

"It's the beginning of everything," I said, closing my eyes into the daydream, thinking of how it were meant to be. "I don't have to be a noble anymore, and the shire can all be free and happy under a fair sheriff."

"Well, you're still a noble," he corrected. "But you don't have to dress like one, if you don't wish."

"Eleanor called me a princess," I told him quiet. "She said it's my duty not just to protect Nottingham, but all of England."

"That's because she wants you with her," he said. "She's very clever like that."

"It doesn't mean it's a lie."

"No. But it also doesn't mean you have to do it. Or even that you can."

I sighed. "I don't want to be noble at all. I just want to be Scarlet."

His breath was in my hair. "Even Scarlet was noble, she just didn't tell anyone. And you protected people even then. You have a very fierce heart, I hope you realize. I can only imagine if we have a baby, you'll be an absolute terror."

I curled up tighter, my heart broken clear and through. I knew I should tell him, say the words, but I couldn't. "Do we have to have babies, Rob?" I asked quiet.

He twisted a little, trying to look at me, but I kept my face away. "No, of course not, not if you don't want to. You don't want to?"

"I can't even imagine it. I'm frightened every time I see babies in the town—that they'll fall or cut themselves or fall sick or *something*. If it were mine I don't think I'd let the thing move, much less grow up. I'd be scared every moment."

He laughed, harder than my pride liked, and I hit him with my good hand. He groaned, but kept laughing. I twisted and hit him again, and he caught my shoulders and twisted me in the bed, falling on top of me, careful of my arm. I went still, and he shifted, lifting some of his weight off. He brushed my hair back. "You can't tell me you don't want to have a baby because you'd *love* it too much."

I scowled. "I can. I don't like being scared."

He kissed my cheek, settling in beside me so we faced each other. "Let's leave it up to God, then. If he wants us to have a child, he'll let us know."

I touched his face. "What will your first action as sheriff be?"

"Besides marrying my only love?" he asked. "Reorganizing taxes."

"Not abolishing?"

"Taxes are necessary; they just don't need to cripple a county," he said. "Protecting the people doesn't mean giving them what they think they want. It means doing what's right for everyone, and not just for a few."

I pushed him back a little to lay on his chest, keeping my injured hand high by his heart. I wondered if his heart could heal my hand the way I always imagined my hands could heal his skin. "Promise me," I whispered to him. "Every night we're married, we'll talk just like this. About anything."

"About everything," he whispered back, putting two fingers light around my wrist. He kissed my hair, and I pressed my lips to his chest. "My heart. My only love."

"I love you too, Robin."

I shut my eyes. No matter what happened in the morning, if my marriage weren't annulled, if Gisbourne hurt me, Rob would come for me. Rob would forsake his position as sheriff, his newfound freedom, even his life for me. And I couldn't let him do it.

My head touched his and I thought, *I love you, Robin. And I'll fight for you.*

I had hours left to think, and I had this heart, this man, and that made me stronger.

Gisbourne thought he knew what it were to not give up. He didn't know the first thing.

CHAPTER

TWENTY-FOUR

—o—

I woke feeling warm and borderless, like my pulse had flooded the surface of the skin, dissolving it, meeting Rob's and melting us together. Blankets were tucked round us, and his heart were beating beneath my ear, taking my heartbeat and echoing it back.

Blinking, I looked up at him. I hadn't slept long; only when I thought of the beginnings of a plan and Rob were snoring quiet did I drift off in his arms. It weren't yet full light out, but the sky were starting to glow and he were sleeping. Still. He'd fallen asleep before me and hadn't woken. I'd have known if he'd woken.

He slept the night through.

I looked at Rob, tempted to slide back into the bed with him, warm on warm, skin on skin. He stirred, and stretched, and looked at me where I stood with his sleepy eyes looking half drunk as he looked at me. It made heat rush over my skin, and I sat on the edge of the bed.

He half rolled over, his arm catching my waist as he beckoned me down to kiss him. I did, shy and soft.

After a moment that felt like a slow, dizzy whirl against his mouth, he broke the kiss, stroking my cheek. "Go get annulled," he told me. "Do you want me to come with you?"

I frowned, tempted. "No. I imagine he wouldn't take to that well."

"Well, by all means, let's keep him happy and kick him out after," he said. He smiled then, like something just came to mind. "I love you," he told me.

I smiled, desperate to keep tears out of my eyes. "I love you too."

"Good. Get on with it; let's make you an honest woman for once." He rolled back in the bed, grinning at me.

I stood, smiling at him over my shoulder. "I ain't never going to be honest, Robin Hood."

He laughed out loud. "Have I ever told you you're a *terrible* liar? Truly. You're awful. Thief I'll never argue with, but liar?"

I were shocked. "I kept enough secrets from you, didn't I?"

He shrugged. "Not saying things and lying about them are very different."

Shaking my head, I couldn't help but laugh. "That weren't what you said when you first found out."

"Get on," he told me, smiling.

"Yes, *Sheriff*," I told him with a curtsy. He laughed at me as he lay in the bed, and I stood in the door a moment, remembering him. Every bit of him. Committing it all to memory where it wouldn't never be taken from me, wouldn't never tarnish or fade.

I went quick to the chapel. The castle priest were there, the very man what wed me, preparing for the morning mass, and he stopped. "My lady Leaford?" he questioned.

Genuflecting before the altar, I crossed myself and looked up at him. "Father, will you counsel me?"

"Of course, child."

He came from the altar down to the pews, seating me in one and sitting beside me. I sucked in a deep breath, and he covered my hands. I nodded once, but the words didn't come.

"What troubles you, child?"

"My marriage," I told him. "My husband."

His hand touched my cheek, looking on the bruises. "He treats you ill."

"No. Well, yes, but that isn't why I came to you."

"No?"

"My husband had much to gain by our marriage. He were elevated, and he gained my lands and my tenants. He has mistreated me, he has threatened to mistreat those dependent on our land, and he has not performed his duty as a husband."

"Duty?" he asked. "You mean, in all this time, he has not consummated the marriage?"

I shook my head slow. "Do I have any recourse in the eyes of the Church?" I asked.

He drew a breath. "The most solemn duty of a husband and wife is to bear fruit," he said. "If he finds himself incapable, you can both petition the Church to have your marriage dissolved."

"He will never agree to it. The marriage is wholly to his advantage," I said.

He nodded slow. "It is possible, but unlikely. An archbishop would be able to do such, but they tend to be persuaded by none but the highest nobility."

If you embrace who you are, you might find a great many tools at your disposal.

Eleanor's words flooded back to me as relief broke like a wave in my chest, and I found myself leaking tears in the chapel for the second time in far too few days.

"Oh, my dear," the priest said, pulling me into his arms. "I'm so sorry. But God will never abandon you to your darkest hour," he told me soft.

I weren't able to tell him that I were thrilled, not heartbroken, so I cried in his arms as the sun climbed higher, pouring in through the stained glass windows, casting the place in shimmering red light.

A princess of England could sway an archbishop. I were the daughter of the Lionheart, the granddaughter of Eleanor of Aquitaine, and if all that stood between Rob and me were learning to speak a bit better and looking the part of a lady, I would learn whatever I had to.

Marian had her future taken from her by the will of

others—the Leafords, Gisbourne, even Prince John. And Scarlet were locked in Sherwood, unable to be with Rob, unable to have a future at all. But I could become more than a silly lady or a lowly thief—I would be a princess of England, and I would use it to steal back the right to my own heart.

—∞—

I went slow to my chambers, steeling my will. When I rounded the corner there I saw two guards in the earl's colors.

"Milady," they greeted.

"Gentlemen."

Standing before the door, I stared at it many long moments. It didn't change what was on the other side of it, waiting for me. I crossed myself, and I prayed. That my bravery would hold through the coming storm. I had my hope; I would be every inch the noble lady I needed to be if it meant thwarting him. And I would dispatch the sheriff—my sheriff—to protect the Leaford lands from Gisbourne if I needed to. He wouldn't win. I would never let him.

"He's not in, my lady," one guard said gentle.

"What?"

"He left last night and he hasn't returned."

I opened the door.

The chamber were empty.

Relief and rage bubbled up in me. Were this a trick? A game? Had he left for Leaford already? If he suspected or knew where I'd been the night before, God only knew how he'd react.

I called for Mary, and she changed my dress in silence.

Perhaps he were drinking somewhere. Surely that didn't count against me.

Feeling along the shutter, I took the last knife I'd hidden there and slid it into my bodice.

I stood in the chamber for a long time, adding a log to the fire to stoke it up, shivery fear climbing inside me with every breath that failed to bring him to our chamber.

Something were desperately wrong, and I didn't know if it were good for me or not.

Time slid by and the sun rose higher. I knew I couldn't miss Eleanor, but I didn't dare risk Gisbourne's wrath. Finally I told Mary to wait for my husband in the chamber and tell him I were attending the queen.

With a shaking sigh, I left the chamber and made for Eleanor's. It were hard to miss; servants were swarming in lines like ants, carrying out her coffers, her furs, the things she would need in the carriage. She were in the center of it all, her hands poised on a bejeweled cane like it were a weapon.

Which, if needed, I were sure would be formidable in her hands.

Her severe face folded when she saw me, breaking into a smile. "My dear," she greeted. I saw one of her ladies cut me a glare for the endearment, but Eleanor didn't care who knew of her like of me. She came to me and hugged me, and one of the women made a sound that sounded much like I had punched her in the belly.

"My lady Eleanor," I greeted. "Can I attend you in any way?"

"Yes," she said. She gestured with her cane to a lush fur cloak, and I picked it up from the coffer, draping it carefully on her shoulders. It attached with a long string of sapphires the size of my fist. "Oh," she said. "That reminds me. I saw this piece and thought of you," she said, casting about for it.

The lady who served us wine the night before handed her what looked like folded velvet. Eleanor nodded her thanks and slowly peeled back the layers of velvet.

It were the largest moonstone I'd ever seen, surrounded by small emeralds, strung on a long silver chain. It stole my breath. "There's quite a bit more green in it than your eyes, but I think the comparison stands," she said. She lifted the chain and slid it easily over my head, and the jewel sank down to sit between my breasts.

I picked it up, marveling. My mouth were dry. "E-Eleanor," I stuttered.

She lifted my chin with her knuckles. "Not a word, my dear. It's quite unbecoming to challenge a gift from a queen."

Water pricked at my eyes, and I nodded. "Thank you," I whispered, terrified of crying in front of her.

"You're welcome. An early Christmas gift."

I couldn't care about jewels and finery, but it were her careless generosity what squeezed round my heart. She thought of me. Something reminded her of my eyes. I flung my arms around her, not minding the pain in my hand to do it. "Stay," I said to her ear. "Please. Stay here."

"Oh," she said in my ear, and the noise sounded twisted and caught. "Oh, my girl, I wish I could. I will return. Very soon, as soon as I can. Things in London are . . . tense. John's going and I cannot leave him . . . well, unattended." She pulled back and pressed my face in her hands. "But you will be welcomed as soon as I convince you to come to London. And we will see each other soon."

I nodded, gulping fast to keep from pouring out water like a spout. "I will come to London. Soon. I fear I may need your help with something."

She smiled. "You shall have it."

She took my hand and I gripped hers in return.

"Come," she said. "Walk me to my carriage."

Nodding again, I took her arm, and the servants made way for us to move.

Eleanor's ladies were flapping orders, their arms flying like bird wings as they said this should go there, that there. Eleanor ignored it all as we walked together to the open carriage door. "You will write to me, of course?"

"If you wish."

"I do. I like a healthy correspondence."

We crossed the open courtyard, and I laughed to see Much and John stumbling from the Great Hall, long-eyed with sleep. They must not have made it to the barn at all.

"Your friends?" she asked.

I nodded. "As close as I've ever had to brothers."

Much tripped and John caught him, and Eleanor chuckled. "It seems we are leaving Nottingham in very good hands."

We were at the coach, and she embraced me once more. "I hope so," I told her.

"I cannot say I regret your discovery, my dear, but I do wish it had happened in less dramatic fashion."

I frowned. "Do you? You had plenty of opportunity to tell me, and you never said a word."

She lifted a shoulder. "Well. I do wish you never found out at all. The secret matters less now that Richard is king, and married, but secrets are often better for staying such." She smiled. "But now you know. And I'm not upset."

"Neither am I," I told her.

"Good. Good-bye, Lady Marian," she said, her voice tripping a bit. "We shall speak soon."

She swallowed and gave me a weak, fond smile, and she took her footman's hand to climb into the carriage.

I crossed my arms around myself, trying to work out how to say good-bye to her, when a scream rang out.

My head jerked, then whipped back to John and Much. They were still in the courtyard, unharmed, looking toward the gauntlet to the lower bailey.

Everyone were. "Protect the queen!" I yelled at her guards. They flung open the carriage door to take her inside and I took off running, skating over the wet, heavy snow with a pounding heart to see what had happened. People were blocking the door to the gauntlet, but I wedged between them even before John started heaving people aside.

I broke through and slipped, slamming into the ground on the walkway of the gauntlet, soaking my dress in snow.

My vision swam, and I rolled to look up as I tried to suck in a breath.

His feet were first. The boots that I knew too well, too still and limp, a cloak licking around them like the tongue of a hell hound. The snap of the fabric were the only sound I could hear. His arms were heavy and straight, his body fully kitted up in black. A rope, wrapped tight to the wall of the guard's walkway above the gauntlet, were wrapped tight around his neck, causing the skin around it to be purple and thick.

Gisbourne's whole face looked swollen and dark, his eyes overwide, glaring at me, accusing me.

I couldn't breathe. I didn't move, still in the snow, numb and unaware. I didn't hear a sound. I didn't see a soul. Just him, hanging there, looking at me.

You were mine, Marian, long before you even knew he existed. Your unassailable loyalty and unshakeable belief should have been for me.

The wind twisted the body a bit, and I saw his hands bound behind him. He twisted back, and his eyes were on me still.

Sudden and desperate I moved, rolling onto my hands and knees to retch. Nothing came, but I kept heaving, my body in deep revolt, trying to purge it all from me.

Arms caught me up, pulling me off the ground, and it were Rob, and the world suddenly lurched back into reality. John and Much seemed to be guarding me, keeping people away, and Rob hugged me tight to him, shouting orders to get Gisbourne down, call for the guards who had been on watch, call for the girl who had seen him first.

"Scarlet," he said to me. "Scarlet, speak to me."

I sucked in a breath, and my insides didn't try to heave it back out. I nodded. "Rob," I said. "Who did this?"

"I don't—" he started, and then a roar could be heard over the crowd.

"Everyone back," Rob ordered, pulling me up through the door to the upper bailey. "I don't want anyone going in there," he said.

"It was *her!*" yelled a voice. The crowd parted, and Rob shifted me behind him as the prince strode forward, throwing a finger at me. John and Much flanked Rob, defending me.

"My lord prince," Rob said, bowing to him. "With deference to your Highness, there is no possible way it was Lady Leaford. He was thrown over the wall, and Lady Leaford likely couldn't have lifted his weight in any situation, but her hand has been severely injured. One-handed, it's impossible that she could have overpowered him in any way. It wasn't her."

Winchester, de Clare, and the other nobles were filling the courtyard. "What's happened?" Winchester asked.

"Lord Leaford has been killed," Rob said.

Winchester's face folded, angry and confused. "And you accuse *Lady* Leaford?" Winchester asked the prince.

The prince strode forward. "Yes."

"Your Highness, there's no proof—" Rob continued, stepping forward like he meant to keep the prince from me.

"*I saw her.*"

Rob's throat worked, and my heart dropped. He was a

sworn servant of the Crown now; he couldn't refute Prince John's word without revoking his new-promised oath. Without giving up the office of sheriff.

"You have the word of a prince of England," Prince John continued. "I command you to hang her as guilty of murder. The murder of her husband, no less, a most heinous crime."

Rob rocked back, and my heart broke. I knew Eleanor would never let John kill me, but Rob wouldn't trust that. Kill me, or give up being sheriff. Hand the position over to someone the prince would appoint, undo all we'd done. Or kill me.

"Your Highness—" Rob started, his voice rough.

"Do it!" the prince screamed.

I cast about the crowd for Eleanor. She were the only one who could intercede now, and I couldn't find her. *Damn*—the guards probably still had her inside. She would never let him do this. I just needed time before Rob were forced to decide.

"Do it, or I will strip you forthwith of your office," Prince John growled. "And you will be punished as a traitor to the Crown."

Death.

Gisbourne's voice floated over the aether to me from the bailey. *He will make you pay for this, Marian.*

This were Prince John's plan—not to kill me, but to take the position back from Rob. He never planned to let us escape from this, never planned to let Rob stay sheriff. And he killed Gisbourne to make it happen.

But I wouldn't let him haunt Rob again. I wouldn't make Rob choose between his life and mine.

I knew he wouldn't hesitate. Given the chance, he would kill Rob. There were only one person here he wouldn't kill. No matter how much he wanted to, no matter what people saw or thought, Eleanor would never forgive him my death, and losing her love were something he wouldn't risk. I were sure of it.

I slid the knife from my back, stepped to the side of Rob, and lunged.

CHAPTER
TWENTY-FIVE

I knew I weren't nearly close enough to actually hurt him, but it weren't the true point anyway. As I lunged at the prince, he stepped back and his guards dove forward, grabbing me and tearing the knife from my hand.

Then the melee started in truth as the tethers of the crowd snapped. I saw Prince John draw his sword and lunge at Rob, who jumped back, unarmed. Another strike, another jump, and I lost him behind people. Much drew his *kattari*—he must have concealed it better than I knew he could—and started swiping, trying to make it to Robin.

John hammered a guard with his fist and easily stole his sword. The wave of people cleared again and I saw Winchester and John both battling to get to Rob, Prince John ahead of them both.

Winchester turned and met the sword of de Clare, and a

vengeful part of me hoped Winchester at least left him something to remember, if not killed him whole.

John got close enough to Robin, catching Rob's eye while
tossing his sword to him. I watched the flash of the steel in the
sky, and Rob reached out and caught it.

My heart leapt, and then I saw Rob's horror-filled, fallen
face. I looked back.

I turned my head just as Prince John pulled his sword from
John's stretched-wide middle. Blood flung out with the sword,
and for a moment, John were still. His arms were still up, like
he were still throwing the sword to Rob. Then they dropped,
and his knees buckled. Like someone took a stick to his legs
they fell from under him, and he crashed into the snow.

His face rolled to me. His arm were out, toward me, and he
coughed, meeting my eyes. I knew I were screaming; I knew
only because my chest hurt like I were screaming, like I were
screaming so hard I couldn't bear to breathe. His cough made
blood spatter his mouth, and the snow, and his cheek. His lips
moved. *Bess.*

I shattered. My legs couldn't hold me, my chest ached for
screaming, my eyes poured so much water I were sure at some
point it had to turn to blood. The guards held me up by my
waist, and that were it, that were all that were real.

The fighting stopped at some point, and I waited for the
guards to let me go, let me go to John, but they didn't. Rob
and Much knelt by his side, but John were still, the second set
of dead eyes to fix me in their gaze that morning.

Much stared at me, wide eyed and wild, saying something, but I couldn't hear it. They put irons on me and made me kneel in the snow, and I fought, desperate, trying to get to John, to Much, to Rob, to my family that had just been broken.

A knight pressed his sword to my throat, and it scraped along my chin before I felt it, before I stopped moving.

Prince John stood before me, but I were senseless. He waved the sword away, but if he were speaking, I couldn't hear it.

His hand cracked across my face. "Mark me!" he growled.

My neck felt boneless, but I looked up at him, trying to hear what he were saying.

"As a traitor, I will bring you to London," he ordered. "You will confess to your motives for trying to assassinate a prince of England, and when I'm satisfied with your confession, you will meet your death."

He were lying. He didn't dare kill me. Rob he would have killed here in the snow, just like he'd done John, but me Eleanor would never forgive. Me he couldn't afford to kill.

Yet at the moment, watching John die on the ground because of me, I wished for death.

"Let me see him," I said, my voice raw and strange, and water started in my eyes fresh. "Let me go to him!"

"Your Highness," Winchester said, coming beside Prince John. "What's the harm in it? She's in chains."

Prince John's eyes never left me. "You can never trust a thief, Winchester. Or a traitor."

"Sheriff," said a soft voice.

Everyone turned to look, and I saw Eleanor standing there, her pale face mottled with pink, her eyes wide. "Yes, your Highness," Rob said.

"There should be a carriage in the lowest bailey that is suitable for securing a prisoner," she said, gravel in her voice. "Perhaps you can see her down to it."

"Not yet," the prince said, and he grabbed my arm, dragging me back to the door to the gauntlet. I let him—I didn't have a bone in my body to stop him, my eyes fixed on John's body in the snow, watching as my soaked skirts skidded over the snow, edging close to his blood. A corner of it caught his blood and spread an ever-lightening red streak in the white snow. Fresh sobs burst through my chest.

He pushed me through the door, grabbing my head and forcing me to look at Gisbourne's body. "Admit it," he growled. "Admit you killed him!"

I kept my mouth shut.

"Admit it!" he bellowed.

"You know I didn't," I said, sniffing back more tears. "You alone know how he died."

He let me drop so he could raise his hand to me again, but it never came down.

"Stop this immediately," Winchester hissed, the only other soul who dared cross the threshold. "There are many things I will watch you do, but strike a woman in chains is not one of them. The sheriff and I will see her to the carriage, but this is finished. *Your Highness.*"

Winchester did not even wait for Prince John's response. He knelt to me and took my hand and waist, helping me up gentle.

"Step aside, Winchester!" the prince snapped.

Winchester did not turn, did not move. "You would do well to remember, my prince, that you are not the king, your nephew is the heir to your brother's throne, and that you are not so much higher than an earl. You are by no means untouchable to me."

Rob came down the gauntlet, and he stood beside me but didn't touch me. His eyes met mine, heavy and dark and blank. His hand reached up, open, to guide me down the gauntlet, and my body jerked. His hands were covered in John's blood.

By the time we reached the second bailey, the world had changed. We made it through the door, and Winchester shut it, and I stared at Rob. "I'm sorry," I said fast. The tears rushed again. "I didn't mean for him to be hurt, Rob, I didn't—how could he—it's my—it's my—"

I couldn't breathe, and I couldn't stop crying. John were dead. Happy John, finally contented John. And Bess knew nothing of it. Bess were alone, and with child, and the sword that run her husband through may as well have been in my hand.

My knees hit the snow-slick stone and Rob were before me. His hands were wet and freezing with snow, but they were clean of blood. They clasped my face. "This is not your fault, Scar." Tears shot out from his eyes. "This is not my fault." His head pressed mine and I knew he felt it like I did, our awful gift to take on pain like greedy children.

"John—*Bess*—" I cried.

"I will take care of her. Of them both."

"Don't come after me, Rob."

He pulled back, looking at me. "Scar, I will have you out within a *week*."

"No. Not at the expense of Nottinghamshire, of being sheriff. Eleanor will protect me as best she can. You know she will. He won't kill me."

"*Scarlet*," he said, and his voice rough running over my skin. "I can't leave you there."

"Yes, you can. Until I find a way."

"Until we both find a way," he told me, staring into my eyes. "And if he harms you, I will deal with the devil himself to get you out of there." He looked up, at Winchester. "Swear to me, Quincy. Swear that you'll watch over her. Keep me informed. *Swear.*"

"I swear."

Robin pulled me forward and kissed me. He tugged me up, holding me still, kissing me again and again, quick desperate things. He held me close and we began walking. We crossed the second bailey and went down to the lowest one. The carriage were already brought forward, which didn't much surprise— word traveled faster amongst the servants than by any other way. There were guards there too, and knights, and I didn't want to find out who were on my side, and who not. I didn't dare cause another soul to be hurt.

Winchester threaded the chains through the bolt in the

floor. He helped me into the seat, and he locked the chains to the bolt with a sorry look to me.

Rob stepped inside the carriage and kissed me, hard and fierce till the tears on our faces touched. Our lips broke but he stayed there still, breathing into me.

I nudged my nose to his cheek. "Last night, Rob—I know we're not meant for much happiness in this awful world, but I will tell myself that last night were the night I married you, and I'll be happy every time I think of it."

"Don't you dare," Rob said. "I will marry you. And I will count the sunsets until I do."

I shut my eyes and cried. I nodded, but I couldn't say another word.

—⁊⁊—

When Rob left, Winchester shut the door and I couldn't mark the time. We started to move sometime after, and the tiny slit of a window showed me snow, and forest, and dark.

I hated it. And I cried. My marriage were over, and the rich shine of being free of Gisbourne were tarnished by everything else I had lost along with it. My home. My love. My friend.

My hope.

But that weren't really the way of it, and that were the worst part. I still had hope. Cruel, bitter, steadfast hope crushed my chest that still hurt for breath; I didn't want it. I wanted to give up, to leave my mind and heart in a bailey in Nottingham Castle as my body went south. I wanted to feel nothing but the blanket of pain and hate swallow me up. I wanted to run backward and lay on the snow with John and stay there, still and frozen and never moving forward again. That would be easy, and lovely, and dark, like the cold woods of Sherwood at night.

The awful thing were faith. Because with everything gone, after a day of horror and hurt, after years of horrors and hurts, the thing I couldn't shake were faith.

I remembered a story that I had heard about the Angevins when I was a girl, and I shut my eyes, trying to remember the pieces of it. It weren't just some legend of the king now, it were a story about my father. About my family.

Richard loved to boast of his devil's blood, begat when one of his ancestors had unknowingly wed a serpent. She bore him eight ugly children, and his curiosity got the better of him. He followed his wife into her weekly bath where he had promised never to disturb her, and found her secret form revealed.

When he confronted her, her heart broke, and she transformed into a dragon and flew above the castle she had built for her husband with her magic. She clung to the spires with her talons and shrieked until the skies grew dark and rained down the tears that she couldn't cry.

For all time she stayed atop the tower, screaming and trembling the earth when the Angevins were born or died, never resting, never failing. Protecting her blood.

That were my blood. The blood of a dragon, a beast, a devil. A woman with supernatural abilities to continue on in the face of pain and betrayal.

The blood that led my father, the Lionheart, to the Holy Land to wage a war for his faith—his vengeance. Vengeance were the darkest side of faith, the thing that claimed violence and fury as holy arrows.

I were lionhearted too. My faith were just as strong.

And I would learn this new side of faith that Eleanor and Richard and the rest of the royal lions claimed. My faith would bring me back to Nottingham. My faith would bring Prince John to his knees before me.

As the carriage pitched and tossed, and the place I were promised to protect faded and the man I loved disappeared, I prayed for faith.

And I vowed vengeance.

ACKNOWLEDGMENTS

Writing a sequel is equal parts evil and exhilaration, and there are many people without whom *Lady Thief* would never have made it over the finish line. First, to my agent, Minju Chang, you're SO amazing. Thank you so much for helping me through the frustrations and difficulties, and always being there to cheer me on. I always feel like we are a team, and that means a lot to me.

Thank you to the entire team at Walker Books. To my editor, Emily Easton—I am so grateful for your insights and for your keen editorial eye. Thank you for making Scarlet who she is today. Thank you to Mary Kate Castellani, for jumping in when needed and providing another very thoughtful perspective on *Lady Thief*. To Laura Whitaker, Beth Eller, Katy Hershberger, Bridget Hartzler, Erica Barmash, and all the people at Bloomsbury/Walker who have championed *Scarlet* and allowed her adventures to continue in *Lady Thief*—I am so grateful. Thank you for all that you've done and continue to do.

The weirdest thing about a debut novel is that it goes from being this somewhat manic dialogue between you and a computer, and becomes this public commodity that so many people experience. It's amazing and it never ceases to astound me, so thank you to the bloggers who helped get my secret little novel out to the world, to the readers who are so passionate about Scar and the idea of a strong girl in fiction, and to the librarians who continue to pass my book to their readers. There wouldn't be a Book Two without you!

Debut year was a crazy thing, but in getting *Scarlet* out there and writing *Lady Thief* I've met some of the people I consider most dear and most crucial to the act of continuing to write. Thank you to the Class of 2k12 and allll of the Apocalypsies, but I have to say there are a few people who need more thanks. Cory Jackson, thank you for reading a super-early draft of *LT* and jump-starting me when I was stuck. Tiffany Schmidt, I owe you my firstborn child for the comments you gave me on a later draft that wasn't working. To Katy Longshore, your books are inspiring and your friendship is more so. To Gina Damico, Gina Rosati, Diana Renn, Kate Burak, and Lynda Mullaly Hunt, for being my Boston authors crew and making visits of all kinds easier. To Hilary Graham for being so cool and being the best partner in crime I could ask for.

The past few years have been really hectic for me, and I wouldn't have made it through without a lot of support from my workplace. Thank you to Meghan, Amy, Paloan, Keith, Alex, Stevi, and especially Paul—you're the best boss ever. Thank you for being so supportive. To Risk, especially Mike and Matt, who have kept me sane on overnights for years. I'll even thank the guys from Engineering (Jason, Scott, and Ermin)—just don't let it go to your heads. And of course, Andrew, we're going to have ants.

There are workplace families, and then there are families that come from working together without money—which I think is more meaningful. To my GLOW girls, you have proven to me that we can do anything (like, literally, anything) and that we can turn around and show young women that they, too, are capable of greatness. Emily, Jenna, and especially Leah, thank you for inspiring me to dream greater, to achieve greater—in a word, glow. (And, you know, for ignoring those 6 a.m. e-mails when I decide to communicate mid–panic attack.) And since I can't miss an opportunity for nonprofit promotion, www.bostonglow.org.

Then there are friends who have always felt like family. Ashley, I would not have survived without that week in Montana, and Gisbourne wouldn't be half the man he is today. Renee, Nacie, Iggy, and Alex, I would cut off my fingers for you. But please don't make me, because they're helpful with the writing.

To Mikey, who wanted to call this *Scarlet 2: Scarleter*, or *Scarlet 2: She'll Cut You*. I'm sorry we didn't go with your titles, but you're the best brother ever. And Kev, who still buys a new copy of my book every few weeks just because. You're the best brother ever. (See what I did there?) I love you both so very much!

Daddy, you've given me everything—including your awful sense of humor. Thank you for hoisting me up on your shoulders and showing me what the world looks like from such a height. I hope this book is a small gesture of my love and gratitude.

To my mum, you and I probably have a little too much fun together. Thank you for always being there for me and for listening to me rant and cry and rant some more. I love being your daughter.